ENEMY VEHICLES FLARED LIKE BONFIRES IN VIOLENT CONFLAGRATIONS

Gary Manning raked the milling al Qaeda combatants with his machine gun as Hawkins methodically executed any gunman who came into his crosshairs.

Having used RPGs to disable every vehicle in the convoy, both Calvin James and Rafael Encizo traded out their rocket launchers for Soviet-era submachine guns. Moving quickly under the cover fire, David McCarter prepared to lead the assault element down the cliff face to overwhelm any resistance.

"Move! Move! Move!" McCarter barked.

As one, the three-man fire team surged forward over the lip of the steep incline. The deployed lines were flung out in front of them. They ran face-first in an Australian-style rappel down the steep incline, one hand running the guideline, the other firing their weapons from the hip using a sling over the shoulder of their firing hand to steady the muzzle.

The loose gravel gave way in miniature avalanches under their feet as they sprinted down the incline, ropes whizzing through the gloves on their hands. The light from burning vehicles cast wild shadows and threw pillars of heat up toward them. It felt as if they were running straight into the open mouth of hell.

DON PENDLETON'S

STONY

AMERICA'S ULTRA-COVERT INTELLIGENCE AGENCY

MAN®

Unified Action

®

A GOLD EAGLE BOOK FROM

WORLDWIDE®

TORONTO • NEW YORK • LONDON
AMSTERDAM • PARIS • SYDNEY • HAMBURG
STOCKHOLM • ATHENS • TOKYO • MILAN
MADRID • WARSAW • BUDAPEST • AUCKLAND

First edition December 2010

ISBN-13: 978-0-373-61994-8

UNIFIED ACTION

Special thanks and acknowledgment to
Nathan Meyer for his contribution to this work.

Printed in U.S.A.

Unified Action

CHAPTER ONE

Michael Klaus understood how the world worked.

The world was predicated on profit. In the end all that mattered was profit, and Klaus had no patience for weaker men who refused the obvious nature of this truth.

There simply wasn't enough to go around. In Klaus's opinion no political system that attempted to address a shortage of equality had worked, and none ever would. The world of haves and have-nots was built on Darwinian fitness where survival was its own justification. Pity, mercy, empathy, justice—these were theoretical concepts that held no place in the jungle lives of humankind.

Michael Klaus would be king of the jungle, by any means necessary.

Klaus stood in front of the floor-to-ceiling windows of his master office suite. He shot the cuffs on a tailored suit and ignored the prostitute as he made his own way out of the lavish room. The lisping Adonis had an envelope of cash and bite marks on his back to remember his visit by. If he was wise and didn't wish to be found floating facedown in the bay, he'd practice discretion.

Outside over the dark waters of the northern Atlantic dark clouds were piling up on the horizon. Klaus could see whitecaps forming from the stiff breeze that was beginning to hit the beach like a company of shock troops. He imagined it was quite cold out there. He didn't know firsthand, since he was inside, secured from the environment, untouchable. Insulated. He preferred things this way. He picked up an ultraslim wireless and pressed the push-to-talk button with a manicured finger adorned with a heavy gold ring.

"Ms. Applebaum, is Mr. Skell waiting for me?"

"Yes, Mr. Klaus," his personal assistant answered immediately. "Shall I send him in?"

"Yes, please."

Klaus believed in impeccable manners. It was part of the charade, part of the mask of civilization he wore the way any ambush predator blended into its background.

He glanced at the Rolex Executive watch on his thin wrist. The heavy walnut door behind him opened and then closed, but Klaus didn't turn around. The corporate magnate remained facing his windows, taking in the view.

"I trust you are well, Mr. Skell?"

"I am, sir," the chief legal officer answered.

On the left of the room a massive aquarium served as a divider between the section of the office suite containing Klaus's desk and a sunken living-room area where more informal negotiations or conversations took place. Skell crossed to this area and helped himself to a tumbler of single-malt Scotch whiskey. He drank it neat, and it went down in a single swallow without a flinch with a practiced flick of his wrist.

"Well?" Klaus asked.

"Have corporate security made an anti-electronic measures sweep?"

"This morning. Would I talk so openly otherwise?" There was a slight undercurrent to Klaus's voice now.

Skell, long used to his employer's moods, sensed it immediately. "I apologize," he said hastily. "We're close now and perhaps the stress is getting to me."

"Perhaps some time alone with all that Thai child porn you've collected?" Klaus offered quietly. "Would that relax you?"

Skell winced at the unsubtle reminder of who was master and who was servant. Klaus turned away from the window and looked at him for the first time. He saw a pudgy, balding man with soft hands, a weak chin and slumped shoulders in a suit as expensive as his own. He also saw a brilliant legal pirate with the eyes of a serial killer.

"Why don't you tell me about our progress?" Klaus offered.

"Everything has gone according to schedule. We found a team of Mossad investigators snooping around in the periphery of our operations but we were able to feed them enough disinformation that they were put onto the wrong track."

"And the Americans?"

"Officially? Quiet. We're still well below their radar."

"Unofficially?"

Skell paused. "There is a…complication," he admitted.

Klaus slowly put his hands behind his back and pursed his lips. Deliberately he walked forward on expensive Italian loafers. He stopped beside his deck and removed a cigarette from a box on the tabletop and lit it. "Go on," he said. His words came out in a cloud of blue smoke.

"Two contractors," Skell began, "working separate aspects of the project. It turns out they were brothers."

"That was an unfortunate oversight on the part of personnel."

"They were working for different companies on different sites. One in Southwest Asian operations, the other at the Santo Domingo office."

As Skell talked Klaus began to move again, trailing cigarette smoke behind him like the front stack on a locomotive. Skell's knuckles were white around the cut-crystal liquor tumbler in his hands as he felt Klaus getting closer. He knew better than to turn around.

"Don't we have software indigenous to our record-keeping system that catches this sort of thing?"

"There was a delay in linking the information." Skell paused slightly. "The employee responsible for such activities has been reprimanded."

Klaus was close enough behind him now that Skell could smell the man's cologne. Fat beads of sweat broke out on the lawyer's bald pate. A heavy hand settled on his right shoulder, then a second fell on his left. Klaus was so close behind him now he could feel the heat of the man's body.

"Did you do the reprimanding yourself, then?" Klaus asked. His face was so close beside Skell that the question was a whisper in the man's ear. Cigarette smoke enveloped his head in a cloud, forcing Skell to cough slightly.

"Yes. Yes, I did."

"Good," Klaus whispered. Abruptly the German turned and walked back across the room toward his desk, where he ground out the cigarette. "Was there a compromise?"

"We believe so."

"And?"

"And I think the two know enough to make them curious, to realize there's a bigger picture, but not enough to make them go to the authorities—yet."

"Fine. You know what to do, then, correct?"

"I'm putting it into motion right now."

Klaus walked back over to the windows and clasped his hands behind his back. He stared out at the ocean now roiling under the windstorm hammering the shore.

"That'll be all."

HALF AN HOUR LATER Skell sat in the back of a plush company limousine. He swallowed a fistful of antacid tablets, two aspirin and a Xanax and washed them down with a swig of bottled water. His hands were clammy from his perspiration, and when the two men got into the back of the limo with him he didn't offer to shake hands.

The first man wore a closely shaved haircut and a shrapnel scar that ran along one jawline. His name was Haight and he'd been a sergeant in the French Foreign Legion for ten years before opting to work freelance.

Haight was tall but lean, whipcord thin and possessing the build of an endurance hunting animal like a greyhound or a cheetah. In contrast, the onyx-skinned man who got in behind him was built like a bear.

Robert Skah Lemis had come up on the hard streets of Santo Domingo the rough way. From gang member to police officer to political assassin, he had excelled in making useful connections. He turned chaotic masses of violent, unorganized individuals into functioning syndicates. Money. Guns. Lawyers. In the Caribbean, Lemis controlled and coordinated these things. It had made him very important to Mr. Skell because it allowed the sweating pedophile to look good for his boss, the unforgiving Mr. Klaus.

Skell blinked behind his glasses, his eyes as beady as they were myopic. Haight smelled like aftershave and Lemis smelled like marijuana. The tip of his tongue looked pink and vaguely sluglike against the fat cupid bow of his pursed lips. A sheen of sweat covered him, casting an unhealthy aurora.

"Here," he said briskly.

He opened a titanium briefcase covered in a thin layer of calfskin and set with gold fixtures. From inside he pulled out two flash drives and handed them to the mercenaries sitting across from him. Both men took great pains to ensure their hands didn't touch Skell's.

As the two middle managers placed the flash drives inside their coat pockets Skell gave them a brief rundown.

"Each flash drive contains information on men we want captured, interrogated and disposed of. Ironically, but unimportant to you, the men are brothers named Smith. One is currently an FBI agent on liaison in the Dominican Republic, and the other is a private military contractor flying unmanned aerial vehicles on surveillance missions in Kyrgyzstan. They learned something they shouldn't have. The details will be provided in the digital briefings.

"Once we've figured out how much they discovered, we won't need them anymore. Put together your teams, arrange transportation, perform the captures, conduct the interrogations, dispose of the bodies. We need this done fast and we are willing to provide you a fifteen percent bonus over and above our normal understandings."

Lemis grinned. His mouth was huge and his white teeth lit up his face like lights on a Christmas tree. "That's good stuff. I'll have the motherfucker wrapped up like candy in a day."

Haight frowned. "My end isn't going to be so tidy. A job like this I'm going to have to use ex-Soviet troops. Bulgarians for the interviews, Russians for the shock troops. I go open market, I can't promise they won't run their mouths off about doing an American to inflate their rep. I go with quiet professionals, I run the risk of getting boys tied in closely with the intelligence services or the syndicates." He leaned back in his seat and shrugged his shoulders. "If we were doing this in Africa it might be a different story…but Kyrgyzstan?"

Skell drew his lips together, forming his mouth into a pout. "Total unit closure?" he suggested.

Haight shook his head. "Too large a crew on this one. I recruit twenty shooters and one or two spooks, then they all turn up missing, I'm fucking done."

"Fine. Use people who can keep their mouth shut. We have ways of dampening down the exposure on the intelligence front." Mentally he adjusted the cost expenditure for the operation. He frowned slightly, then decided it was obviously still cost-effective given the alternative.

Once the American dollar had been devalued the resulting profit margin from Mr. Klaus's currency speculation would be so considerable that a few million-dollar bribes to Russian generals at the old Kremlin would hardly be missed.

CHAPTER TWO

Southern Caribbean

The NA-265—60 Saberliner Jet cut through the air at well over 500 mph. Below the forty-four-foot wingspan wisps of clouds obscured the view of the Caribbean Ocean. To the west the sun was setting in an explosion of reddish-yellow light.

The civilian jet was flown by a skeleton crew of three pilots from the Central Intelligence Agency's clandestine service, while in the passenger area the three operators of Able Team lounged after being picked up after a mission in the Uruguay capital of Montevideo.

Big, blond and built like a nightclub bouncer, Carl Lyons reclined in one of the plush seats and stared out the window. Wearing civilian clothes and tan, thick-soled hiking boots, he looked rumpled, dirty and tired. One knee of his jeans was stained with blood splatter and his hands smelled like cordite. He set down his can of soda and crossed one size-twelve boot over his knee.

He noticed absentmindedly that the toe and tread of his boot were flecked with brain matter. He turned to look at the mustached, sandy-haired man sprawled in the seat across the narrow aisle from him.

"You think you used enough Semtex in that last satchel charge?" Lyons asked, voice dry.

Hermann Schwarz shrugged as he opened a can of soda. He took a long drink, then shrugged again.

"Don't know," he admitted. "I mean, the door came open. Right?"

"Every ass clown in that FARC hit squad came out the opening looking like fruit in a blender," Rosario Blancanales pointed out.

"Did I tell 'em to carry a suitcase full of grenades?" Schwarz countered.

"Barb's going to be pissed we didn't recover any intelligence artifacts," Lyons pointed out. The leader of Able Team referred to Barbara Price, the mission controller at their organizational headquarters, Stony Man Farm.

"I'm really more of an engineer and less of an archaeologist," Schwarz answered.

"Who said anything about archaeologists?" Lyons demanded.

"It was a play on the dual use of the term 'artifact' you mentioned," Blancanales explained.

"Thank you," Schwarz said.

"It was also stupid and obvious," Blancanales continued.

"Thank you," Lyons said.

The digital speakers of the Saberliner's PA system cut on and the pilot's voice, sounding well modulated and distant, cut in. "I got an alert from HQ," the woman said. "You have a fragmentation order. Please access the communications display in your table."

"Speaking of Mama Bear…" Blancanales grinned.

Reaching out a single blunt finger, Lyons jabbed it into the console button. A section of the desktop slid back to reveal a recessed screen and keyboard. A red light next to a digital camera blinked on and the blank image on the screen snapped into resolution, revealing the attractive features of the honey-blond Stony Man mission controller, Barbara Price.

"Good work in Uruguay," Price said. "I've got something new for you."

From behind the television Blancanales snorted in laughter. "I wish she'd knock it off already with all the chitchat and get to business."

"No shit," Schwarz muttered.

Lyons scowled in their direction out of habit. "Go ahead, Barb," he said.

"Hal just got a request through the Justice Department," Price started, referencing Hal Brognola, the director of the Sensitive Operations Group which oversaw Stony Man Farm and its teams. "An investigative liaison for the FBI assigned to the Dominican Republic went missing twelve hours ago."

"I'm not tracking," Lyons said with a frown. "This doesn't sound like an Able operation." Looking down, he saw the blood splatter on his boot. "At all," he added.

"We have three major problems," Price began.

"Here it comes," Schwarz said.

"One, the agent's mission was twofold. Ostensibly he was helping with money-laundering operations used by international drug cartels. For that assignment he was given a Dominican counterpart. Partway into that investigation he came across evidence of corruption within the nation's security services."

"Gasp." Blancanales shook his head.

"He was instructed to keep a low profile and to build a file to be turned over to the State Department. He went to meet a confidential informant and failed to make his last two check-ins."

"Surely the Feds have protocols for that?" Lyons pointed out.

"They do," Price answered. "The problem is that six hours ago police forces opened fire on an eighteen-year-old boy in a Santo Domingo ghetto. The police claimed the boy was resisting arrest, but witnesses claim he was unarmed. It turned out the boy was the son of the president's chief political opponent."

"Uh-oh," Schwarz said. "The plot thickens."

"Street gangs loyal to the opposition party immediately began rioting. The government responded with force and the unrest has now spread to all major parts of the city. The consulate is locked down. Nonessential personnel have been choppered out to Navy ships offshore. The city is locked down under martial law and the State Department has declared the Dominican a nonpermissive area."

"Meaning no unescorted diplomats or government personnel," Lyons finished.

"The government has refused to give sanction to any retrievals or investigations by us until the civil unrest has been contained," Price said.

"And all the evidence wiped clean," Blancanales added.

"Your pilot has been given her new flight instructions. You'll touch down at the auxiliary executive airport just outside of town. To clear customs you'll have to come out of this plane without the gear you used in Uruguay. Someone from the consulate will be waiting for you. Carmen has just sent the coordinates to a joint CIA/DEA safehouse to Schwarz's BlackBerry. Go there, equip and go over what files we got on the missing agent's case."

"Sounds good," Lyons said and nodded.

"Remember," Price added. "We have no Dominican liaison for you. We do not have permission to operate. The city is locked with riots and under martial law. As far as we are concerned, the FBI's contacts in Santo Domingo are compromised. This is going to be hairy."

Schwarz looked at his teammates. "What's new?" he asked.

Stony Man Farm, Virginia

INSIDE THE communications center of the underground Annex, Barbara Price clicked off the screen to the communications relay station and slowly turned in her chair. She saw Aaron "Bear" Kurtzman, leader of the Stony Man cyberteam, waiting for her. The burly man was sitting comfortably in a motorized wheelchair outfitted with an array of computer uplinks and interfaces.

There were two steaming mugs of coffee in his huge paws. He leaned forward and handed one to Price, who took it gratefully. She sipped at the coffee and looked up in surprise.

"This is great!" she sputtered. "*You* made this?"

Kurtzman grinned from behind his mug, suddenly self-conscious. "Yeah…I really don't know what happened."

"Is Phoenix in the conference room?"

"McCarter and James are," Kurtzman replied. Price rose and began walking. "The rest of them are at the equipment cages getting gear ready for the airlift."

"Good," Price said, exiting the communications center.

Kurtzman followed the woman as she strode quickly

down the hallway, pulling an iPhone free. Carmen Delahunt, the red-haired ex–FBI agent, came up and offered Price a form.

"Requisitions needs your signature for the AT-4s," the woman explained.

Price shifted her phone to the crook of her shoulder and scrawled her name across the form. On the phone the connection clicked into place.

"Go for Brognola," Hal Brognola said in his usual gruff voice.

"What are you doing?" Price asked.

She began walking again and the motor of Kurtzman's chair whined as he followed her down the hall.

"Trying to ram our budget past the cabinet," he replied. "You realize we use more ammunition than the entire United States Marine Corps in a year?"

"Even now?"

"Even now," the big Fed said drolly. "What can I do for you? Able en route?"

"Able's scrambling for the Dominican," she confirmed.

She spun on her heel and shoved open the door to the Annex conference room, barging in to see Phoenix Force leader David McCarter and team medic Calvin James waiting for her.

"Phoenix?" Brognola demanded.

"That's why I'm calling," Price replied.

She pointed a finger at Kurtzman, then at the wall and the tech administrator worked a sequence on his chair-mounted keyboard. Instantly the plasma wall monitor sparked into life and went to its default setting of a global atlas.

"What do you need?"

On the screen the geographical image was overlaid with two thin red lines, one for latitude and one for longitude. Wherever the two lines intersected, a box formed, capturing the terrain and political information of any spot on the planet. Kurtzman worked a mouseball on his keyboard.

"Before I scramble Phoenix," Price continued, "I need to know if I'm going to get overflight permission from Uzbekistan or if we have to get a plane capable of maintaining enough altitude to avoid detection during the insertion."

"Just a second," Brognola said. "Let me call a general at Stratcom to sense the general impression before I try to get it authorized."

"I'll hold," Price said.

Calvin James, former Navy SEAL, turned toward the Phoenix Force leader, David McCarter. "We're going to Kyrgyzstan."

McCarter, a former British Special Air Service commando, shook his head. "Nah, Tajikistan. They've been having problems north of Kabul lately."

"Kyrgyzstan," James replied stubbornly.

"Twenty spot on it?"

"Done." James shook the fox-faced Briton's hand.

On the screen the lat and long lines settled over central Asia. The political lines showing the border of Kyrgyzstan with China on the right and Tajikistan on the south and Kazakhstan to the north and west showed up. Then the mountain range in the southeast of Kyrgyzstan was pulled up in vivid relief reading.

"Pay up, limey." James smirked.

McCarter scowled good-naturedly. "I'll get you in a bit."

"You're worse than Hawkins about paying up."

"All right," Price interrupted. "While I'm waiting for Hal to check this angle, we'll move forward. This operation is a supplementation to an operational focus initiated by Joint Special Operations Command. We're going to be performing direct-action missions based on information fed us by the Intelligence Support Activity," Price explained, referencing the Pentagon unit tasked specifically with providing tactical information to special operations forces independent of civilian intelligence agencies. "What do you know about Kyrgyzstan?"

James shrugged. "There are clashes going on between progovernment and opposition forces. The government is threatening to balkanize, making the whole area highly unstable. There've been increased activity of extremist groups in the area. Most especially the Islamic Movement of Uzbekistan, or IMU, a terror group with direct links to al Qaeda."

"Those are our boys," Price said. "We have good intel they're planning attacks on U.S. government facilities in the region. JSOC has had to shift too many assets south into Pakistan because of increased Taliban activity in the northwest border region there. They asked if we could send you boys to war."

McCarter sat up. "Straight fights?"

"Is anything you do straight?" Kurtzman asked.

McCarter looked at him. "I'm not quite sure how to take that, mate." He paused, then lifted an eyebrow. "Are you flirting with me, Bear?"

"Yes. Yes, I am," Kurtzman said and nodded.

"If we're done playing eHarmony.com do you think we could get back to the briefing?" Price asked.

"We're going after bad guys?" James asked.

"Hunter-killer operation, search and destroy," Price confirmed.

"I'm so happy," McCarter replied.

Santo Domingo, Dominican Republic

THE SABERLINER BANKED hard as it made its approach.

Out their windows the members of Able Team could see several columns of thick, black smoke roiling up as the city burned. Dominican politics started at the street level and worked its way up. Public housing units and neighborhoods were carved into voting districts, and political workers utilized street gangs and corrupt police to intimidate voters and manipulate precincts.

Democracy in the Dominican Republic, much like ghetto-level law enforcement, was an exercise in violence, bribery and fraudulent activity on such a widespread scale that it was endemic to the nation.

The smooth, well-modulated voice of the pilot broke over the speaker. "I just received permission to land at the executive auxiliary airport," she informed them. "But I've been advised that customs has shut down the gates as a result of the rioting."

"Damn it," Lyons muttered. "Nothing can ever be simple." He paused. "Ever."

Blancanales turned toward the speaker and addressed the pilot. "How soon can you do a turn-around and be in the air?" he asked.

There was a pause then a slight buzz of feedback as the pilot opened the channel again. "Ten or fifteen minutes," she replied. "Just long enough for the ground crews to turn the plane around. There are no other planes scheduled ahead of us." She clicked off then added, voice dry, "We're apparently the only 'executives' stupid enough to land in Santo Domingo in the middle of chaotic civil unrest."

"I don't suppose you have, um...*contingency* items on board?" Schwarz asked.

"We're not that kind of ride, gentlemen," she answered. "We get things done by flying under the radar."

"Ha-ha." Lyons scowled.

CHAPTER THREE

With a bemused expression Hermann Schwarz watched the Saberliner take off. Beside him Blancanales was engaged in a rapid-fire exchange with an airport official while Carl Lyons stood off a short distance, big arms folded over a massive chest, scowl firmly in place.

The Dominican Republic had the feel of a hell zone, Schwarz reflected. He'd seen plenty of Third World trouble spots in his time, first with the military and then with Stony Man. The air was thick with humidity, heavy with equatorial-influenced heat. The smell of smoke from structure fires floated on the air with a greasy, acrid stench that was impossible to mistake.

He could hear the sounds of people rioting just blocks from his location, the dull roar punctuated by shrill staccato of police and emergency vehicle sirens. Occasionally there was the bark of firearms, sometimes even the sharp boom of a gasoline tank going up. The city was still reeling from two hurricanes that had blown ashore this season alone. Political corruption had only delayed and diluted the response. Private aid companies such as UNICEF and the Red Cross had been forced to use UN peacekeepers to deliver food and medicine. Some organizations had even been forced to hire private military companies to ensure delivery to areas deemed too hostile for UN security platoons.

Sometimes the Dominican military helped; sometimes they exacerbated the problems. Likewise with the police, the government bureaucrats and even the street warlords.

Schwarz snorted himself out of his reflection with sardonic cynicism. A flying cockroach the size of a Ping-Pong ball buzzed his head. He turned away and spit onto the concrete.

"Hot," he said.

Lyons nodded. "Sun's going down," the Able Team leader said. Both men were waiting to see if Rosario "Politician" Blancanales would successfully work his special brand of magic on the airport official. If not, things were going to get increasingly difficult. "You make the crew at the gate?" Lyons asked.

Schwarz nodded without turning around. "Sure. Port authority patrolmen. M-16s and maybe a two-way radio."

The customs force was parked at an employee access gate about fifty yards from where Able Team stood next to an upgraded Quonset hut hangar. Three police officers with a sergeant of the guard had parked a white soft-top Land Rover next to the chain-link gate.

The men ran to a type, tall and whipcord-lean with very dark skin. Their weapons were held casually and their uniforms, loose British-style tan jungle khakis, were reasonably maintained. Just beyond them a long asphalt road ran along a boulder-and-ballast dike across a swampy stretch of land before entering a rundown neighborhood.

Schwarz gestured with his chin toward the urban buildup beyond the garbage-strewn marsh before slapping at a mosquito on his neck. "You wanna take the back road?"

"Seems wise," Lyons agreed. "We go out the front gate into the shopping district, we're only going to run into more patrols and checkpoints."

"Gangs are going to run the neighborhoods. Might be just as bad," Schwarz pointed out.

"Gangs won't cause as much trouble in the long run," Lyons countered. "With the dead bodies and all," he added.

Schwarz smirked. "Thanks for clearing that up. For a moment I thought you meant they'd be able to trace all the bibles we'd be handing out back to the Farm."

Lyons ignored him, turned back toward the gate. His eyes narrowed as he sized the men up. "I'd rather bribe 'em," he admitted.

"The safehouse'll have operational funds but for now we're fresh off the plane. We either get out of this gate or we fail. It's one or the other."

"Don't I know," Lyons said. "I just hope Hal's contacts will pull through."

"Maybe if the government wasn't under siege…" Schwarz trailed off.

"I guess if I don't like it I can always go back to being a cop." Lyons turned his head and spit on a beetle longer than his thumb as it scurried by on the concrete. The air was so damp from the humidity he felt as if he was being water boarded.

"Our target is out there," Schwarz reminded him. "I kinda doubt they're going to let us just track him down. I got long odds on us getting our ticket out that gate."

Lyons nodded. He lifted one fist the size of a canned ham and squeezed it with his other hand. The knuckles popped like gunshots. "There's an American in trouble," the ex–LAPD detective said. "Bad day to be a Dominican customs cop."

"Have you seen this place?" Schwarz grunted. "Every day is a bad day for those poor sons of bitches."

Blancanales nodded, then thanked the minor bureaucrat he was addressing. The man walked away and Blancanales came toward them. He looked jaunty and upbeat as he approached, but that was just the man's basic personality. Lyons knew before the stocky Puerto Rican said anything that it was a wash.

"Did Barb call us?" Blancanales asked without preamble.

"No updates, no frag orders, no reprieves," Schwarz answered. "We either give here or roll out that gate, brother."

"Oh, we're going out that gate," Lyons said.

Kyrgyzstan
0430 am local time

THE ISOSCELES-TRIANGLE-shaped delta aircraft streaked across central Asian airspace. Four pulse detonation engines hammered the flying wedge forward at Mach 5. Normally staffed with two flight officers, one pilot and one reconnaissance officer, the converted aircraft was piloted by Stony Man ace Jack Grimaldi, who flew solo on this mission.

Cameras, sensors, remote imagers and central processing units had been removed and the body retrofitted to provide a drop platform for airborne insertion. In the dark, claustrophobic hold Phoenix Force waited, attached to oxygen until the GPS system alerted them to their proximity to the jump zone.

A tiny red light blinked once, then shifted to amber. Inside the transport chamber the five commandos felt the airframe shudder under the stress of declining speed. The oxygen system was pumping pure oxygen into the Phoenix Force operators, flushing nitrogen from their blood systems in preparation for the drop to offset hypoxia complications.

On the instrument panel the jump light clicked over from amber to green. Grimaldi reached out and flipped the toggle switch, activating the hydraulic ramp. Within seconds the team was gone into the central Asian night.

The five black figures were invisible against the dark backdrop of the night sky. Unit commander David McCarter, himself a jumpmaster from the elite British Special Air Service, kept a close eye on the plunging members of his team.

Using his altimeter as a guide, McCarter gave the signal to disengage from supplemental oxygen. The air that high above the black-and-gray checkerboard of the landscape was chill as the commandos breathed it in.

At the predetermined altitude McCarter gave the signal and the loose circle of paratroopers broke away, turning into corkscrew spiral led by the British soldier. The black silk parachute of combat diver Rafael Encizo billowed up and popped open to begin the deployment sequence.

The four other members of Phoenix dropped past the paragliding Cuban-American and in quick succession ex–Navy SEAL Calvin James, then Canadian special forces veteran Gary Manning pulled their ripcords. McCarter and T. J. Hawkins dropped below the rest before the Texan and former Delta Force operator deployed his own parachute.

McCarter turned in his free fall and yanked his own ripcord. His chute unfurled and snapped open, jerking him up short. Arrayed behind and above him the team continued its descent in a long, staggered but symmetrical line.

McCarter led the paragliding procession using his wrist-mounted GPS unit to guide the team down to a narrow plateau on a ridge of low, sparsely wooded hills set above a road.

He used his time under the canopy to do a last-minute reconnaissance of the area as he dropped. Off to the northeast he was able to clearly distinguish a long line of headlights coming from the northwest. He felt a certain grim satisfaction as he realized his prey was heading directly toward the guns of his team.

He flared the chute as he touched down, then absorbed the impact up through the soles of his old Russian army boots. McCarter, like the rest of Phoenix Force, was dressed in a motley collection of drab, local civilian garb and Soviet-era Russian army uniform items. Their weapons were Russian, their faces covered in beards, and their equipment from explosives to communications and medical items were common black market items available in the arms bazaars of Armenian criminal syndicates.

Moving quickly, McCarter turned and began collecting his chute, rolling it into a tight ball as the rest of his men landed around him. Hawkins quickly unzipped an SVD sniper rifle from its cushioned carryall and powered up the illumination optics on the night scope.

As the other three members began to cache the drop

gear, Hawkins went to the edge of the windswept gravel landing zone to pull security while McCarter worked his scrambled communications uplink.

"Phoenix Actual to Stony Farm," he barked.

"Go for Stony," Price replied immediately.

"We're on the ground and initiating movement to target," McCarter informed the woman.

"Good copy," Price acknowledged. "We have eyes on," she assured the field commander.

Above their heads the Stony Man's own Keyhole satellite had spun into geosynchronous orbit and the NASA cameras began focusing tightly on the broken terrain with a lens capability so powerful it could read the license plate of a speeding vehicle at night. The ghostly white figures of Phoenix Force appeared on Price's heads-up display back in the Virginia command and control center.

On the stark, exposed finger of the central Asian topography McCarter turned as his team cached the last of their jump gear and began to assemble and ready their primary weapons. Besides Hawkins and his SVD sniper rifle, the massive, thickly muscled frame of Gary Manning was adorned with a 7.62 mm RPK machine gun. The short fire-plug profile of Rafael Encizo came up behind the Canadian, a Type 50 submachine gun his hands. The compact weapon was a prolific Chinese knock-off of the Soviet-era PPSh-41 SMG, and Encizo used it to supplement the RPG-7 launcher he carried along with a sling of HE rockets.

Calvin James was the second half of Phoenix Force's rocket team. He was also armed with an RPG-7 and Type 50. For his part David McCarter would be using a cut-down AKS-74 outfitted with a black market M-203 40 mm grenade launcher.

"We're ready to roll," Manning informed McCarter.

McCarter nodded, then spoke into his uplink. "How we looking out there, Hawk?"

"All clear on the approach route," he answered.

"Copy. Bound forward one hundred yards into overwatch and will move into position."

"Hawk out."

"Let's go," McCarter ordered.

The four-man assault squad fell into a loose Ranger file with McCarter leading and Manning with his machine gun bringing up the rear. For McCarter the movement to target held a surreal quality. The stark, denuded geography seemed like a moonscape through the filtering lens of their commercial night-vision goggles. Each footfall sent puffs of pale dust billowing up, and there was the constant companion of high-altitude wind.

Around them the bare tops of hills rising from a lightly wooded river valley sat like a twisting barrier to the grasslands just beyond, stretching all the way toward the Chinese border.

Moving quickly, the team linked up with Hawkins and moved into position above a narrow switchback in an ancient dirt road carved out decades ago through the low mountains. McCarter called a halt and the team took three minutes to drink water from their canteens.

Once again Hawkins with his telescopic lens was dispatched to the periphery of the formation to provide security as the other four members of Phoenix Force prepped the assault site. Wooden-handled Soviet entrenching tools quickly hacked narrow holes into the side of the earth. Belay pinions were shoved in and buried, forming dead man hangs that allowed the team to deploy their rappel ropes.

"I've got the scout vehicle at the bottom of the canyon," Hawkins said, breaking radio silence.

McCarter narrowed his eyes and turned his ear into the chill bite of the wind. On the air he could clearly make out the throaty growls of heavy engines climbing a steep grade in low gear. "Copy," he told Hawkins. Turning back toward his teammates, he gave terse directions. "We have initial eyes on. Snap into ropes and ready weapons."

Without comment all four commandos snapped their ropes into the D-ring carabiners of their rappel harnesses. Once locked into their drop rigs, Calvin James and Rafael Encizo quickly laid out several warheads and primed their RPGs. Beside them Gary Manning methodically dropped down the folding legs on his machine gun's bipod and settled into position on the flank of the hit squad, poised to pour 7.62 mm rounds down the steep incline and onto the road below.

There was a harsh metallic click as he racked the bolt and chambered the first round on his belt. "Terrorist surprise package hot," he declared in a soft self-satisfied voice.

McCarter grunted in response and slid home a high-explosive 40 mm grenade into his M-203 launcher. Once he was locked and loaded he pulled his Combat Personal Data Assistant out from a Cordura and Kevlar pouch. The CPDA had a commercial housing that on initial inspection hid the electronic upgrades provided by Stony Man's technical section.

McCarter turned his head away from the bite of the

omnipresent and icy breeze, bringing his finger up to key his mic. "Stony, you have eyes over target?"

"Affirmative," Price replied.

"Send signal to my hand unit for final confirmation," McCarter instructed.

Having given his instructions, McCarter held up the CPDA and opened the screen to the digital feed. So far every aspect of their intelligence had been correct, but he wanted to have absolute confirmation that he wasn't accidentally taking down a civilian caravan before he turned Phoenix Force loose on the line of vehicles below.

On his screen the satellite feed appeared, the line of vehicles appearing as white outlines against the cold dark of the Kyrgyzstan geography. The hoods of the trucks glowed slightly from the reflected heat of the hardworking engines and the headlights flashed in hard shards of illuminations. With all the reflected light McCarter was able to clearly pick out the six vehicles of the convoy.

Two commercial four-wheel-drive pickups ran at the front of the vehicle line, followed by three Russian army five-ton trucks with canvas sheaths over the rear storage compartments. The final big truck was uncovered, leaving the several men of the gun crew exposed. Four men in loose turban-style headgear manned a 20 mm antiaircraft gun.

McCarter felt like purring as he clicked his push-to-talk button on the com uplink. "I have visual confirmation of target," he told Stony Man.

"You are cleared to engage," Barbara Price informed him.

CHAPTER FOUR

Dominican Republic

Able Team was a direct-action unit that identified its targets and went forward until enemy combatants had been neutralized in one fashion or another. Capable of stealth and subterfuge, the team was a trio of extremely fit, extremely confident special operators used to sizing up all manner of opposition—soldiers, police, criminals and spies. It wasn't hard to identify the hard-eyed Carl Lyons and more laconic features of Rosario Blancanales and Hermann Schwarz as experienced ass kickers.

The sun was low in the sky, radiating heat like a flamethrower, and the humidity was so thick it felt like a hanging curtain as Able Team approached the customs police in a loose triangle with Lyons at the front.

Recognizing the potential for trouble, the four guards dropped hands to the grips of weapons and stiffened their posture. The leader of the group, an extremely dark-skinned islander with a seemingly fleshless skull, threw a half-smoked cigarette to the ground and let it smolder.

As the three Stony Man operatives approached, Blancanales and Schwarz drifted out a few steps to the side, turning their approach wedge in a softly enveloping semicircle that kept the bodies of the customs officers trapped between themselves and the frame of their vehicle.

Sensing trouble but seeing no weapons, the officer took a step forward and opened his mouth to bark an order.

Lyons lifted up a meaty fist and snapped it forward down his center line in an old-school karate punch. The first two knuckles of his fist slammed into the custom officer's chin, his jaw hanging loose as he prepared to speak. The hinge joint where the jawbone joined the skull was rammed backward, mauling the nerves centered there. The officer went down like a pole-axed steer in a Chicago stockyard, instantly unconscious.

Hermann Schwarz moved in close to his target, his limbs tracing predetermined combative patterns. His left hand slapped the barrel of his man's weapon to one side, his right hand snapping once in a short jab to the man's solar plexus that doubled him over, followed by a hook that took the man flush along his temple and dropped him instantly.

On the opposite side of Lyons from Schwarz, ex–Special Forces soldier Rosario Blancanales hammered into his own opponent. The Puerto Rican commando slammed his left hand against the forestock of the man's rifle, pushing it hard into the startled Dominican's chest and trapping it against the torso.

Caught by surprise, the man's first instinct was to clutch his weapon even more tightly, slowing his response to the attack. Immediately, Blancanales snapped the edge of his right hand into the side of the Dominican's neck, striking the officer along his carotid sinus. The man's eyes rolled upward until only whites showed and he crumpled to the ground at his feet.

The final officer had time to swing a clumsy over-hand buttstroke toward Lyons, who deflected it with the palm of his hand before catching the overmatched soldier on the angle of his chin with a powerful boxer's hook that dropped him.

"Let's go," Lyons snapped, jumping to work.

Quickly they used the downed men's own handcuffs to secure them before stripping weapons, a cell phone, vehicle ignition keys and an ancient Motorola handheld walkie-talkie from the checkpoint officers.

"Do you think three white dudes in a government-marked jeep will be suspicious?" Schwarz asked, voice wry, as he fired up the vehicle.

"Speak for yourself, Mr. White Guy," Blancanales said as he jumped in the back seat and pushed the police weapons out of obvious sight.

"Just try to look official until we can get a different ride," Lyons said.

Schwarz pushed the accelerator down and gunned the jeep down the asphalt service road running behind the airport and toward Santo Domingo. Beside him Lyons was using thick fingers to triangulate a GPS-guided route on the screen of his CPDA.

Ahead of them a line of aluminum-and-clapboard shanties formed a labyrinthine barrier on the outskirts of the town. Beyond this ramshackle slum in the more built-up areas of the city, columns of brown-and-black smoke rose and the wail of sirens could be easily picked out, punctuated by the sharp reports of gunfire. Forming a backdrop to this was an audible sound of the rioting mobs forming a sort of human white noise that under-lined and overlaid everything else.

Santo Domingo was a city on fire.

Working on his navigational program, Lyons snarled in disgust and shoved the CPDA away. "The damn thing only wants to give me obvious thoroughfare," he explained, voice terse with frustration. "We roll down main avenues and we're going to hit crowds and riot police every fifty fucking yards."

"Oh, now you don't want to be obvious?" Blancanales called out from the back seat.

Schwarz reached the end of the service lane and swerved off onto a side road to avoid running into any official traffic working checkpoints or coming from the opposite direction.

He swerved to avoid a stray dog and ran the vehicle through a rut into a long shallow puddle of polluted ditch water. They entered a winding street of the shanty slum and were immediately forced to slow because of the people milling around. Though not rioting, this group of citizens was clearly anxious about the situation and crowded the sides of the street.

A sea of dark faces turned in surprise toward the three men in the jeep. Dogs barked as bystanders pointed with open curiosity at the sight. Other vehicles, freight trucks, minibikes and taxis, began to clog the road, slowing Schwarz's speed.

Lyons mulled over his situation as Schwarz expertly guided the vehicle through the narrow twisting lanes. Groups of young males, some openly carrying machetes, began to appear on street corners.

"We've still got five miles to go to the docks," Blancanales pointed out. "We're going to be playing Russian roulette in a couple of minutes once we get into the industrial and merchant areas," Blancanales continued. "I don't mind putting a couple of this regime's bully boys to sleep to get a ride, but I don't think a gun battle is going to be productive."

"I'm open to suggestions," Lyons said, hooded eyes watching the crowds and vehicles for any sign of a threat.

"Why don't we take a taxi?" Schwarz offered.

"We don't have any cash and I didn't think to rob those clowns from the airport," Lyons replied.

"We barter?"

"What? Not weapons?" Lyons demanded.

"Why not? You said it yourself—we either do what we have to do to save the American or we go home now. We've been put in an imperfect situation. We can either keep a moral high ground or, you know, actually succeed at the goddamn mission."

"We got a cell phone," Blancanales leaned forward and pointed out. "I can use that and the lead officer's pistol to get us a ride, I think. If you want, I can use my pocket knife to juke the fire pin so that it looks all right but will snap when fired."

"I doubt they'll even look as long as there are bullets in the clip," Schwarz argued. "If you want we could just toss the recoil spring altogether. No harm no foul…sort of." He grinned through his mustache.

Lyons nodded once. "Let's do it."

Within half a block of deciding to act, Blancanales had expertly sabotaged the 9 mm pistol. When they found a driver in a battered silver Kia Sophia taxi three minutes later, Blancanales was forced to add the keys to the jeep into the mix but Able Team had secured a driver.

They quickly pulled down a narrow dirt lane overhung with laundry and the curious eyes of the slum's inhabitants. Using their own lightweight jackets as makeshift covers for their longer weapons, Able Team left the government jeep behind and piled into the cramped confines of the taxi.

The driver was in his sixties, scar-faced, with arthritis-gnarled hands and flawless British-accented English. The man watched his passengers with a wary eye but quickly navigated the car away from the scene.

Within seconds Able Team was driving into the heart of an urban firestorm of riots and military police units.

Kyrgyzstan

ABOVE THE CENTRAL ASIAN HILLS clouds began to form, casting dark shadows on the already dark terrain. On the ridgeline above the narrow mountain road Phoenix Force lay in wait, five ambush predators waiting for their quarry.

Weapon muzzles tracked the approach as gleaming headlights appeared on the twisting road. The engines snarled as the vehicle operators ground the gears up the steep grade.

Watching through his night-vision goggles, McCarter felt a professional satisfaction as he surveyed his ambush site. It was a perfect amalgamation of satellite imagery and tactical experience. It was a lethal kill box.

The operation was designed to neutralize an informational node terrorist cell propagating chaos and unrest in underdeveloped and weak countries. The traveling team were graduates of al Qaeda training camps in the former Taliban-controlled Afghanistan. The command-and-control instructors educated local radicals in logistics, administration, financing and target selection, ruthlessly turning clumsy, disorganized gangs of killers into streamlined, corporate models of murderous efficiency.

Phoenix Force was about to execute their own lessons in murderous efficiency.

"Wait for my call," McCarter said smoothly. "On my call, strike our predetermined targets."

"Copy," Hawkins answered.

"Copy," Encizo acknowledged.

"Copy," James echoed.

"Copy," Manning finished.

Below the ex–SAS commando the terrorist convoy ground past. He watched the scout vehicles crawl past his position, close enough now to see the glow of the occupants' cigarettes. Fifty yards down the line, the last truck brought up the rear. The convoy commander had allowed the rough terrain to cause his drivers to bunch up too closely together.

It was a fundamental mistake McCarter intended to exploit.

Slowly, McCarter lifted the butt of his AKS and nestled it into his shoulder. His trigger hand found the curve of his 30-round magazine and his finger lay on the smooth metal curve of the M 203's trigger as his free hand grasped the grenade launcher by its grooved tube.

To either side of him he could feel the men of his unit tensed and poised for his command, ready to unleash a heavy curtain of hellfire on the terrorists below him. He moved his boot slightly and dislodged a stone.

The pebble slid free of the initial lip of the ledge and slid downhill, dislodging a miniature avalanche of gravel that petered out halfway down the incline grade. McCarter let the pent-up air in his lungs escape in a slow hiss as he squeezed his trigger.

The recoil of the shot rocked his carbine back into his shoulder as the round discharged with its signature bloop sound. As the first-strike signal, McCarter had reserved the right to call his target on site instead of taking an assigned target as they'd discussed in their mission workup.

Due to the heavy firepower potential of the 20 mm antiaircraft gun in the last truck, he made the decision to put his first HEDP into it. With surprise, aggression of action, command of terrain and superior training Phoenix Force held the upper hand in the conventional military ambush. If there was any possible game changer then it was the heavy weapon serving as the convoy tail gun.

His round arched into the night, its velocity low enough that he could just trace the arc of its movement as it sailed out across the length of a soccer field toward the truck.

In the next instant there was a flash of light, followed by the thump of the HE round going off. Then men started screaming as fire rolled up in a brilliant orange ball toward the sky and the battle began.

Keyed to the actions of their team leader, both Calvin James and Rafael Encizo reacted instantly, triggering their RPG-7s within breaths of each other. The twin warheads streaked out from the overhang in flashes of ignition fire on traverses almost 180 degrees apart. Encizo fired his round toward the hood and cab of the rear truck already struck by McCarter's 40 mm round, while James angled his into the undercarriage of the lead pickup.

The RPG rounds struck the convoy almost simultaneously. The rockets hammered home with ruthless force. James's round was an inch low and struck the hard gravel road exactly between the front and rear driver's-side tires. The round detonated, spreading a lethal umbrella of shrapnel and flame that first shredded then ignited the vehicle's fuel tank.

The secondary explosion was massive, picking up the light sports utility vehicle and its armed tribesmen and flipping them upside down in a bonfire of orange flame and roiling black smoke. Bodies spun like pinwheels as limbs were ripped free and thrown next to scorched torsos.

Encizo's round cut across the distance at a sharp angle with a screaming, swooshing sound as distinct as any human voice. The rocket skipped off the angled hood of the old Soviet-era truck and skimmed into the windshield. Flames shot out the truck cab through windows in all four directions.

The expanding concussion wave of the exploding RPG warhead ripped back through the dash and hammered into the truck's massive engine block, igniting the vehicle's fluids.

With two well-placed applications of ballistic high explosives, Phoenix Force had effectively pinned the convoy in place on the narrow mountain road. The remaining terrorist troops were left with nowhere to run, no where to escape, and the surrounding terrain made a counterattack virtually impossible.

Manning opened up with his RPK, the weapon hammering out a long burst of 7.62 mm ComBloc rounds that he stitched down the exposed side of the trapped vehicles from one burning truck to the next. His rounds perforated the thin metal of the light-skinned trucks, hammering out divots and burrowing into scrambling, screaming, frantic flesh. His burst broke bones, opened wounds and split skulls as the hapless terrorists twisted and danced under the withering fire.

On the opposite end of the spectrum Hawkins turned his sniper optics on, the nighttime target range as brilliantly lit as a summer day in his home state of Texas. He fired, rode the recoil, adjusted his aim and fired again with an industrial efficiency so smooth it was almost appalling.

First he killed the drivers, then he allowed himself the luxury of picking out a diversity of targets, even killing a struggling terrorist for no other reason than to spare the burning man an agonizing death. Once he saw a terrified and panicked gray-bearded elder desperately attempting to work the buttons on his sat phone. Hawkins used the 4-power magnification of his PSO-1 telescopic sight to put a single 7.62 mm round from his Dragunov SVD through the man's thick, low forehead.

Blood rushed like a river from a cracked dam as the man crumpled and fell away, his satellite phone dropping to the ground from lifeless fingers.

"On ropes!" McCarter shouted.

Both Encizo and James fired their second volley and Phoenix Force prepared to launch its final assault on the convoy.

CHAPTER FIVE

Dominican Republic

The cabdriver was skilled and as interested in avoiding trouble as Able Team. He circumnavigated the trouble spots and police checkpoints throughout the city until he was able to drop them off within blocks of their objective.

Moving quickly down narrow alleys and across vacant lots, Lyons led the team by as surreptitious a route as possible under the circumstances. The U.S. government safehouse was a single-bedroom walkup in an older building set above a fruit warehouse.

The locals watched them with open curiosity, and Lyons noticed the prolific presence of machetes immediately.

"Blending in is going to be a problem," Schwarz noted, voice dry.

"You think?" Blancanales replied, equally sarcastic.

"Could be one of the problems our missing agent had," Lyons pointed out.

"Only in the tourist-heavy areas would he have been able to blend in," Schwarz agreed. "Screw it, we ain't gonna be invisible so we might as well get inside and gear up."

"True," Lyons said. "I was tired of all this sneaking around anyway."

Blancanales rolled his eyes in humor as the team crossed the busy street and approached the outside staircase leading to the safehouse.

Lyons's apprehension grew as he moved closer to the building. If elements within the Dominican government were responsible for the agent's disappearance, then they would have the resources to keep the location under surveillance.

Seeming to read his mind as they crossed the cracked sidewalk, Blancanales spoke up. "According to the Farm, this place isn't believed to be compromised."

"Virginia is a long way from here," Lyons replied evenly, his eyes searching the rooftops.

From a few blocks over there was a sudden burst of weapons fire, and in response the crowd loitering on the street grew animated.

"Fuck it," Schwarz said. "A police patrol could come by at any minute. We need to get out of sight for a while."

"Let's go." Lyons turned his head and spit. "Just to be safe, Pol," he said, "why don't you hang at the bottom of the stair while we check the place out—watch our six, see if anything shakes loose."

"You got it, amigo," Blancanales said.

The former Green Beret peeled off from his friends and wandered down toward the end of a foul-smelling alley toward where an ancient Chevy flatbed delivery truck was parked next to a row of overflowing garbage cans.

Lyons walked forward. The staircase was an ancient, weathered structure obviously decades old. It ran up a story then doubled back under a covered flight of steps, where it ended at an awning-overhung porch. The door set there was dark. From inside the alley the sounds of the street, of automobiles, conversations and blaring radios was muted and sounded farther away by some trick of acoustics.

Lyons moved up the staircase slowly, making little noise. Taking his lead, Schwarz followed his example. Below them Blancanales glanced up, established their position, then scanned the area for signs of trouble.

At the door Lyons paused and looked down. He frowned at what he saw and ran a finger over the door latch, noting the scratches obvious on the faceplate. His proximity sense clanged like a submarine klaxon.

He turned his head on a neck as muscled as a professional boxer's and put one big, thick finger to his lips in warning. Schwarz nodded once, hand poised on the railing. With his other he alerted Blancanales that something was amiss.

Carl Lyons reached out slowly and pushed against the unlatched door. It swung open to reveal a short, dark entranceway. The light of the setting Caribbean sun pushed a cluster of shadows backward. From farther within the apartment the Able Team operatives heard the slight sound of movement. Lyons closed his right hand into a massive rock-hard fist and stepped softly forward.

Schwarz slid slowly forward behind Lyons, turning sideways into a loose karate stance. Moving quietly, the two men penetrated the apartment safehouse. Schwarz saw a modestly furnished but modern space. It boasted a flat-screen television on a far wall next to a window, curtains drawn, which faced the street outside. The TV was the center piece of a loose half circle of furniture including a couch and chairs next to a pedestrian dining set.

Beyond that space was a small kitchen, and running past the open service areas of the apartment was a hallway, leading, presumably to bedrooms and living spaces in the rear of the government residence.

Just behind a closed door down the hallway the sounds of movement were clearly audible now. Schwarz pulled his face into a frowning mask. Common sense suggested that if the intruder was Dominican police or intelligence, the perpetrator would not have inserted without backup.

Having discovered no one serving overwatch either outside the building or inside, all indications pointed toward some other unknown and likely criminal actor. Which raised a lot more questions than it answered, both Lyons and Schwarz realized. They also realized common sense dictated that their unseen adversaries would be equipped with firearms.

Walking heel-toe and rolling their weight forward to avoid making any noise, the two men tested the floorboards for telltale squeaks before each step. From behind the closed door all movement suddenly ceased. Instantly the hyperprimed commandos froze, ears straining to catch any sound.

The figure came through the doorway like a hurricane touching shore. The door flew open, triggering immediate action from Lyons and Schwarz. Schwarz twisted and dived, rolling over one shoulder and out of the hall. He came to his feet like an acrobat and reached for one of the wooden dining-room chairs standing near at hand.

Reacting without thinking, Carl Lyons sprang forward and off to one side, desperately trying to create and exploit an angle in the tight kill box of the narrow apartment hallway.

The figure swung around the frame of the open door in a swift buttonhook maneuver. Lyons had an impression of a short dark figure with a slight build, hands wrapped around the butt of a black automatic pistol.

He struck the hardwood floor, spun over one shoulder and came up inside the interloper's extended arm. He twisted at the waist as he rose and lashed out with his arm, striking the figure's nearest elbow with a heel-of-the-palm strike.

The grunt was feminine, and Lyons was stunned to realize his assailant was female. His strike threw her arms to the side and the hands holding a Glock pistol struck the wall. He reacted instantly, striking downward with a knife-edge blow that hammered into the woman's wrist and knocked the gun to the floor.

With surprising reflexes the perpetrator spun and slammed a knee into the ex–LAPD detective's groin. He rolled one of his thighs inward to block the blow. Fingers raked at his eyes. He responded with a windmilling block followed by a straight punch like a power jab.

The woman threw herself backward, avoiding the blow easily. She catapulted into the bedroom she'd just emerged from. Lyons surged forward, following hard on her heels. She did a back handstand, then came down in a crouch. Her hands flew to where her pant leg met the top of her dark hiking boot.

Realizing she was grabbing for a holdout weapon, Lyons scrambled to close the difference. Even as he lunged he knew he wasn't going to make it in time. The figure came out of her crouch with a silver Detonics .45-caliber automatic in her gloved hands.

Kyrgyzstan

ENEMY VEHICLES FLARED like bonfires in violent conflagrations. Gary Manning raked the milling al Qaeda combatants with his machine gun as Hawkins methodically executed every gunman who came into his crosshairs.

Having used RPGs to disable every vehicle in the convoy, both Calvin James and Rafael Encizo traded their rocket launchers for Soviet-era submachine guns. Moving quickly under the cover fire, David McCarter prepared to lead the assault element down the cliff face to overwhelm any resistance.

"Move! Move! Move!" McCarter barked.

As one, the three-man fire team surged forward over the lip of the incline. The deployed lines were flung out in front of them. They ran face-first in an Australian-style rappel down the steep incline, one hand running the guideline, the other firing their weapons from the hip using a sling over the shoulder of their firing hand to steady the muzzle.

The loose gravel gave way in miniature avalanches under their feet as they sprinted down, the incline ropes whizzing through the gloves on their hand. The light from burning vehicles cast wild shadows and threw pillars of heat up toward them. It felt as if they were running straight into the open mouth of hell.

A figure with an AKM assault rifle appeared out of the smoke. Encizo shifted his muzzle across his front and caught the man with a short burst in the torso, putting him down. Without missing a stride, the Cuban-American combat diver vaulted the body and came off his rope onto the road.

McCarter ran up beside him, his AKS nestled in his shoulder and spitting bullets with a staccato burst. Another bearded terrorist absorbed the burst and crumpled. James came off his rope and took up his sector of fire, providing security on the far flank.

"Be advised," Barbara Price's voice cut in. "We have too much ground smoke and ambient heat for orbital imagery. We have no eyes at the moment."

"Copy," McCarter acknowledged. He turned toward Encizo and James. "Let's start at the lead vehicle and work our way down."

From above them Manning's machine gun had fallen silent. Hawkins's sniper rifle barked once, then was still.

At every vehicle they found dead terrorists and burning corpses. The ambush had been unleashed with brutal efficiency, leaving no survivors after the initial assault. Satisfied, McCarter informed Stony Man, then called his overwatch element down to the road.

"We're ready for phase bravo," he said simply. A burning truck at his back cast his sharp features in a slightly diabolical light. "Form up and let's roll."

Immediately, Phoenix Force formed a loose Ranger file, each soldier putting twenty yards between themselves. Calvin James, in the lead, took a GPS reading, noted the time and then set out up the center of the road at a fast clip.

For the next phase of the operation Phoenix Force would conduct an overland march for movement to target. To keep cover of darkness, they would have to maintain a tight pace. Their margin of error had been whittled down to a very slender gap.

In the hands of the IMU terrorists was an American contractor tasked with controlling Predator drones in the border region.

With terrorist reinforcements stopped while still en route, Phoenix Force was now prepared to make the overland hike to the location and free the American contractor who was being held hostage.

James set a rugged pace, leading the men straight up the road until they had crested the rise and started down the other side. Using a pace count perfected over long years of patrol and special reconnaissance missions he led them three miles before reorientating himself and cutting cross-country.

Following James's navigation, while McCarter doubled checked the GPS landmarks, Phoenix Force cut across the rugged terrain. As they dropped in altitude from the high mountain pass, sparse vegetation gave way to temperate forest. Saw grass and chokeberry bushes became interspersed with stands of thick dogwood and copses of coniferous trees, providing good cover for their movements as they drew closer to their target.

Finally, James called a halt at the team's predetermined rally point. The group huddled close together in the lee of a stand of tamarack pines. Below them an adobe-style walled compound was set on a stretch of valley floor in the middle of a small village. The road they had followed for part of their insertion after the ambush cut in from the west and ran directly through the hamlet. This late at night the only lights showing came from the compound. Overhead a low-pressure front had rolled in and stacked up like dirty cotton candy against the mountains.

Hawkins adjusted the ambient light levels on the passive receiver of his sniper scope, bringing the compound into a starker relief. Beside him Gary Manning had swapped out his night-vision goggles for IR binoculars, allowing him greater ocular clarity of the target site.

"I got three sentries," the Canadian muttered softly.

"That's my count," Hawkins confirmed. "Two at the east-facing driveway gate and one walking the wall to the rear of the compound."

McCarter keyed his com set. "You still have eyes or has the pressure front cut us off?"

"Be advised," Price replied immediately, "cloud cover has obscured our imagery."

"Understood." McCarter clicked off. "Any sign of the hostage?"

"Negative," Hawkins said.

"If the intel is spot-on, then he's down in the basement," Manning added, still scanning the scene with his IR binoculars.

"Shaking thing to bet a life on," James said.

"I agree," McCarter replied. "I think we're going to have infiltrate silent and identify before we commence with the takedown."

"The approaches are rough, just like the satellite showed. Coming down the hill on the far side will bring a damn avalanche down with us," Encizo put in.

"Yep," McCarter agreed. "I was hoping once we got on location we'd catch a break." He eyed the steep terrain surrounding them and funneling downward toward the terrorist compound and village. It was unforgiving. "But it looks like our luck is holding true to form."

"Straight down the road?" James asked.

"Straight down the road," McCarter answered.

Dominican Republic

CARL LYONS FLUNG himself to one side, and the Detonics Combat Master went off like a hand cannon in the confined space. The heavy .45-caliber slug snapped through the air and burned down the hallway before burying itself in a wall.

Hermann Schwarz spun around the wall and threw the chair in a rough lob. It arced out and landed, bouncing awkwardly. The interloper jerked back, flinching away from the flying furniture.

Lyons used the seconds to readjust himself and leap onto the masked figure. His hand caught her wrist just behind where the gun butt filled her palm. He surged forward, snapping his elbow around and driving it into the side of her head.

The masked female slumped under the blow, stunned. The compact automatic dropped out of her hand and fell loudly on the floor. Schwarz rushed into the room ready to back Lyons up. He looked down and saw the sprawled figure on the floor as Lyons pushed himself up.

"She go night-night?" he asked.

"Like a baby," Lyons replied, and picked up the pistol.

Out in the front room they heard the door being thrown open violently. Lyons spun and lifted his handgun.

"We're fine, Pol," Schwarz called out.

"Glad to hear it," Blancanales replied. "Guess I jumped to the wrong conclusion after seeing you walk into a building right before there's a gunshot." Blancanales walked in and looked down at the unconscious figure on the ground. "*Dios mios,* Ironman, we don't have time for you to start dating."

"You're getting to be a real old lady," Lyons muttered.

"Speaking of ladies," Schwarz said, "maybe we could ask this one some questions?"

"Suits me." Lyons nodded, and stuck the gun behind his back. "Let's get her up and put her in a chair."

Blancanales took her mask off to check the extent of Lyons's blow, and an attractive woman with mahogany skin and Caribbean features was revealed. Her head was covered with close-cropped, tight-knit rows of dark hair pulled back severely from her handsome face. Her temple was swelling where it had made contact with the sharp end of Lyons's elbow.

The woman came awake, still dazed while the three men pushed her down into a deep, comfortable chair in the living room that was so soft it would be impossible to quickly rise from. She sought to argue and perhaps fight, but Lyons laconically showed her her own pistol and she sat quietly, shooting daggers with her eyes.

"Anything?" Lyons asked after Blancanales had finished searching her.

The Puerco Rican nodded and held up empty hands. "Nothing."

Lyons nodded. "Check the room she was tossing," he instructed.

The big ex-cop regarded his prisoner while Blancanales moved back to the bedroom where they had first jumped the thief. Schwarz moved behind the woman and took her hands up, rolling her fingers across a glass he had taken from the kitchen, then setting it just out of reach on the table.

The woman squawked in protest at the liberty taken and spit out a long line of vulgarities. Lyons smirked in admiration at her profane grasp of the English language.

"Nice. You kiss your mother with that mouth?"

"My mother's dead, you *Yaquis* pig-screwing bastard!" the woman snapped.

Lyons didn't believe her for a second. "Everyone's got a hard luck story, sister. What's your name?"

"None of your business."

"Sure, you break into the house of my friend, try to steal stuff, and it's none of my business. But that's fine, little girl, we'll know who you are in a moment."

At the kitchen table Schwarz was quickly mixing a small amount of commercial glue taken from desk supplies in the apartment with common tap water. He worked methodically while the computer next to him began warming up.

"Where's your badge?" the woman demanded, trying to turn the tables.

Lyons smiled at her and lifted one big, blunt finger to his lips. "Sshh. You felt my badge upside your head just a minute ago."

"Someone will have heard that pistol shot," she warned. "They will call the police."

"In this neighborhood? In the middle of a riot? For a car backfire?" Lyons shook his head gently and the girl slumped into the chair.

Blancanales came back into the room carrying a black canvas backpack. "She found the safe," he said, and dumped her pack out onto the table next to where Schwarz was working.

"She crack it?" Lyons demanded.

"Nope, but she would have," Blancanales answered. "I found this."

The Puerto Rican Special Forces veteran lifted out a black electronic device the size of a commercial Pocketbook computer with two coaxial cables dangling from it. The implement was a top-of-the-line digital safecracker. Lyons let out a long, slow whistle of appreciation.

"That's not exactly gear I would associate with a common street burglar," he said.

The woman looked away. From the kitchen table behind her Schwarz scanned his fingerprint sample into the safehouse computer. "I'm sending it through now," he said into his com link.

The Stony Man supercomputers would compute a match at speeds that far outstripped the power of the field station equipment.

"Why don't you save me some time, lady," Lyons snapped. "No one's buying the burglar act."

"Who are you?" the woman asked, voice steady.

Lyons opened his mouth to reply but was interrupted by Schwarz, the man's voice thick with sardonic irony.

"Who are we, Ms. Felicity Castillo?" Schwarz laughed. "As of now, we're your contacts." He turned toward Lyons. "She's one of ours."

Lyons got a look of disgust on his face. "I already hate this fucking town."

CHAPTER SIX

Kyrgyzstan

"Phoenix to Stony Man," McCarter said. There was only silence in answer. Surprised by the lack of response, McCarter put his finger up against his communications device, tapping it slightly. "Stony?" he repeated.

There was still no answer. He looked over to where Calvin James squatted in the dark, weapon at the ready. James looked at him expectantly and the Briton nodded once.

"Phoenix to Stony," James tried. The medic shook his head. "Nothing."

Each of the remaining team members attempted to make contact, but none of their geo-sat uplinks were working. In the space of a heartbeat Phoenix Force found itself cut off from the outside world.

McCarter turned toward the hulking form of Gary Manning. "Jammer?"

The big Canadian Special Forces veteran nodded his head slowly. "Sure. It's possible. But it'd have to be a little more upscale than we'd expect from a crew of local clowns like the ones we're supposed to hit. I suppose it's just as possible we have low-earth-orbit interference."

"The plot deepens," Encizo muttered.

"We still going to make the meet?" Hawkins asked.

McCarter nodded. "I'll put Hawkins out on flank in an overwatch position. Manning will move forward, then set up the machine gun for a secondary angle of fire. The rest of us will go in paranoid."

"Let's do it," James agreed.

Phoenix Force moved out in a slow accordion formation toward their RZ, or rendezvous point. U.S. intelligence had set up a meeting with a local indigenous asset who would provide them with materials and transportation their rapid response infiltration had made impossible to bring with them.

In this case a local smuggler friendly to Western money had agreed to supply them with a heavy-bodied diesel engine truck of the type used by local military units. Calvin James carried a fanny pack filled with local currency in the sum of eighteen thousand U.S. dollars.

Such pay-to-play operations were inherently dangerous for obvious reasons, but were common in tribal regions removed from the influence of a centralized government. Cold hard cash had become as much of a tool in the paramilitary operators' arsenal as carbines and shape charges.

The three-man fire team consisting of McCarter, James and Encizo slid into position behind a screen of sturdy mountain shrubs with oily, cold-resistant leaves and sticklike branches. Ahead of them they saw the old truck sitting beside the dirt road that eventually led into town.

The night was silent except for the wind through the pines. Nothing moved out beyond their perimeter. McCarter lifted his weapon and utilized his night scope in precise patterns, covering vectors in a methodical manner. He could detect no sign of obvious human presence.

James leaned in close and whispered into the Briton's ear. "You see the driver door is open?"

McCarter nodded. A bar of shadow separated the gloomy metal gray of the door from the body of the cab. The hair on the back of the ex–SAS commando's neck began to rise in almost preternatural warning.

"Feeling hinky," he muttered.

"Big time," James agreed.

Encizo shifted his weight and leaned in toward the other men. "I'll slide up and check it out."

McCarter frowned as he realized the exposure the man was vulnerable to, but then nodded. If the plan was going to unfold, they needed the truck. Giving up on the truck at this juncture meant giving up on the hostage. He wasn't willing to do that until he had exhausted every possibility.

Encizo carefully rotated his Soviet-era submachine gun around on its sling until it hung muzzle down across his back. He pulled his silenced pistol from a shoulder holster on his web gear and silently disappeared into the dark.

McCarter waited patiently, James at his side. The two men scanned the darkness as clouds began to gather overhead, further obscuring the terrain. Long, tense minutes later James quietly nudged McCarter with his elbow.

The Phoenix Force leader turned away from his survey of the far side of the roads and watched the dark shadow of Rafael Encizo slide out of the ditch next to the back of the truck. Both men gripped their weapons tightly.

Encizo moved like water flowing over the ground, staying low to present a subdued silhouette as he edged toward the front of the big truck. Carefully using his free hand to peel back the canvas tarp covering the cargo bed of the five-ton vehicle, he held his position, peering inside. Satisfied, he gently lowered the edge of the tarp back into place and crept forward.

Moving in silent increments he approached the open door to the vehicle cab. The blunt muzzle of his pistol silencer led the way like a hunting dog on point. He reached up with his free hand and made contact with the truck, checking for trip wires or other obvious booby traps.

Suddenly he put a combat foot on the running board and stepped up, swinging the door open and leveling the pistol. Behind him McCarter and James tensed, mentally prepared for a sudden hellstorm of gunfire.

Encizo froze for a moment in the open doorway, his broad-shouldered back orientated toward his teammates, making it impossible for them to see past him. After a long, pregnant pause, the Cuban turned and hauled something out of the truck before jumping down.

McCarter swore silently as he saw the limp body strike the hard-packed dirt road like a sack of loose meat. His eyes ran over the corpse with an expert forensic eye. The head was obviously concave on one side, either from a point-blank firearm shot or some blunt instrument.

If the ambush was going to come it was going to come now, he realized. His finger took up the slack on the smooth metal curve of his trigger. Beside him he felt James stiffen in readiness. Across the little clearing Encizo had taken a knee with his back to the truck. His pistol was back in its holster and his submachine gun was now up and ready in his hands.

Nothing happened.

Slowly, McCarter felt his adrenaline begin to bleed off as they weren't hit. After a minute he tapped James. When the ex-SEAL turned toward him he gave the man the hand-and-arm signal for a perimeter sweep. Instantly, James stepped backward into the tree at the bottom of the defilade and began a 360-degree search of the rendezvous zone.

McCarter rose into a crouch and jogged over to where Encizo waited by the corpse. The bulk of the ancient five-ton truck loomed above them. As he drew closer he saw the bloody hole that filled the left side of their contact's face.

If a bullet had entered through the driver's window it would have struck the truck occupant in just such a fashion, he realized.

"Is this our guy?" Encizo asked him.

"Don't know," McCarter whispered back. "We had location, time and code exchanges."

Both men turned at the same time, weapons ready. Calvin James appeared in front of them, then squatted. "It's clear out to seventy-five yards in these woods. Beyond that anyone watching us would either be down the road or up in elevation."

Encizo got up and investigated the vehicle cab as McCarter shook the corpse down for any useful information. James, a trained medic and forensic investigator, performed a cursory inspection of the major head wound.

"Low velocity, larger caliber."

"Pistol?"

"Almost certainly. Maybe one of your favorites—a Browning Hi-Power or even a .45 with a silencer."

"How can you tell a silencer?" McCarter asked as he pulled several items out of the dead man's clothes.

"Can't be one hundred percent sure," James admitted. "But the entrance wound was pretty damn traumatic for there to be no exit wound. That suggests a soft-nosed slug with a subsonic load."

"High-end electronic jammers and silencer kills?" McCarter grumbled. "We stepping on someone else's toes?"

"Chinese?" James offered.

"Chinese gear beating Bear's electronics?" McCarter shook his head. "Not a chance."

"Curioser and curioser," James replied.

"Hey, guys," Encizo said from the cab. "Get a load of this."

Dominican Republic

THE WOMAN SPUN in the chair, obviously surprised by Schwarz's revelation.

The Stony Man operative smirked back at her. "Let's keep it simple," the Able Team electronics genius said. "Skip your transient codes and go right to your mother parole." He paused, then said, "India Delta Six."

The woman, tension draining from her limbs, frowned and sighed. "Delta India Nine," she replied.

"I was almost shot by one of our own stringers?" Lyons demanded. "Christ, that happens too often. Fine. Where the hell's Smith?"

The woman turned back and looked at him. "I don't know. He never showed up to our meet. I went to the secondary rendezvous and he didn't show for that, either. I began to suspect the security service for the government had realized he was more than a law-enforcement liaison and did away with him."

"So you broke into this place?" Schwarz asked.

"I've been here before," she replied. "It seemed the most obvious place he would have kept information about me. I wanted to erase my trail before internal security followed up on me."

"What was the last thing he was working on?" Lyons demanded.

"A meet for tonight with a middleman for some third party. Maybe about drugs, maybe weapons. Either way he thought it would get him a lead into which elements within this regime were working both sides of the street."

Lyons frowned, locked eyes with Schwarz over the top of the woman's head. "I guess we know where we go next," he said.

Schwarz nodded.

Stony Man Farm, Virginia

INSIDE THE computer center, Professor Huntington Wethers let out a long, low whistle and set his cold pipe down on the desktop next to his keyboard. A tall, laconic black man with almost gaunt features and salt-and-pepper hair, he was the ultimate academic.

He preformed his tasks of research, logistics and information networking with methodical, almost mechanical efficiency. He was not an artist making wild leaps of intuition like his younger counterpart on the cyberteam, Akira Tokaido. Rather he crossed his t's and dotted his i's like a probate lawyer until every fact or isolated bit of information was accounted for and placed neatly into its appropriate box before being checked off.

Wethers made connections, he found links, he built bridges one binary bit at a time between data streams until scrambled mosaics became crystal-clear pictures. In his usual understated way, he had made another connection.

"Bear?" Wethers asked over one bony shoulder.

From beside the bubbling coffeepot where he was assembling a table of organizational equipment for the field teams Kurtzman looked up. "Go ahead, Hunt," he growled. "You got something?"

"I have a rather odd connection between what our teams are doing," Wethers answered.

Curiosity piqued, Kurtzman maneuvered his wheelchair out from behind his desk and toward the former college professor. "Between the Caribbean and central Asia? A connection? Do tell."

"Could be a fluke," Wethers warned. "One of those odd coincidences people use to justify a belief in fate."

Kurtzman rolled up next to him and grunted. "No such thing as coincidences in our world. What do you have?"

"Our missing FBI agent in Santo Domingo and our missing contractor in Kyrgyzstan?"

"Okay?"

"They're brothers."

Carmen Delahunt burst into the room through the door leading to the communications center. "We've got a problem," she said without preamble. "We just lost our uplink with Phoenix."

"Weather?" Kurtzman asked.

"Weather shouldn't have been a problem. I ran a forensic diagnostic on the signal and I got shadow chatter in the low-end megahertz range."

"Crap," Kurtzman swore.

"High-end jammers," Wethers agreed.

Kyrgyzstan

MCCARTER MOVED IN a crouch through the graveyard. Behind him three other members of Phoenix Force were spread out in a loose wedge formation, weapons up. Above them, hidden on the ridge, Hawkins tracked their progress from a sniper overwatch position.

McCarter dodged in and out of headstones, skirting graves torn open by artillery rounds. He averted his gaze from mummified husks of old corpses and tried not step on any of the skeletal remains that lay scattered like children's toys. Rafael Encizo muttered something low and in Spanish under his breath as his foot came down in a spot of a decomposing corpse.

In five minutes everything had gone to shit.

The high-altitude wind had stacked eastern storm clouds up on the elevated geography behind them and a cold rain had begun to fall. In the same instant contact with their communication satellite had vanished. Then as they made their initial approach into the village they had realized a battle had just occurred within the small populated area.

They were now operating blindly in an extremely hazardous environment. The thought of abandoning the mission had never been discussed. There was still a hostage out there in the middle of this mess.

The falling rain was a blanket of white noise. The Phoenix Force warriors remained ghostly figures as they traversed the cemetery. The weight of their weapons were reassuring in their hands. They breathed in the humid air, feeding their bodies through the exertion.

The first rifle crack was muted and distant. Mc-Carter went down to one knee behind a headstone. Instantly, James did the same, followed by Manning and Encizo.

The Briton strained his ears against the muffling effect of the heavy rain. He heard another single shot of rifle caliber. A burst of submachine gun fire answered it, and McCarter saw the flash of muzzle fire flare out of the dark rectangle of a window in the second story of a compound ahead of them.

McCarter quickly ascertained that none of the fire was being directed toward their position.

"What the hell is going on?"

"Internal coup for command?" James offered in a whisper. "Could be a blood feud, I guess. Everything is tribal politics this far up in the mountains."

McCarter nodded. "Let's try to use the chaos to our advantage."

They were about fifty yards from the edge of the settlement where thatch and mud hovels surrounded the more built-up areas in a loose ring broken by animal pens. McCarter wiped rain water out of his eyes and looked toward the irrigation ditch that had been his original infiltration route.

He scowled. He wasn't bursting with anticipation to slide into the muddy, waist-deep water of the ditch. Another burst of submachine gun fire came from the compound's second story and was answered by two controlled single shots.

He rose from behind the headstone and began moving toward the village proper. Behind him his teammates rose and followed, keeping their formation loose and broken but still maintaining overlapping fields of fire.

The team dodged the open graves, artillery craters and headstones like runners navigating hurdles on the quarter-mile track. The soaked ground swallowed up the impact of their footsteps, spraying water with every step they took.

McCarter reached the round wall of a mud hovel and went around one side of it. He peeked out and saw an unpaved alley running deeper into the village. Bullet holes riddled the wall of one long, low, mud-brick building. A mongrel lay, shot dead, in the weeds beside it.

"I'm going to move forward then wave you up once it's clear," he instructed James. The ex-SEAL nodded as Encizo and Manning took up defensive positions to secure the Briton's infiltration.

McCarter pushed forward. The alley ran past the back of the compound several blocks up. Trash bins lay overturned in the muddy street and rubbish was heaped everywhere. McCarter stayed close to one side of the building and edged his way carefully into the street. His eyes squinted against the rain, searching windows and doorways for any sign of movement.

There was no more gunfire. The rain was even louder adjacent to the structures of the village. It hammered onto shanty roofs of corrugated tin and ran off into makeshift gutters, forming rushing waterfalls that splashed out into the street every few yards. McCarter wiped water from his eyes and stalked farther into the tangle of dank and twisting streets.

He crossed an open area between two one-story buildings and sensed motion. He spun, bringing up his carbine. A black-and-white goat on the end of a frayed rope looked up and bleated at him. The little animal's fur was matted down with exposure to the rain. There was a little hutch built behind the staked goat. From the doorway of the hutch a slender arm and hand sprawled in the mud. There was a bracelet of hammered metal around the delicate wrist and the fingers had frozen in rigor mortis.

McCarter looked up the street in both directions but saw nothing. He crouched and reached across with his left hand to his right boot and pulled a Gerber Guardian straight blade from his boot sheath. He stepped into the pen, ignoring the squish of mud and shit in the straw under his feet.

The animal bleated again and McCarter shushed it reflexively. He reached down and slid the double-edged blade into the loop of twine around the animal's neck. He flicked his wrist and severed the rope. The goat walked to the edge of the pen and began munching on the straw that had been out of its reach before.

McCarter slowly sank to one knee. He slid the Gerber back into its boot sheath and bent forward, looking into the hutch. The shadows were deep in the tiny space. He saw the arm running back into the dark. McCarter blinked and the shadow resolved into the shape of a woman.

She was young and dead, with opaque eyes staring out at him. There was a bloody open gash in his forehead where a bullet had punched in. He looked away.

McCarter rose slowly out of his crouch. He heard a man call out several streets over and he froze. The language was French. Someone farther out from that answered him in the same language. Anger made McCarter grit his teeth. He swallowed a lump of bile that had formed like a rock in his throat.

Despite his anger he was more concerned by the mystery of the European voice. He had to keep his mind on the operation, focus his thoughts.

The men who had murdered this woman were human, just like him. They were killers, just like him. But they were nothing like him, nor he anything like them. To reduce violence to an evil unto itself, without regard to the circumstances that spawned it, was a philosophical arrogance McCarter could not stomach.

Securing his grip on the butt of his pistol, he walked over to the edge of the animal pen between the two houses and looked out into the narrow street. The incessant rain dimpled the puddles with the weight of its falling drops. He opened a little gate and stepped out into the street, leaving it open behind him.

He crouched, turned and made eye contact with James, who nodded. As his Phoenix Force colleagues shuffled forward behind him he hunted the darkness for unfamiliar shapes. The team had stumbled onto the middle of something, he knew, and he needed to get a handle on it and fast.

Once Phoenix Force was in position he began to move toward the compound, walking quickly with his weapon ready. He reached the edge of a round, one-story silo and looked carefully around it. A short passageway between buildings linked the main street with the secondary alley McCarter now navigated.

About twenty yards down a man stood with his back to McCarter. The ex–SAS commando narrowed his eyes in suspicion. The man wasn't dressed like a rough mountain tribesman. He wore a night suit bristling with all the paraphernalia and accoutrements of the modern special-operations soldier. For some reason only night-vision goggles were missing.

McCarter lifted his carbine in a slow, smooth gesture. He straightened his arm and placed the sights squarely on the occipital lobe of the terrorist soldier's skull. His finger curled around the trigger of the carbine and took up the slack.

The combatant looked to his left and lifted a fist above his head in some prearranged signal. McCarter shuffled sideways across the narrow mouth of the alley, his weapon tracking the man's back with every step as he moved.

Once on the other side of the alleyway, McCarter slid around a corner and put his back against the wall and turned his face back toward the dirt lane he had just crossed. He drew the Beretta 92-F in an even, deliberate motion. He held the pistol up so that the muzzle was poised beside the hard plane of his cheek bone. He bent slightly at the knee and crouched before risking a glance around the edge of the building.

He looked over to where James was crouched motionless behind cover. He put a finger to his lips in a pantomime for quiet then pointed at his own eyes and at the European operative. James nodded once.

McCarter prepared for his kill.

CHAPTER SEVEN

Dominican Republic

The sawmill squatted on the banks of the Ozama River. Silent as a mausoleum, the building stood surrounded by warehouses and industrial structures now fallen dark, or burned to rubble in the wake of successive riots and civil unrest. Rain fell, dirty gray from the sky.

Rosario Blancanales drew his mouth into a tight line. He scanned the building and the area around it through his night-vision goggles, searching for telltale smeary silhouettes in the monochromatic green of the high-tech device. He saw nothing. The sounds of traffic came to him from the other areas of the city, muted across the distance. Close by, his ears detected only the whisper of cold wind skipping across the polluted river.

Outfitted from the cache at the safehouse, Able Team had arrived at the meeting set up by the missing FBI agent.

Next to the Puerto Rican Special Forces veteran, Lyons scrutinized the building, determining his approach. To the rear of the building loading docks with big roll-up bay doors sat shut and locked.

On the side of the building closest to him stood a maintenance door set on a short flight of concrete steps. Off in the distance, Lyons heard the soft thump-thump of a relief agency helicopter cruising low over the city.

Lyons again scanned the area through his goggles.

Santo Domingo was a city locked down under martial law, threatened by civil unrest and criminal gangs threatening to overrun their squalid ghettos. Police units patrolled in armored personnel carriers, and army checkpoints secured every major road and highway leading into the city.

Able Team had taken a grave risk by going armed into the streets of a supposedly allied nation dealing with the threat of a violent insurrection. An insurrection with increasingly apparent ties to the worldwide narcotics syndicates. Moving incognito had proved nearly impossible.

Lyons moved forward, scrambling out of the empty drainage ditch running parallel to the abandoned sawmill's main building. He approached a chain-link fence and dropped down, removing wire cutters from his combat harness. With deft, practiced movements Lyons snipped an opening and bent back one edge.

Blancanales held the wire up while Schwarz remained outside the building to provide security and surveillance.

Lyons slid through head first and popped up on the other side. Blancanales crawled through and they began their approach. Traveling in a wide crescent designed to take them as far as possible from the silent street, Lyons approached the single maintenance entrance on the building's side. He scanned the triple row of windows set above the building's ground floor for any sign of movement. As he neared the building Lyons pulled a Glock 17 from his shoulder rig. The weapon had come from the safehouse armory but was not his first choice in handguns.

Lyons crab-walked up the short flight of concrete stairs leading to the door, clicking the selector switch off safety on his pistol as he moved. Behind him Blancanales tracked the muzzle of his own pistol through zones of fire.

Reaching the door, Lyons pulled a lock-pick gun from a cargo pocket and slid it expertly home into the lock as Blancanales maintained security.

The ex–LAPD detective squeezed the trigger on the lock device and heard the bolt securing the door snap back. Replacing the lock-pick gun, Lyons put a hand on the door, holding his 9 mm pistol up and ready. He looked over at Blancanales, who nodded wordlessly.

Before he moved, Lyons took a final scan of his surroundings. The industrial wasteland was eerily still. Taking a breath, he turned the handle and pulled open the door.

Stony Man Farm, Virginia

BARBARA PRICE CRADLED her phone next to her ear and took the clipboard and pen from the Farm's head of security, a former Marine, Buck Greene. On the other end of the com link Hal Brognola queried Price further.

"There has to be more than that, Barb," he said.

"I know, Hal," she said into the phone. Signing the requisition form, she nodded once to Greene and handed the clipboard back. "We don't have any other connection besides the fact that the two men were brothers. No other link. Just seems strange."

"All right," Brognola relented. "I'll call the director and see if anything about the man's brother came forward during the agent's security background checks."

"Great," Price said. "When you get it, just shoot it to Delahunt on her email. We'll feed it into Wethers's search from there. I was thinking that for the brother to get his job as a civilian contractor flying those drones he had to have been in the military, right? Air Force or Army."

Seeing where she was going, Brognola grunted his agreement. "Right. I'll check to see if the other brother had some military time before joining the FBI. But how are we doing with commo for Phoenix Force?"

"We're almost positive it's a high-end electronics jammer, but whose, we can't say yet. Bear's working on trying to get a relay station from Bagram he can para-drop in to try to outboost the hostile signal." Price paused. "No promises, though."

"Fine. Keep me up to date and I'll try to shake something loose on these two brothers for you."

"Thanks, Hal," she said, and hung up.

Price looked down at the cell in her hand and frowned. Both Phoenix Force and Able Team had been scrambled at the last minute on these operations, a situation ripe for intervention by that bastard Murphy and his immutable law. There had been no time for advance homework or advance preparations, and she prayed to heaven it wasn't going to cost her the lives of her men in the field.

Dominican Republic

LYONS STEPPED THROUGH the black mouth of the open door and into the darkened interior of the building. He shuffled smoothly to one side and sank into a tight crouch, pistol up. Blancanales stepped through and let the door swing shut behind him. Lyons quickly scanned the hall in both directions. It was empty. Rising, he began moving down the corridor toward the rear of the building. Covering their rear, Blancanales followed.

The sawmill was oppressively still and quiet around them. The perimeter hallway ran the length of the structure, with doors leading to the building's interior spaced at intervals along the inside wall. At the far end of the hallway Lyons could make out the heavy steel of a fire door that would open up onto stairs.

The intelligence of the building layout had been spotty. Aaron Kurtzman had been unable to pull up engineer blueprints during his rushed info search. All Lyons knew was that according to Smith's contact the FBI agent was supposed to tag along with a minor street crook and the man's bodyguards to a meet in an office suite on the second floor.

The sound of his breath loud in his own ears, Lyons entered the stairwell. He craned his neck, looking upward. Nothing moved on the stairs or crouched in the gloomy landings. He tracked his scanning vision with the muzzle of the Glock 17. The hair on the back of Lyons's neck stood up like the hackles of a dog.

Blancanales put his shoulder at a right angle to the big ex-cop's back, his own weapon up.

There was a smell of dust and disuse hanging heavy in the air. Faintly beneath that was the slight odor of machine oil coming up from the sawmill floor. Lyons's straining ears detected only the beating of his own heart. He placed the reinforced soles of his boots carefully on the first metal rung of the building's skeletal framed staircase and began to climb.

He edged around the curve of the stair, Blancanales right behind him. The raised grip of the pistol's butt tight in his palm, he kept his Weaver stance tight, ready to react to the slightest motion. Smith's contact was an established veteran of life as a hunted man. Security this apparently lax was inexplicable in such a man.

Reaching the second-floor landing, Lyons snuggled up tight against the fire door on that level as Blancanales took a position. He pressed his back against wall beside the door handle. The seal of the landing door was too tight for him to use a fiber optics surveillance cable bore scope. The heavy steel door effectively muted any potential sound coming from the second-floor hallway.

Gritting his teeth, Lyons nodded once and Blancanales pulled open the door. The ex-cop darted his head around the edge. He was met with silence and darkness. The hallway ran for several yards, office doors on one side, dark windows facing the parking lot on the other. The hall turned in a L-break at the far end toward the front of the building.

Lyons moved down the center of the hallway, ready to drop prone or respond with deadly fire at the slightest threat. Behind him Blancanales edged into the hallway, weapon up.

CHAPTER EIGHT

Kyrgyzstan

In the street a second black-clad European had joined his partner. This one held an ancient AKS submachine gun and together the two men jogged quickly up the alley toward McCarter's position. McCarter ducked his head back around the edge of the building. He skipped several steps to the side and slid into the recessed arch of a doorway. The two combatants had now cut McCarter off from the rest of Phoenix Force.

As the men rounded the corner he could hear them talking to one another in low, excited voices. Both of them turned down the alley in the direction of the IMU compound and McCarter's hiding spot.

McCarter stepped out of the doorway and into the rain and leveled his Beretta 92-F as the men stumbled up against each other in surprise at his sudden appearance. The pistol spit a single time even as McCarter extended his arm, and the terrorist holding the AKS went down. The rain had plastered the gunman's shirt to his muscular frame, and McCarter could clearly see where the blunt round smashed into the prominent ridge of the man's sternum and punched through it.

The terrorist fighter tripped over backward under the impact, going down. He dropped his submachine gun and it fell across his legs as he went down. Beside him the second SKS-armed terrorist struggled to bring his longer weapon to bear as McCarter swiveled at the hips and brought the Beretta around at point-blank range.

The man's eyes were startlingly white as they bulged outward in his terror. The two men were so close McCarter could see the yellowing of the man's sclera and the bright red blood vessels in the eye there. McCarter's round powered through his face at the bridge of the nose with a loud smack that sounded wet and sharp even in the falling rain.

The yellow-tinged eyes rolled up backward in his face and the man sagged into the mud. His weapon dropped from limp fingers and fell to the ground. The combatant crumpled over and dropped face-first into the muck.

Even as the second gunmen fell, McCarter spun, weapon ready and tracking for any witnesses to the executions. He heard no alarm, saw no movement and took no fire. He quickly lowered his gun and went to one knee in the muck where the corpses were pouring blood from their ragged wounds.

James raced over and reached down with his left hand, snatching one of the dead men up by his shirt collar. He dragged the body over to the edge of the narrow street and laid him against the lee of the building before quickly returning to the center of the alley to retrieve the second gunman. While McCarter guarded his actions on one side, Encizo and Manning took the other. He hauled the limp corpse over and placed it beside its brother against the building.

James looked around. Seeing what he wanted, he looped the AKM over one shoulder and grabbed up several overturned trash bins. Without preamble he covered the bodies with soggy garbage and then placed the empty cans over them. The camouflage would only withstand the most rudimentary of inspections, but he hoped that anyone simply looking down the alley in the rain and dark would miss the bodies.

McCarter took the AKS into his hands and began to jog down the alley in the direction of the compound.

THE COMPOUND FORMED one side of the center of the Kyrgyzstan village. On the other side of the compound was the walled mosque of mud brick and the accompanying *madrassa*, or religious school. A long, low building had a Kyrgyzstan flag hanging limply and either side of the street on the fourth side of the village square was taken up by the most prosperous of the village stockyard vendors.

The Phoenix warriors moved forward, suspicious at the absence of civilian locals moving around in response to the gunfire. The corpses of the Europeans had provided little intelligence.

McCarter peeked around the back of a combination gas station and mechanic's garage. The station bore the logo of a Russian company, which was unsurprising given the company's dominance in the region, most especially in nearby former Soviet republics.

During McCarter's approach more sporadic gunfire had sounded, triggering another burst from the compound's second floor. The team moved carefully toward the garage positioned beside the compound across from the mosque. A mess of fifty-five-gallon oil drums had been placed haphazardly in back of the building and McCarter wound his way into these as he approached the structure.

Rainwater shimmered in oily rainbows on the lids

of the barrels and they felt greasy under his touch. A dim yellow bulb burned above the back door to the garage. The door sagged on its ancient hinges and its paint peeled badly. The knob was burnished metal that looked slick from the continuous rainfall.

McCarter carefully wound his way through the barrels and toward the door. Manning sank to one knee and brought his heavy machine gun up to cover their rear approach as Encizo and James fanned out. Somewhere on the elevation beyond the village boundary Hawkins tracked their progress through his sniper scope.

As he moved, the Phoenix Force leader constantly reevaluated his understanding of the situation. Such analytical skills had been the margin between life and death for McCarter many times in the past. The IMU terrorists had taken over control of the village and used it as a staging area for their operations. Now a force of European commandos had entered the village and initiated hostilities.

McCarter doubted the Europeans were government agents on some related mission of counterterror or hostage rescue. There were no supporting helicopters or other aircraft. Such a frontal assault seemed far more likely to get a hostage executed than rescued. Rather, what they had witnessed so far had all the hallmarks of a frontal infantry attack designed for pure attrition.

McCarter could find no good reason for why Europeans would want to capture and hold an extremist village in the central Asian mountain. It was unsurprising that IMU security formations inside the village amounted to little more than a well-armed street gang. What was strange was the complete lack of evidence of Kyrgyzstan national forces other than the craters left by artillery rounds. Had the regional commander completely abdicated control to tribal elements?

A burst of fire erupted from inside the garage. The sound of a Kalashnikov firing was unmistakable to McCarter. A flurry of rounds struck the wall along the second story of the compound. Bullets tore into the clay-brick structure already tattooed with the scars of weapons fire. A window was shattered and glass tinkled.

Come on, McCarter thought. He signaled Encizo.

The Cuban rose out of his crouch behind the oil barrel and began jogging across the short distance to the back door. The submachine gun was up and held tight in his fists. A short burst of submachine gun fire lashed out from the compound in answer and raked the side of the building.

As the rounds struck the garage Encizo ran up and kicked the flimsy door off its moorings. The door exploded inward off its hinges, splintering under the impact of the combat diver's big boot tread. Leading with his AKS submachine gun, he burst into the building.

A 1980s red Toyota hatchback was up on the racks above a service pit. Its windows were busted out and its frame riddled with stray machine-gun fire. Encizo ducked down underneath the raised vehicle to get a better look inside the unlit garage bay.

He saw two men hunkered down behind the concrete walls on either side of a bullet-riddled service bay door. They spun, bringing up AKM assault rifles as he burst in on them. Their expressions were almost comically startled.

McCarter raked them both with ComBloc rounds from the Soviet submachine gun. He stitched a line of slugs across one terrorist gunman's chest.

The racket of his firing was deafening in the confined space of the room. Shell casings arched out of the weapon's oversize ejection port and spilled across the floor. They bounced across the oil-stained concrete and rolled into the open mouth of the service pit under the red Toyota. The muzzle on the submachine climbed with the recoil of Encizo's continuous blasts, and the tail end of his burst buried four slugs in the second terrorist fighter's head.

James came in through the shattered doorway and curled around the jamb to cover Encizo's entry. A wild tribesman with an AKM was running forward, trying to get a bead on the attacking Encizo. James's subgun rattled in his hands and the man went down hard. The gloom was so deep in the room that each burst of automatic gunfire lit up the room like a strobe light, casting weird shadows across bullet-pocked walls and the dimpled metal body of the red Toyota.

The terrorist's skull bounced crudely off the wall, leaving a smear of crimson syrup and gray brain matter clinging to the wall as he slid down. Encizo eased up on the trigger of the subgun and turned the weapon back on the first terrorist. Blood leaked out of his slack mouth and trickled down both sides of his chin.

James fired a neat 3-round burst into him then turned and repeated the procedure with the second terrorist. A glass bottle half full of grain alcohol slid out of the dead man's hand and rattled on the floor. Liquor rushed out of the bottle and mixed with the growing pools of red.

The stink of burned cordite filled James's nose. Smoke trailed up from the muzzle of the submachine gun as beside him Encizo shifted his eyes around the room.

Outside in the street they heard Manning suddenly open up with his machine gun.

Dominican Republic

BLANCANALES MOVED as silently as his considerable skills allowed, but to his own adrenaline-enhanced ears, his footfalls echoed loudly. Just in front of him, reaching the bend in the hallway, Lyons took a rapid look around the corner. Along this stretch, doorways marked both sides of the hall at intermittent lengths.

Halfway down the hallway he picked out a crumpled form through his night-vision goggles. From the green smear under the still shape, Lyons could tell the figure had lost a lot of blood, and recently, as the signature still held a good amount of heat. Instinctively, Lyons snapped his line of sight upward, scanning the corridor for any sign of movement. Seeing none, Lyons slid around the corner and into the passage, Blancanales creeping along behind him.

The heat register could only mean the downed figure was either still alive or had been struck down just minutes before. Keeping low, Lyons moved forward. His nostrils flared under the saddle of the night-vision goggles. The reek of cordite was heavy on the stale air of the abandoned sawmill.

Coming up to the body, Lyons looked it over quickly, poised to strike at the first sign of movement. Blancanales sidled up next to him, primed for combat, and regarded the corpse.

"Stay frosty, Gadgets," Blancanales subvocalized into his throat mike to Schwarz. "We've found body count."

"Copy," Schwarz replied from his overwatch position outside the sawmill. "No movement yet on the perimeter."

"Out," Blancanales acknowledged.

In front of them the figure remained still. Reaching out with his free hand, Lyons felt for a pulse on the neck but found none. He peered down, straining to make out facial features in the ambivalent light of the NVGs. The figure was male. Thick dreadlocks framed a full beard that fell across a broad swell of chest. He was dressed in street clothes. There was a folding-stock paratrooper model AKS-74 trapped under the man's body.

Lyons touched the barrel. The metal was cool. The weapon had not been fired. Keeping his eyes up, scanning the hallway, Lyons used his fingers to probe the corpse, trying to ascertain the source of his injuries. The face was intact, the torso clear of wounds. Frowning, Lyons felt the back of the man's head.

His fingers came away wet.

The location on the back of the head was called the medulla oblongata, Latin for "stem of the rose." Put simply, it was the place where the spinal cord merged with the back of skull. It was the collective location for all of the nerves of the central nervous system. The hypothalamus hung there like a grape cluster, regulating breath and the beating of the heart. In the special-operations community, a shot to the medulla oblongata was known as "popping the grape" and was a preferred method of neutralizing subjects from behind.

This hadn't been a sloppy assassination. The dead man had been coolly dispatched from up close and personal by someone with the nerves of a professional killer.

Lyons rose and stepped over the corpse. The man had been killed directly in front of a door on the outer side of the hallway. Intelligence hadn't been specific as to which office on the second floor was Smith's destination.

Lyons put his hand on the office door. Behind him Blancanales eased into position, weapon up. Lyons pushed against the door and it swung open easily under his touch.

Lyons glided into the room, pistol tracking ahead of him.

The space was a reception area leading, presumably, to a private office farther back. The room had been stripped of furniture when the last owners of the building had pulled out ahead of increasing violence and the folding of the timber market to Colombian interests. There were no pictures on the walls, no furniture or filing cabinets set up. Overhead, exposed wiring hung down like snakes from a ceiling stripped bare of light fixtures.

Bodies lay scattered around the room like the discarded toys of spoiled children. Through the heat-sensitive NVGs, the walls looked as if they had been splattered with fluorescent paint from the spilled blood. The reek of cordite was overwhelming in the tightly confined space. Spent shell casings pressed up against Lyons's feet as he moved through the room. Four corpses were tossed with careless abandon around the enclosure.

Blancanales stepped in and squatted by the door frame, his weapon up.

More of the folding-stock AKS-74s lay in hands quickly cooling in death. The office was a stinking abattoir filled with the stench of torn flesh and the copper tang of pooling blood. Lyons kept his eyes trained on the doorway leading into the inner recesses of the suite. His silent recon had revealed a surprising turn of events. It was time to adapt, to improvise, to overcome. Carefully, Lyons crouched. He secured an assault rifle by its pistol grip, tugging it free from its owner's dead fingers.

Tucking the skeletal buttstock into his hip, Lyons ensured the safety was disengaged. Once outfitted, he holstered his handgun. Safely tucking his pistol away freed his hands, and Lyons snapped down the folding stock of the paratrooper carbine to make it more manageable in the enclosed environment. Things were ugly now. Able Team had been thrown a bloody curve ball, and he was determined to take it in stride.

There was an IR penlight built into the goggles. When activated, it shone like a flashlight in the lenses of the night-vision device, visible only in the infrared spectrum. Using it, Lyons quickly determined that none of the dead was the FBI agent Smith.

Lyons stood, slowly unfolding from the crouch he had used to navigate the room. The soles of his boots were tacky with blood. Keeping the AKS tight against his torso, he padded toward the door to the inner office.

Behind the office door came the end of the line. Secrecy and stealth became superfluous the instant he crossed through that final door. Lyons had every reason to suspect that he would find the corpse of Smith inside. What he was less certain of, given the freshness of the kills, was whether or not he would find Smith's murderer, in there as well.

Standing just off at an angle in front of the office door, Lyons surveyed it as carefully as he could through his NVGs. The door was closed. That seemed wrong.

Once the principal had been taken out, and considering the mess in the outer chamber, why go to the trouble of carefully closing a door behind you as you left?

The ex-cop made his decision. Stepping forward, he rose up high on the ball of one foot and brought his right knee up to his chest where he held the AKS at port arms. Exhaling sharply through his nose, Lyons snapped his curled leg out with explosive power. He thrust through on the breaching kick, his big foot slamming into the door just inside of the door handle, even with where the bolt ran in the lock housing.

The door popped open under the sharp force and swung wildly back. Lyons recoiled off to one side in an attempt to avoid any return fire from inside the room. After a heartbeat he tucked in behind the muzzle of his appropriated AKS and moved rapidly through the entrance. He swept the rifle muzzle around as he entered the room, his feet moving in a shuffling motion. His eyes sought the corners of the room, seeing the contents of the chamber first in terms of motion, second in broad details of shape. He felt a breeze on his face, smelled the damp pollution stink of the Ozama River bisecting Santo Domingo.

CHAPTER NINE

Kyrgyzstan

Bullets suddenly poured through the wooden door leading into the side office of the garage. James threw himself down and forward. He hit the ground hard and rolled across his back to drop into the service pit. He landed in the little concrete hole on his feet. He brought his submachine gun up above his head and fired a blind burst of suppressive fire as he moved toward the front edge of the pit. Instantly, Encizo was beside him.

The little weapon shook and stuttered in the Cuban's hands as he came up against the pit wall. Bullets from inside the garage office tore through the flimsy door and shot around the room, ringing off the Toyota's frame, hitting walls and whistling through blown-out windows.

James's weapon jerked in his hand as the last round fired and the bolt snapped open. He tossed the submachine gun to the side and drew his side arm. Beside him Encizo rested the carbine barrel on the floor of the garage and trained the sights on the bullet-perforated office door.

There was an even chance the gunmen on the other side of the door were so worked up that they'd rush through in an attempt to finish him off. There was also every chance the weapon operator was nowhere near that gutsy.

Encizo heard a voice shout something out from across the street in the mosque. A higher-pitched voice answered from inside the garage office. James shifted his feet and looked around, trying to ascertain if any other terrorist troops were in a position to direct the actions of the man in the office or to draw down on Encizo and himself.

Outside the sudden rain was falling in sheets with such force that the raindrops bounced when they hit the ground. Water flooded the narrow ditches beside the street and stood in a shallow lake across the square. Vision was obscured in the dark at ten yards and everything beyond twenty was a blur. Only the flash of muzzle fire would be visible from across the street.

McCarter shouted something the engaged men couldn't hear but then was drowned out by the roar of Manning's machine gun.

James watched the door in the sudden lull. He tried to peek through the bullet holes to see into the room beyond but the angle was wrong. He decided to fix that. He aimed carefully down the barrel of the carbine. He tightened his hand on the pistol grip and forced air in a steady stream out of his nose.

He squeezed the trigger.

The carbine roared in his hand and a muzzle-flash spilled from the barrel. The gun jerked back against his grip, and James automatically adjusted for the recoil pressure. The big slugs struck the ratty, bullet-riddled door in the lock mechanism and blew apart the handle.

A fist-size hole appeared in the door and the bullet

snapped the latch cleanly. The kinetic force shoved the door open. It swung inward on its hinges and Encizo caught a glimpse of a filthy desk and an ancient vending machine. He saw the startled gunman lying on the floor.

The terrorist was young and the Chinese Type 56 assault rifle he was trying to aim looked ridiculously large against his slight, bony frame. The IMU terrorist looked at James from where he was stretched out on the floor, his eyes as big as saucers as the man opened fire.

The bullet struck a tattered office chair in the backrest. The big slugs tore through the chair and sent it tumbling across the room, spinning out of control the way a strong wind teases a loose feather. James shifted and fired the carbine again. A hole the size of a fifty-cent piece appeared in the side of the vending machine, and the sound of the impact was like a baseball bat on a countertop.

The terrorist shrieked in surprise and dropped his weapon. Behind him a second man appeared, only to be killed by Encizo. Scrambling frantically to his feet, the first terrorist dived toward the office door and out into the rain. James worked his jaw grimly, attempting to pop his ears from the ringing the gunfire had left in them. He felt like someone afflicted with tinnitus. Then he shot the fleeing terrorist between the shoulder blades.

Next to him Encizo slid down behind the protective cover of the service pit to avoid any return fire from outside the building. He lifted the still hot carbine away from his body. He ejected the magazine, looked at the count and shoved it back home.

James briefly thought about securing one of the AKMs from the terrorists he'd shot and then decided against risking the potential exposure. He wrapped the slack from his rifle sling around one arm and crawled up out of the service pit.

Outside, McCarter slid up next to the open back door of the garage and peered cautiously out into the rain. Beside him Manning had driven back a fire team of black-suited Europeans from the alley approach to the IMU compound. Inside he heard James call out a status check and answered in turn.

He looked out into the rain.

The heavy downpour did not give up its secrets easily. McCarter knew it only made sense that, if the unknown combatants wanted to take whoever was holed up inside the compound, they would surround the building.

But the terrorists facing them were unprofessional, lacked good communications and were uncoordinated. Now Phoenix Force had found itself in the midst of a chaotic battlefield with enemies on all sides. If not for the life of the American contractor, McCarter would have withdrawn long ago.

Again McCarter peered out into the rain as Manning shifted position, hunting rooftops then doorways and second-story windows. The buildings directly behind the IMU compound were open-air structures with thatched roofs with livestock pens placed at the back of them.

A huge pile of raw white cotton was heaped loosely like hay under a tin roof. McCarter crouched down, holding his weapon at port arms, and slid forward. He took up a position among the oil barrels lined up on the opposite side of the door from the direction of his approach to the garage.

The terrorist sniper in the stockyard strolled around a thick center pillar. His rifle, a battered old Soviet SVD 7.62 mm Dragunov sniper rifle, was fitted with a PSO-1 telescopic sight offering a 4-power magnification. The man was dressed in camouflage he'd scrounged somewhere and held his rifle casually under one arm while he rolled a cigarette with his hands.

Obviously the gunman had attributed the gunfire he'd heard from inside the garage as more attacks centered on the compound. McCarter leveled his weapon across the top of an oil barrel. The Phoenix Force leader quickly lowered the rear sights and set his point of aim. The range was right at fifty yards and over such a short distance the high-caliber round was bound to rise only slightly if at all.

McCarter watched the man dip his head and light the cigarette using a burnished silver Ronson lighter. McCarter took a quick check of the area around the man to make sure he was alone. He nestled the rifle buttstock into his shoulder and settled into a comfortable firing position.

The man's skin was a burnished brown so deep it seemed copper. McCarter settled the open sights of his gun on the prominent ridge of the tall, lanky man's Adam's apple.

ON THE BRIDGE above the village T. J. Hawkins welded his cheek to the buttstock of his weapon. His eye narrowed as he peered through his scope. The barks and pops of gunfire echoed up sharply through the rain.

He tracked his team's progress from eight hundred yards away, picking their movements out through his sniper optics. Twice he killed men in their pathway, putting high-velocity rounds center mass before the wandering targets could engage his brethren.

The ground under him turned soggy from runoff, and he began to shiver slightly from the exposure as he lost body heat. He never missed.

Dominican Republic

A LARGE DESK dominated the middle of the room, a dark hulk in Lyons's goggles. The top of it glowed with a dripping luminescence. Behind the desk a body cooled as the night breeze blew in through a window blown to shards. Moving carefully, his nerves crackling with the electricity of potential danger, Lyons checked the corpse.

He reached down and unceremoniously yanked the dangling head up by a shock of greasy hair. In the IR enhancement light, the bland features of some unknown man looked back up at him. The middle-aged man's eyes bulged sightless from his death-slackened face. Bloody holes the size of coins riddled the man's chest, ruining an expensive suit.

Lyons was too late.

Disgusted, Lyons put a boot on the edge of the office chair and kicked it over in frustration. It slid a few inches and then toppled. The heavy, loose form of the body slipped out onto the floor with all the deftness of a sopping wet bag of cement.

Lyons cursed. Cursed again. Out of a professional habit of carefulness, he quickly looked around on the floor for Smith's laptop or any other effects. Nothing. The place had been stripped clean of all but the dead, stinking meat.

No sign told him if Smith, the FBI agent, had been here or not.

Now that he was sure of the meeting outcome, Lyons knew he had to exit the scene as quickly as possible. The abandoned sawmill had become red-hot. Too hot for a foreigner packing a military arsenal on Dominican soil in a time of civil unrest and martial law. He had to get out of there, retreat to his safehouse and contact Brognola for further instructions.

"We good?" he asked his teammates.

"Copy, clear on perimeter," Schwarz said.

"Copy, clear on interior," Blancanales echoed.

Suddenly, Lyons froze. Some faint sound on the periphery of his hearing came to him. He cocked his head to the side, tense.

He couldn't recapture the sound now that he was actively listening. In the graveyard silence that surrounded him, Lyons couldn't be sure he'd heard anything to begin with. It was unsettling. He knew it hadn't been Blancanales. He slowly sank onto one knee by the sprawled corpse of the unknown black marketer and ran an expert hand over the man's dead body, fishing through his pockets.

Nothing.

Lyons turned and stood. It was then that the necessary angle of vision was correct and the battery light from the man's satellite phone burned green, now obvious in the gloomy room. Lyons frowned again, head cocked, listening for any sound coming from outside the office.

He heard nothing to give him pause, knowing Blancanales was holding security, and turned his attention back to the satellite phone. The man's phone was a good catch—not the same as his laptop, to be sure, but still good. It seemed hard to believe that professional operators capable of a hit of this magnitude could have possibly missed it.

Still, though the takedown had all the earmarks of top-line training, it could have been anyone, though. Drug teams trained by foreign mercenaries, internal security services for the Dominicans. The list of potential players in the Caribbean was long.

Lyons picked up the sat phone. It was sticky with the dead man's blood. Lyons powered the device off and placed it in a pocket of his shirt before he stepped around the desk and moved through the open door into the outer office chamber. The bodies of the dead bodyguards still lay sprawled around in haphazard disarray.

After years of experience, Lyons had a critical, almost gifted, eye for crime-scene forensics. He was able to re-create the events of even the most horrific battle by the position of corpses, spent shell casings and blood spatter. In this case, rushed for time, he was unable to conclude whether this butcher's work had been done by a coordinated team or a single, talented professional.

Lyons moved carefully through the room. He held his appropriated AKS at the ready as he approached the door. His feeling of disquiet had not subsided. He couldn't place his unease, and that made it all the more bothersome. He stalked forward, pausing at the door leading out into the hall.

"You get anything?" Blancanales asked from his security position.

Lyons shook his head, then said, "Maybe. Not much. A phone. Let's get out of here."

The Puerto Rican rose to his feet, cocked his head to one side, sensed nothing, moved forward.

All hell broke loose when he stepped through the door and entered the hall. The ex–Green Beret felt as if he had moved into a field of static electricity. The hair on his arms and the back of his neck lifted straight up as cold squirts of adrenaline surged into his body. The soldier reacted instantly, without conscious thought, throwing himself to the floor.

Behind him Lyons dropped to one knee and leaned back in the doorway, sweeping up the barrel of his AKS and triggering a blast toward a shadowed motion.

The unmistakable pneumatic cough of a sound-suppressed weapon firing on fully automatic assaulted Lyons's ears across the short distance. Shell casings clattered onto the linoleum floor, mixing with the sound of a weapon bolt leveraging back and forth rapidly. Lyons felt the angry whine of bullets fill the space where his head and chest had been only a heartbeat before.

From the floor Blancanales, now pinned down, returned fire, cursing in Spanish.

Lyons targeted diagonally across and down the office hall, firing his rifle with practiced, instinctive ease. He let the recoil of the carbine stuttering in his strong grip carry him back through the doorway behind him in a tight roll. From his belly Lyons thrust his muzzle around the doorjamb and arced the weapon back and forth as he laid down quick suppressive blasts.

"Roll clear!" he shouted.

Blancanales hopped backward over the body in the hall, the front of his clothes soaking red with blood. Lyons shouted across the link to Schwarz, "We have contact! Secure our six!"

"Copy!" Schwarz answered immediately.

The carbine rounds were deafening in the confined space, and his ears rang painfully from the noise. Lyons reached up and jerked his night-vision goggles down so that they dangled from the rubber strap around his neck. He heard the bullets from his assailant's answering burst smack into the Sheetrock of the outer wall with audible smacks that rang louder than the muzzle-braked weapon's own firing cycle.

Blancanales burned several shots down the hall toward the enemy muzzle-blast as he scooted backward for the cover of an office door.

From the impacts, Lyons determined the shooter was using a submachine gun and not an assault rifle, though he was hard-pressed to identify caliber with the suppressor in use. Lyons scrambled backward and rested his rifle barrel across the still warm corpse of another dead bodyguard. If there was more than one assassin out there, and they were determined to get him, they would either fire and maneuver to breach the room door, or possibly use grenades to clear him out. He wasn't looking forward to either possibility.

"What the hell did you get yourself into, Smith?" he wondered out loud.

Kyrgyzstan

MCCARTER EASED THE AIR out of his lungs and took up the play in his rifle trigger.

It would be a clean shot, he knew. The terrorist sniper looked over toward the back of the IMU compound and blew out twin jets of gray cigarette smoke through his nostrils. The end of the cigarette glowed cherry-red as the gunman inhaled. He settled his shoulder against the worn wood of the big central pillar and made himself comfortable. He plucked the cigarette from his lips with a free hand and carefully knocked off ashes.

McCarter squeezed the trigger.

The rifle recoiled smoothly into his shoulder, but McCarter knew as soon as he had pulled the trigger that his shot was off. The wood of the pillar to the right of the gunman's head exploded as McCarter's round struck.

McCarter snarled. The front sight had been dinged at some point, throwing off his aim. The man sprang back from the post, dropping his cigarette and swinging up the Dragunov. The skin of his face turned ashen and he squatted into a crouch, looking instinctively toward the compound to see where the shot had come from.

McCarter rose off one knee from behind the oil barrel and tried to compensate for the damaged sight by using Kentucky windage. Before McCarter pulled the trigger again, catching the sniper in profile, a round struck the man high in the left shoulder.

The terrorist was driven up hard against the pillar and spun halfway around. Blood blossomed and instantly stained his uniform scarlet. Face caught in a stricken mask, the terrorist looked out into the heavy rain from his position under the roof and realized just how exposed he was.

McCarter realized instantly that the terrorist had found himself in Hawkins's crosshairs and sent out a silent word of thanks. More than ever he found his lack of communication ability frustrating.

Working mop-up, McCarter squeezed the trigger on his weapon again as the man threw himself to the ground, mortally wounded. McCarter's shot tore through the open air where the man had been crouching. McCarter cursed again, disgusted. From that angle he could no longer fire on the man and remain crouched behind the oil barrels.

McCarter rose, triggering the damaged rifle again and again in sloppy semiautomatic blasts of rifle fire. The wounded terrorist saw McCarter's muzzle-flashes and tried to pick up the long-barreled Dragunov and bring it to bear. McCarter pulled the trigger on his carbine three times, striking the downed terrorist once in the hip and once in the lower back.

The IMU terrorist spasmed like a fish in the bottom of a boat, then lay still, his eyes wide open and blindly staring. Blood began to quickly pool around his motionless body and it rolled straight toward the pile of raw cotton, staining it bright red along the bottom.

McCarter, disgusted by the battered carbine, threw the weapon down and drew his Beretta. He scrambled out from behind the tangle of oil barrels and trotted into the alley. He was only a few short yards from the compound's back door now.

Out on the elevation Hawkins fired his weapon, shifted and pulled the trigger twice.

CHAPTER TEN

In front of McCarter two dead IMU gunmen tumbled to the ground, the backs of their heads cratered. Gary Manning fired a long, ragged burst down the alley behind the team, driving back a three-man squad of the night-suited fighters.

Two IMU terrorists jogged out of the downpour, their weapons up and ready, but they seemed more curious than aware that they were walking into potential danger. James, emerging from the garage, snarled and went to one knee in the middle of the alley. He brought his weapon up in a two-fisted grip and dropped the men from twenty yards.

They splashed down dead onto the wet street and McCarter rose from his crouch. He began jogging quickly toward the men. One of them had been armed with a more modern AKS-74 with a folding stock, which McCarter intended to make his own. McCarter reached the dead men and bent down. His hand grasped the assault rifle and he pulled it out of the slack grip of the dead terrorist soldier. He slid his pistol away before holding the rifle up to inspect it.

"Let's go!" he snapped, nerves humming with adrenaline. "Let's take this place down." He turned and rushed toward the rear entrance of the compound.

From down the alley he heard someone shout, and then another voice joined in. He covered the muddy ground like a sprinting racer, running hard with the AKS-74 up and at the ready. He looked upward and saw the rear of the compound clearly. The building surface was pockmarked with bullet holes and not a single window remained unbroken.

He scanned the building for the door and saw it had been shot a dozen times but still held on its hinges and latch. He put his head down like a running back breaking through a defensive line and charged the doorway. A second before he struck the door he turned his shoulder down and bore the brunt across his back.

Gunfire burst out on all sides of his approach. James and Encizo utilized their submachine guns at point-blank range as Manning switched out ammunition belts on his primary weapon.

With James hard behind him McCarter heard a burst of machine-gun fire from behind him as he hit the door. There was a pop and the sound of wood tearing as he crashed through the structure. His foot tangled up with the bottom lip of the doorway and he fell heavily on his side astride the broken door.

James hurtled his form and buttonhooked around the door frame, weapon up. McCarter hissed in pain as his already bruised and abused body absorbed more blunt trauma. He pushed himself up and scooted to the side, away from the opening. Bullets, like angry hornets, buzzed through the gaping doorway and slapped into the walls.

Encizo fired over the crouching form of Manning as the Canadian snapped back his charging handle and armed his machine gun. Then the RPK opened up and pushed a wall of suppressive fire down the alley behind them.

McCarter rose out of his crouch and saw he was in a small, tight room. There were garbage cans lined up against the wall and several old mop buckets on wheels. Black rubber boots were arranged against one wall and greasy aprons hung from metal hooks.

McCarter brought up the AKS. He looked over his shoulder at the open door. The room was black, and the gloom from outside was a bar of lighter gray in comparison to the cavelike dark of the little antechamber. McCarter squinted and turned back toward a pair of swinging doors that led off the back dock and deeper into the compound.

James shrugged his submachine gun into his shoulder and covered the door. Encizo entered the room, his weapon up, as well, followed by Manning, who was spraying suppressive fire from his hip.

"Let's go!" the giant Canadian shouted. "More of the Europeans just hit the street!"

A machine gun erupted outside and a wall of bullets sailed in through the door. The rounds struck the mops and tore into the garbage cans, scattering them across the floor. Gouges of wood paneling ripped out of the wall, and coat hooks were torn off their housings.

Manning jumped forward and away from the opening. McCarter pushed through the swinging door and entered a large kitchen with a long metal table running the length of the room between sets of ovens and microwaves. Pots and pans hung from racks overhead and the shelf under the table contained more of the same. Across the room a second set of swinging doors hung still, leading deeper into the front of the main compound building. Behind McCarter, James took a pair of quick steps and leaped up onto the metal table, sliding across it and landing on the other side.

He had no intention of trying to hold the gunmen off if they chose to assault the building now. It was a hopeless task and he would only become bogged down. Speed of movement and aggression were the only things that could save Phoenix Force now.

McCarter pushed his way through the swinging kitchen doors and into the dining room, which ran from the food-preparation area out to about three-quarters of the way toward the front wall of the compound. The big room was filled with tables and chairs of dark wood. There was an empty fireplace against the wall, and several comfortable chairs formed a sitting area in front of two windows that were now blown into splinters.

Through the shattered glass McCarter could clearly see the wall running around the mosque directly across the village square. Two men jogged out of the front gate, one holding an RPK machine gun and the other a green ammo box. They headed quickly toward the government offices on the other end of the square. McCarter signaled Encizo to cover the area.

He turned and looked across the low wooden wall that served as a divider between the dining and lounge areas and the common area where a narrow staircase ran up to the second floor.

A man in traditional headdress and cloth vest appeared in the window, his hands filled with a Kalashnikov. Encizo and James reacted as one, scything the man in crisscrossing streams of fire that shredded his flesh.

As the mutilated man fell, a grenade arced through the window and bounced off the floor.

Dominican Republic

THERE WAS SILENCE for a long moment. Lyons's head raced through strategies and options. If the assassin's intent had merely been to escape, then why had he bothered to stay behind or try to take Lyons out? If the unknown assailant was armed for a quiet kill, then that would indicate that he was probably not carrying ordnance much heavier than the silenced SMG being used now.

Using the slight lull to his advantage, Blancanales performed a reverse low crawl until he had reached the relative safety of a doorway. He looked over at Lyons, who nodded back.

"We're still clear outside," Schwarz said over the com link. "I'm going to clear your insertion route."

"Copy," Blancanales subvocalized.

Lyons maneuvered the barrel of his AKS out the entrance and triggered an exploratory blast, conducting a recon by fire. Precious seconds ticked away.

Suddenly, Lyons's aggressive burst was answered with a tightly controlled salvo. Bullets tore into the wooden doorjamb and broke up the floor in front of his weapon. Lyons ducked back; he had seen what he needed and had found a way to exploit his heavier armament.

The gunman had taken position across, and two doors down, the hall from the room where Lyons was now trapped. From that location the gunmen controlled the fields of fire up and down the hall, preventing Lyons from leaving the office without exposing himself to withering short-range fire.

Again Lyons triggered a long, ragged blast. He tore apart the door of the office directly opposite him, then ran his large-caliber rounds down the hall to pour a flurry of lead through the ambusher's door. Tracer fire lit up the hallway with surrealistic strips of light like laser blasts in some low-budget science fiction movie. Blancanales directed his own fire toward the threat in deadly synchronicity.

Lyons could smell his own sweat and the hot oil of his AKS-74. The heavy dust hanging in the air, kicked up by the automatic weapons fire, choked him. His ears rang and, over everything else, even the fever pitch of excitement, was the sharp smell of burning cordite.

"Moving!" the big ex–LAPD detective yelled.

Lyons ducked back around as the gunman triggered an answering burst from his SMG. Lyons heard the smaller caliber rounds strike the wall outside his door, saw how they failed to penetrate the building materials. It confirmed his suspicions that his adversary's weapon was no more than a 9 mm SMG. Blancanales expertly redirected his weapon around Lyons's movements.

Lyons snarled, gathering himself, and thrust his weapon out the office door a final time. He triggered the AKS, and the assault rifle bucked in his hands as he sprinted through the doorway hard behind his covering fire. His rounds fell like sledge hammers around the door to the room of his ambusher. Hot gases warmed his wrists as the bolt of his weapon snapped open and shut, open and shut as he carried his burst out to an improbable length even as he raced forward.

Two steps from the office door directly opposite the room he was in, Lyons's magazine ran dry and the bolt locked open. Without hesitation Lyons flung the empty weapon down and dived forward. The big man's hard shoulder struck the door. Already riddled with 5.45

mm bullets, the flimsy construction was no match for Lyons's heavy frame and he burst through it into the room.

He went down with his forward momentum, landing on the shoulder he had used as a battering ram and somersaulting over it smoothly. He came up on one knee and swung his second AKS carbine off his shoulder, leveling it at the wall separating his position from the gunman's.

Outside Blancanales worked the trigger on his weapon furiously, keeping the hidden gunman pinned down.

Lyons triggered his weapon from the waist, raking the weapon back and forth in a tight, low Z-pattern. The battlefield rounds chewed through plywood, Sheetrock and insulation with ease, bursting out the other side with terminal velocity.

Still firing, Lyons smoothly uncoiled out of his combat crouch, keeping his weapon angled downward to better catch an enemy likely pinned against the floor. His intentions were merciless. Momentum and an attacker's aggression were with Lyons now. Coming to his feet, he shifted the AKS pistol grip from his right to his left hand. His magazine came up dry as he shifted his weight back toward the shattered door to the room.

The butt of Lyons's pistol filled the palm of his free hand as he fired the last rounds through the looted AKS. He was moving, lethally graceful, back out the door to the room. His feet pirouetted through a complicated series of choreographed steps as he moved in a tight Weaver stance.

"Moving!" he warned in a loud command.

Out in the hall, smoke from weapons fire and dust billowed in the gloom. Lyons stepped out long and lunged forward, sinking to one knee as he came to the edge of his ambusher's door. He made no attempt to slow his momentum but instead let it carry him down to the floor. He breached the edge of the enemy door, letting the barrel of the pistol lead the way. He caught the image of a dark-clad form sprawled out on the floor of the room. Behind him Blancanales shuffled up the hall, weapon up.

The 9 mm pistol coughed in a double tap, catching the downed figure in the shoulder and head. Blood splashed up and the figure's skull mushroomed out, snapping to the side on a slack neck as brain matter splattered out and struck a section of bullet-riddled wall.

Lyons popped up, returned to his feet. He moved into the room, weapon poised, ready to react to even the slightest motion or perceived movement. After the frenzied action and brutal cacophony of the gun battle, the sudden return of silence and still felt deafening, almost oppressive. Approaching the dead man, Lyons narrowed his eyes, trying to quickly take in details. Muzzle-flash had ruined his night vision.

Frustrated, Lyons snuggled his NVGs back into position and turned the IR penlight on. The room returned to view in the familiar monochromatic greenish tint. As Blancanales entered the room, Lyons looked over at the dead gunman's weapon.

From its unique silhouette Lyons instantly recognized the subgun as a PP-19 Bizon. Built on a shortened AKS-74 receiver, it had the signature cylindrical high-capacity magazine attached under the grip and the AKS folding buttstock. The weapon was usually associated with Russian federal police or army troops, but international arms merchants had been turning up with them more and more as the Russian economy went through its series of hiccups.

"Bizon," Blancanales grunted. "Odd. Last intelligence estimates had a big shipment of them coming out of Kyrgyzstan."

"Kyrgyzstan?" Lyons echoed as he rolled the dead man over and cursed. Any hopes for identification were gone. The man's face held all the structural integrity of mush. "Where Phoenix is operating?"

"Yep," Blancanales confirmed. He lifted his hand to his earjack. "Schwarz, we've cleared the threat. Let's rally up here."

"Copy," Schwarz answered. "I'm on the staircase now."

Lyons knew he didn't have a lot of time. In a city locked down under martial law, the sound of the assault rifle he had been forced to use would draw unwanted attention very quickly. Lyons patted the dead man down, finding a leather wallet filled with U.S. dollars but devoid of personal identification. The man had no phone or laptop.

"You think that stringer set us up?" he asked Blancanales as Schwarz entered the room.

"Could be," Blancanales allowed. "But it was a pretty lousy setup with all those other operators and a lone gunmen. It doesn't really add up."

Lyons grunted his agreement as Schwarz moved forward and pulled a thin, flat-faced Nikon digital camera from one of the carriers on his harness. He clicked off the IR light and settled his own NVGs on his forehead.

Working quickly, the Able Team electronics genius turned the camera on and opened the lens protector.

Without preamble he grabbed the doughy-fleshed hand of the dead man by his index finger. Cradling the Nikon securely in his palm, Schwarz rolled the man's finger across the lens facing of the camera as carefully as any police desk sergeant at a big city precinct house.

Schwarz held the camera up, letting the dead killer's hand drop unceremoniously. It struck the uncarpeted floor with a dull clap as Schwarz pointed the Nikon at a blank stretch of wall unmarred by his penetrating gunfire.

"Flash," he warned, and his teammates closed their eyes against the flash as he snapped a picture. Later, he would download the snapshot digitally and send it to Stony Man for analysis. If the shooter was a leftover bodyguard, fine. If he was something else, then Able Team desperately needed to know.

"Let's roll the hell out of here," Lyons said.

Upon returning to the Santo Domingo safehouse Schwarz immediately downloaded his picture of the dead assassin's fingerprint and emailed it through an encrypted, anonymous server along with a brief sitrep, to a Stony Man capable site. Kurtzman would be accessing all federal and international databanks in an effort to find a match.

Somewhere in the city, foreign operators controlled by an agent of Michael Klaus's named Lemis noted the failure of their hit team to make contact and a clock started ticking.

CHAPTER ELEVEN

Kyrgyzstan

"Grenade!" McCarter called out as he rolled away from the blast zone.

James and Encizo peeled off from each other like basketball guards running a full court press. McCarter went down and covered as the explosion ripped through the room. He felt a dozen impacts on his body armor and stinging pain along his exposed arm as shrapnel sliced into him.

He went deaf for a moment and rose, turning and seeing only a cloud of black smoke. He saw Encizo, the man's face a mask of blood, stumble out of the cloud. James, amazingly unhurt, emerged a second later, mouth twisted in a scream McCarter couldn't hear. The ex-SEAL flung himself on the Cuban and knocked him to the ground.

Intuitively understanding the situation, McCarter swiveled and his ears popped. Suddenly he could hear the chatter of weapons fire as two IMU terrorists entered behind the grenade, guns blazing.

He tore off the top of the skull of the first man, who dropped immediately. Gary Manning emerged through the team's breach point firing his RPK from the hip and tore the second attacker apart.

Encizo bounced up and gestured toward McCarter, telling him to move.

The Briton crossed out of the common eating area through an opening in the dividing wall and into the front living area. He checked over his shoulder to make sure terrorist gunmen hadn't breached into the kitchen behind him.

He took a couple of tentative steps toward the stairs, AKS at the ready head, still spinning from the blast. He looked over his shoulder back out the front and saw the first machine-gun crew had halted before reaching the far compound structures. In the lee of a bullet-perforated pickup they had set up a hasty fighting position. Their own RPK sat on its bipod with the muzzle trained on the front of the compound.

"Christ!" McCarter snarled.

He moved quickly to the foot of the stairs and stopped. A terrorist lay sprawled head down on the first couple of steps. His left eye and part of his forehead had been blown away at such close range that McCarter could see the powder burns. The gunman's blood covered the floor and McCarter realized he was standing in it.

McCarter hesitated before entering the kill zone of the stairs, despite the pressing matter of time. It was too reckless, too needlessly suicidal. He crouched beside the front desk, holding up the AKS muzzle. He constantly shifted his gaze from the kitchen doors to the front of the compound and then back to the stairs.

From the front of the building McCarter heard an excited shouting break out from the gate to the mosque. The assistant gunner shouted back at the men behind the wall, and McCarter knew what was coming even though he didn't understand the language.

The RPK opened up. Red tracer fire poured through the open window and smashed into the dining room of the compound. Rounds struck tables and splintered chairs. Bullets clawed into the faded wallpaper and knocked pictures off the walls. Bullets blew chunks of mortar off the cooking fireplace and punched through chairs, sending stuffing into the air.

McCarter snapped. The stupid sons of bitches, he thought. He popped up and set his elbows down on some random box. It wasn't their trying to kill him that had finally pissed him off. It was the godawful disrespect they were showing him by being so blatantly stupid.

He centered his rear and front sights, puffed out a breath and squeezed the trigger. The bolt cycled once and tossed the spent shell out onto the floor. Out in the courtyard the machine gunner slummed dead, a coffee-cup-size chunk of his forehead jutted out from his skull.

The assistant gunner shrieked and leaped to his feet. He spun, slipping in the mud, and tried to scramble for the protection of the pickup. McCarter put a single round through his neck, sending him tumbling ass over teakettle to the muddy wet ground.

Screams and shouts of outrage erupted from the terrorist fighting positions in the mosque and government office building. Arcs of automatic weapons fire streamed out of the two locations and began striking the front of the compound.

As one, Phoenix Force answered the attack, throwing curtains of lead through the breach to drive the IMU gunmen back.

Behind them McCarter spun around in the dead terrorist's blood and moved over to the front of the stair.

Bullets tore into the lobby behind him. He stuck his head around the corner of the compound stairs and then ducked back quickly. He had seen nothing.

McCarter gritted his teeth when he got no response and forced himself to turn the blind corner. He had come far and suffered much in the short time he had been in this hellhole of a country. He had to turn the corner and he knew it.

He held his AKS to the ready but down as he slid around the corner and onto the stair. He moved slowly, eyes peering up into the murky stretch of the staircase. Behind him the team held down anchor as he penetrated further. He placed his feet carefully around the terrorist corpse so as not to trip. The soles of his boots were thick with bloody mud and left messy footprints on the old wood.

McCarter took each step carefully, peering into the shadowed gloom. There was not the slightest hint of motion from the upper story. If he was caught on these stairs he was dead. He could see the railing at the top of the staircase and caught a glimpse of the walls beyond it on the second-floor landing.

He stepped up past the dead terrorist soldier's feet and climbed a few more steps. The creaking of the old wood seemed ridiculously loud given the cacophony of automatic weapons fire that had just tore up the downstairs level. McCarter eased himself up another step.

Now he could see the tops of doorways breaking the line of the wall through the banister railing around the landing. None of them stood open. He went up several more steps and noticed the haze of gun smoke hanging in the thick, humid air.

His head cleared the landing and he stopped, taking

everything in. There were eight rooms on the floor, each with its door shut closed. The walls showed scorch marks from tracer fire, and bullets pockmarked the flower-pattern wallpaper. Lying next to the railing a second terrorist gunmen lay facedown in his own blood. At the end of the landing a window set over the compound's front doors had been blown out. A pile of loose shell casings lay under it alongside empty magazines for what McCarter thought might be an Uzi submachine gun.

The figure cut across his vision from left to right. Not a IMU in the traditional baggy shirt and trousers with black headdress, but a night-suited commando with a silenced weapon. The figure turned, face covered by balaclava hood and the moment stretched out into a freeze frame of realization and reaction.

The figure lifted his high-tech bull pup assault rifle as he dived forward but McCarter was an instant faster. His first blast caught the man low and shattered the rifle in his hand. His second burst hammered through the figure's throat, almost decapitating him.

The figure spun and fell.

McCarter climbed the rest of the way up the stairs and fully onto the landing. He nudged the body of the terrorist at the top of the stairs, making sure he was dead. The confined hall reeked of cordite and the fresh slaughtered stink of the dead terrorist gunmen.

Encizo appeared at the foot of the stairs, weapon ready. McCarter held up a hand, then put a finger to his lips.

McCarter could hear voices from outside through the broken window. He backed out of the center of the hall and over toward one side of the landing in case he was silhouetting himself to any gunmen outside.

A voice called out from behind a door in French, the voice sharp. McCarter's French was weak but good enough to know what was about to happen. He twisted at the waist, eyes never leaving the door, and called down to Encizo as the Cuban combat diver came up the staircase behind him.

"It's on," he warned.

McCarter crossed to the door, hugging the wall. Encizo lay the muzzle of his weapon over the lip of the stair. Below them more gunfire was breaking out.

The door ripped open and a tall figure in black fatigues and balaclava emerged, holding an identical bull pup SMG to the first figure. The combatant was primed and ready to go, but the doorway was a vertical coffin for him, trapped as he was in both McCarter's and Encizo's gun sights.

They shot him down, the rounds driving him back into the room. McCarter followed his gunfire in, charging forward, seizing the initiative. A figure moved. It was armed, so McCarter put six rounds into it. The figure fell and the room door rebounded off the inside wall and snapped closed.

Encizo charged up the final stairs, cutting the angle on the doorway to cover McCarter as the Briton held ready. They looked at each other, silent across the dead body on the floor between them. Encizo nodded once.

McCarter turned the knob on the door and it unlatched with a greasy click. He put his fingertips against the wooden shape and gently pushed. It swung open under his touch while Encizo kept himself poised.

McCarter lowered his weapon to his hip, holding the AKS-74 so that the muzzle was pointed down. He stepped out into the bar of light directly in front of the open door. He could make out a shape against the far wall of the little room. The compound room's single bed had been overturned, as had its dresser.

There was blood on the floor in a spreading puddle. The commando figure lay still. The body under the window shifted. A voice faint and so weak it quavered spoke out in English.

"Who's there?"

Stony Man Farm

BARBARA PRICE MOVED through the door and into the communications center in a whirlwind of activity. Her fingers hammered out messages on her secured Black-Berry and she cut a connection on her cell phone as she stopped in front of Kurtzman's desk.

"We have uplink with Phoenix yet?" she asked without preamble.

"Negative," Kurtzman admitted. "The jammer is just too close to ground zero."

Price cursed in frustration, then automatically answered her phone when it rang again half a second later.

"Go for Price," she said.

"Barb, Hal," Brognola said. "I've got a lead on the Smith brothers."

"Excellent. Finally some good news. What have you got?"

"I've got the Air Force and a private intelligence contractor named Ze."

"The French outfit?" she asked.

"Exactly. Former para colonel recruiting ex-Legionnaires and French naval special-operations troops."

"Go on?"

"Both of our boys did six years in the Air Force. One flying drones out of the base in Las Vegas, the other as a security police officer with time in Afghanistan and Iraq."

"Okay."

"They get out and both go to work for Ze. One flying aerial drones used on the poppy interdiction program in the Afghanistan-Pakistan border region, the other working convoy security from Kandahar to Kabul. Two years ago they're both working a contract out of Bagram. Then bang, the drone pilot quits and goes to work for another contractor, this time in Tajikistan. The other brother quits and goes to the FBI Academy."

"Okay, seems pretty aboveboard."

"Sure, but at the time they quit, the Pentagon opened up a review of contractor activities in that area with guess who as the primary focus…"

"Ze?"

"Bingo. There are allegations of Ze working hand in hand with Iranian intelligence on a cash-for-play operation, feeding NATO troop information to handlers. But that's not all. On their last mission in-country both brothers were assigned on a two-day surveillance operation in a place called el-Kabar along the border."

"Okay."

"It gets spooky," Brognola explained. "It seems every contractor who worked that station has been killed in the last eighteen months."

"So the chances of two brothers half a world apart both going missing isn't a coincidence—it's a pattern," Price said.

"Exactly."

Dominican Republic

LYONS DRANK A SODA and made himself a sandwich from the pickings in the refrigerator. He surveyed his surroundings from every window in the place, looked in closets and behind closed doors until he felt like he knew the layout of the place well enough to navigate it in the dark, under fire if need be.

Schwarz leaned back in the chair at the table. One hand maneuvered his mouse pad and keyboard while the other tapped absently on the pistol grip of his weapon. Across the room Blancanales watched the street through the window.

"You got anything yet?" Lyons demanded for the tenth time in almost as many minutes.

"I'm getting a download right now," Schwarz replied. "Unbunch your panties."

"Ironman gets real cranky when people shoot at him and he doesn't know why," Blancanales drawled from the window.

"Sometimes I even get cranky when I know why they're shooting at me," Lyons muttered. "But if we can ditch the stand-up routine maybe Gadgets can tell us who in the hell we'll be shooting next."

"Gotta respect a man with a passion for his work," Schwarz said.

"Gadgets," Lyons warned.

"Fine!" Schwarz moaned. "The guy has a Interpol sheet. Former Legionnaire working for a private security firm called Ze."

"What the hell does that have to do with Smith?" Blancanales asked.

"According to Barb, he used to work for 'em, too."

"That's a harsh severance package," Blancanales added.

"Doesn't help us with our problem, though," Schwarz said. "Hell, even if Carl hadn't killed him, it looks like Smith never showed up to that meet."

"So what do we do next, then?" Blancanales asked.

"We take it from the top," Lyons said. "We retrace Smith's steps as best we can. Barb's sent us his reports on running his contacts in the government and on the street. We hit everyone, make some noise till something shakes loose."

"The people in the government he was investigating will get nervous, start shooting. The crooks'll try to keep things quiet, start shooting. If this Ze corp doesn't want what Smith knows out, they'll start shooting." Schwarz ticked off the options in a laundry list of potential murder suspects.

"Good," Lyons replied. "Then we shoot back and clear the whole mess up."

CHAPTER TWELVE

Lyons entered the casino.

Located just outside the main city where the tourist industry provided a level of security normal Dominicans could never enjoy, it was so filled with foreigners that Able Team was able to move undetected.

He stepped to the side just inside the door and let his eyes adjust to the dark casino interior. The place was full, but not crowded and he heard the spinning of roulette wheels and the dissonance of slot machines over the more general noise of the crowd.

Behind him first Blancanales then Schwarz followed him into the resort. They wandered to separate areas, keeping each other in sight.

Lyons let his gaze slide across the crowd. He kept his thoughts as unfocused and bland as the neutral expression on his face. He wasn't looking for anything specific, simply soaking in details, waiting to see if his inner radar picked up any blips. He surveyed the casino from payout cage to bar. Then from security desk to the table games.

Blancanales took up a position at a little bar off the main floor. Schwarz stood an unassuming sentry at a row of slot machines.

The guards Lyons saw looked hard alert. Tourists meant money and that meant keeping the overweight, sunburned and drunken hosts safe from pickpockets and local bully boys. The unrest in the streets would only add to their level of alertness.

He saw a fat man with two blondes, each supporting improbably large breast implants, on either one of his arms. He saw a nervous-looking Asian puffing away on his cigarettes as the dealer turned over cards and took his chips. The man was tall for an Asian. A broad-shouldered guy with obsidian skin and dreadlocks leaned against an elegantly decorated pillar fiddling with a thick gold bracelet.

The casino was a strange mix, influenced by the youth club in the basement of the property, as well as the gaming floor. There were moneyed clients mixing with the partygoers, young and old. The place was neither a dive nor too high end. There was a fair mix of Americans and Europeans. Lyons nodded to himself. This was a good establishment to go unnoticed in, and he understood why Smith had chosen it as a drop point and meet place.

Lyons checked the time on his Rolex Submariner watch. There was no inscription on the back, nothing to give him away. Lyons knew who it was from, and that was enough.

Lyons walked over to the bar. He watched pretty girls in revealing dresses or the sexy cocktail waitresses as a cover for his perpetual surveillance. He ordered a beer in a pint glass. He left the bartender a tip and took his beer to the casino cage, where he changed some cash into chips with the help of a brunette in a low-cut uniform and too much eye shadow.

Lyons shook his chips loosely in his hand and strolled toward the roulette table. He preferred blackjack but he wasn't here on vacation. Roulette was a sucker's bet, but it was company money, so what the hell. He'd do it the way Smith wanted. As Lyons approached the table, he idly second-guessed himself, wondering if his decision to come unarmed was wise. He was still operating under his journalist cover and a weapons charge by overzealous police troops could unravel the whole operation at this point.

Lyons eased up to the table and made eye contact with the croupier before put the equivalent of a twenty-five-dollar token on Black 8.

Smith had made his last call from an emergency drop cutout phone and not from the Santo Domingo station line. There had been no explanation for this irregularity, and Lyons had chosen to follow Smith's lead in avoiding usual channels. Lyons's paranoia was omnidirectional and hard earned.

The croupier called out Red 23 as the winner and took Lyons's money. Lyons slid another chip onto Black 8 to replace the one he had lost. The big-shouldered guy with the dreadlocks wandered over to watch the wheel. The fat man said something and the two blondes barked laughter like trained seals at a talent show. The wheel spun and the white ball jumped and bounced its way across the device. After a moment the ball settled into one of the slots and the croupier called Red 11 the winner.

Lyons had to admit the casino protocol was a wise setup despite the seeming cinematic feel of the practice. The principal could remain anonymous in the crowd, surveying the environment. The contact was making no discernable moves that threatened exposure if he was under surveillance. Either party could simply walk from the scene without commotion if something seemed askew.

Blancanales surveyed the casino from behind his drink while Schwarz methodically plunked dollar tokens into the machine. If it was going to happen, Lyons knew, it was going to happen soon.

Kyrgyzstan

TWO IMU TERRORISTS lay dead, sprawled across the floor in the middle of the room a pool of red. The wall of the compound room behind them had been splattered with their blood like the canvas of an impressionist painter. Flies were thick in the room. They stirred and lifted in a black cloud from the corpses in lazy protest as McCarter entered.

Suddenly a dark figure darted out of a far corner, weapon going to his shoulder. McCarter spun, his own weapon up and tracking.

Eight hundred yards away T. J. Hawkins held the target window in his crosshairs. The powerful scope brought the interior of the room into vivid relief through his sniper optics. His reaction was automatic. The rifle bucked against his shoulder.

In the room McCarter threw himself backward, clearing the man's angle of fire. His finger tightened on his trigger even as the man's head jerked to one side, leaving a red mist in the air. The man crumpled at the knees and dropped to the floor, dead.

McCarter let out a pent-up breath and stepped farther into the room. Wedged between the two dead terrorists, Smith looked up at him from the floor.

"I'm here to get you out," McCarter said.

The contractor looked up at him through heavily lidded eyes. His left arm had swollen to the point that the skin seemed almost ready to burst open like some piece of overripe fruit.

"What happened?" McCarter asked.

"Infection set in."

"Can you move?"

"Not really. Being sick slowed me down. I took a round to the gut when those guys came in and killed the IMU shooters. I thought *they* were the rescue team. At first anyway."

Encizo appeared in the door, smoke curling up from his barrel. He nodded toward Smith, then spoke to McCarter. "We've created a lull," he said. "But this place is lousy with IMU pricks. Even with the ones those French bastards killed." He met McCarter's eyes. "Time is a factor."

McCarter nodded, then said quietly, "I need Cal." Encizo disappeared from the doorway. McCarter moved in closer and knelt beside Smith. "Let me see."

Smith let the hand holding the bloody cloth over his lower abdomen fall away. Blue-green flies buzzed between the two operators. McCarter frowned but forced himself to suppress any outward reaction. He looked away from the glistening blue-gray coil of Smith's intestine and out the window.

"It's bad," he admitted.

"I don't suppose you have a medevac waiting?" Smith smiled. His voice was a whisper and his skin was appallingly ashen.

"The other team brought jammers. I got a Chinook coming to get us, but we're out of com link and the weather has us socked in."

"What's up?" James asked, appearing in the doorway.

McCarter simply nodded toward the injured Smith. James surveyed the man, his face betraying nothing. He knelt and ran a head-to-toe assessment, then stood and went to the bed on the far side of the room. He grabbed up a pillow and pulled the case off, turning it inside out. He pulled his Gerber knife out and began slicing the sheets from the bed into strips.

Smith watched McCarter with dull eyes as he took a first-aid kit and added it to his assembled supplies. He took went to the door to the room and opened it wide, giving him a view out into the hallway from where Smith was propped against the wall.

McCarter took up a position by the window, watching outside. In the hallway the rest of Phoenix covered the staircase. Manning set up his RPK down the stairwell while the other two secured his flanks.

Moving back over to Smith, McCarter passed in front of the room's only window, which faced the mosque across the street from the compound. Gunfire erupted from the structure and struck the wall outside, and McCarter dropped quickly. Rounds from an assault rifle struck the compound outside the window again. Several bullets, including a green tracer round, buzzed into the room.

"That was sloppy of me," McCarter muttered.

"Sure was," James agreed. "They sound pissed off."

"Yeah, me, too," McCarter muttered. "But I saw a team of those Europeans out there, as well as IMU bad boys. Those guys don't give up." He squatted on his knees beside the gravely wounded American. He looked up at him and tried to smile as he set his rifle on the floor.

"Don't tell me about sloppy," he slurred. "I'm the one with the bullet in them."

McCarter grunted and tried to smile. He picked up a mini-Uzi and popped the magazine, checking how full it was. He reinserted the magazine into the pistol grip well and carefully placed the weapon on Smith's leg below his wound.

James pulled a pair of white latex gloves out of his little field kit and put them on. It was probably a losing battle to try to keep the wound clean in this kind of environment, but he was going to at least make the effort.

"This is going to hurt," he warned.

Smith closed his eyes and nodded briefly. A stream of automatic-weapons fire arched through the window above their heads and poured into the room. It hurtled into the open door and rattled it on its frame. McCarter ignored the fire but shot a look toward the now ruined door to the room. There was a burst of return fire as Encizo sprayed out the window, cursing in Spanish.

James spun the cap on top of the little bottle of hydrogen peroxide open with his thumb. The cap came loose and shot across the room, bouncing off the dresser and hitting the floor. He didn't warn Smith again but instead simply upended the bottle and poured the disinfectant over his wound.

Smith gasped at the sudden pain. His eyes shot open wide and he made as if to sit up but McCarter put a gentle hand on his shoulder, easing him back down. The hydrogen peroxide bubbled and became a white froth over the area of exposed flesh. It made a sound almost like a sizzle.

McCarter waited for Smith to regain his composure while James diligently worked.

"Is there an exit wound?" he asked.

The private contractor agent shook his head. "The French team won't give up," he said suddenly. "Klaus is stubborn."

"Tell me about Klaus," McCarter said while James continued working.

"He heads the conglomerate that owns Ze, who the French work for. I thought I got away with something in Afghanistan but it seems I'm wrong."

"How so?"

"Provisional authority in Iraq shipped railroad cars full of money into the Green Zone. Some of them came up missing."

"Klaus?"

"Klaus and his contractors with Ze. I was working on a drone surveillance program. I caught the movement on a digital feed I sent to my brother. Then the contractors got hit transporting the money. I followed the insurgents with the drone, saw them bury the money then hit them with a Hellfire missile."

"Klaus wants his money back," McCarter said.

Smith nodded. "My brother and I covered the incident up and left Ze. It seems Klaus has put two and two together. Now he wants his money and any witnesses to his crime eliminated."

James waved his hand and shooed flies away before taking gauze dressings and placing them across the wound where they stuck and immediately turned red. He gave the hall outside another quick check when he was finished. A burst of heavy gunfire echoed in a rattling cacophony.

Manning saw the top of a head breach the lip of the stairs, followed almost instantly by a pair of widespread brown, almost black, eyes. The big Canadian centered his open sights on the IMU terrorist. The man struggled to bring up a battered AN-94 in the narrow confines of the staircase and twist it over the edge and fire on McCarter.

The Stony Man operative pulled the trigger on the machine gun. The gun snarled and 7.62 mm ComBloc bullets dug up gouges out of the hall floor as Manning walked his burst onto his target. The IMU soldier's right elbow came up sharply behind his head as he tried to pull the AN-94 back and then shove it forward and return fire. Splinters of wood, logged in nearby Tajikistan, tore off and spun through the air.

The first of two bullets struck the man in the crown of his head and knocked him back. A red cloud of bloody spray haloed the man's head and then he dropped out of sight. Manning waited, machine gun poised.

James continued to work feverishly. He had to move Smith but if he moved the contractor before he bandaged him then he would trail his guts out like confetti. He was very worried his efforts wouldn't matter anyway.

As McCarter peered out the window, James placed the folded pillowcase he had taken off Smith's bed over the bloody gauze bandages. He turned and picked up a length of sheet he'd cut in strips. Outside Manning heard something on the stair and picked up the RPK and fired a burst into the opening. His rounds tore into the wooden railing of the banister, chipping wood and snapping support struts.

James encouraged Smith to lean forward, which the contractor did, moaning low with the pain. He looped

Get FREE BOOKS and a FREE GIFT when you play the...

LAS VEGAS

GAME

Just scratch off the gold box with a coin. Then check below to see the gifts you get!

YES! I have scratched off the gold box. Please send me my **2 FREE BOOKS** and **gift for which I qualify.** I understand that I am under no obligation to purchase any books as explained on the back of this card.

366 ADL E4CE	166 ADL E4CE

FIRST NAME   LAST NAME

ADDRESS

APT.#   CITY

STATE/PROV.   ZIP/POSTAL CODE

7	7	7	Worth TWO FREE BOOKS plus a BONUS Mystery Gift!
🍒	🍒	🍒	Worth TWO FREE BOOKS!
🔔	🔔	♣	TRY AGAIN!

Offer limited to one per household and not valid to current subscribers of Gold Eagle® books. All orders subject to approval. Please allow 4 to 6 weeks for delivery.

If offer card is missing write to: The Reader Service, P.O. Box 1867, Buffalo NY 14240-1867

BUSINESS REPLY MAIL
FIRST-CLASS MAIL   PERMIT NO. 717   BUFFALO, NY

POSTAGE WILL BE PAID BY ADDRESSEE

THE READER SERVICE
PO BOX 1867
BUFFALO NY 14240-9952

NO POSTAGE
NECESSARY
IF MAILED
IN THE
UNITED STATES

the ends of the cloth strip around the man's torso and then helped him lean back.

"They're coming," McCarter whispered tersely. "Tie those sheet ends into place the best you can."

The knee of James's pants had become stiff with dried mud, but kneeling in Smith's blood had moistened the material again and it clung to his skin with a warm, slimy sensation as he rose in a combat crouch.

Keeping away from the window and watching the hall, McCarter picked his AKS-74 up again and ducked under the sling so that it hung off his shoulder and down across his body with the pistol grip dangling by his right hip. Once he had situated the folding stock carbine he called out to Encizo.

"What can you see?"

"I see a bunch of those IMU bastards, nothing on the Ze team. But it seems like the terrorists are dividing their forces. I call the situation a push."

He eyed the staircase outside the door to Smith's room. He had no illusions. Smith was unstable and couldn't be moved. He had no place to move him to or any means of transportation anyway. The private contractor was going to die in this stinking compound room.

His mind raced, cold logic fight with emotion and his own warrior's ethics. Mission creep had set in. The information Ze seemed willing to kill for was vital to the U.S. government, if only to prevent yet another cancer of corruption from emerging within the halls of power. McCarter believed this with true conviction and without question. Smith would have to give up his information. Beside him, James waved a few fat flies away from his face.

"If we can hold out long enough I believe my extraction team will arrive shortly, but I have no com-link now."

"Okay," Smith whispered. His voice sounded wet; it almost gurgled. McCarter looked at James, who shook his head slightly. Short of a hospital there was nothing to be done.

"But you know why Ze is here. I need you to tell me what you found and where it is."

"Business first?" He tried to laugh.

McCarter heard the hurt in his voice and risked a look over at the man. A stray round shot into the room. He barely flinched. Smith looked ghastly. He shifted his head and fixed him with a stare. His eyes were glassy.

"Who are you?" he asked.

McCarter glanced away from the dying man and back toward the open door. Operational security demanded he lie, but Smith was dying. It seemed sadistic to lie to a dying man when asking for his trust.

Outside an RPG round slammed into the building.

CHAPTER THIRTEEN

Dominican Republic

Lyons eyed his watch and then slid another chip onto Black 8. He almost wanted to place another bet just to make things interesting, but he was afraid the diversion could potentially throw off his contact. Smith didn't know him by sight, so any variation from the established contact routine would be stupid. The Asian, eyes glassy, left the blackjack dealer and stumbled up to the table as Lyons lost again. Two security guards in well-fitting jackets watched the table, seemingly bored. They were joined by a third after a moment.

Lyons put his chip down on Black 8 again. The guy with the dreadlocks ordered a drink from a passing cocktail waitress. The Asian changed cash into chips at the table and lit another cigarette. One of the blondes had moved behind the fat man and was whispering into his ear while she pressed her breasts up against his sweating back. Her friend leaned in beside him, hand in his lap under the table as he played.

"Red 4," the dealer said.

Lyons put his chip on Black 8 once more.

"Final time," he said.

There was a tense moment when the Asian man began throwing hundred-dollar chips across the board, but he didn't play Black 8 and Lyons relaxed as the croupier called an end to bets. This was it, Lyons reflected. The time for the meet in the prescribed manner was past. Smith hadn't shown. Another lead had dried up.

Lyons watched the roulette ball bounce around the revolving wheel. He smelled cigarette smoke and the sweat rolling off the Asian. Perfume and alcohol were copious scents as he watched the roulette ball hit Green 00.

Throwing a chip down for the croupier, Lyons rose.

It seemed he could feel the weight of the sniper's crosshairs on his exposed back, even though he knew that was ridiculous. Smith hadn't shown, but that didn't necessarily mean the meet location had been compromised.

Across the casino floor Blancanales finished his drink and left a tip for the bartender. Schwarz pumped the last of his coins into the slot machine and waved off a cocktail waitress.

Lyons was sure Smith had found trouble. He was working on a top-level asset itching to roll over on Dominican government corruption. When Ze operatives had shown up out of his past he had avoided his station command, used asymmetrical communications and now had missed a last-chance emergency meet. Lyons frowned as he walked. This was bullshit.

He walked outside and flipped open his regular cell phone. He hit a number on his speed dial while hailing a taxi driver in a sleek green Volvo. Blancanales and Schwarz joined him.

"That was a waste of time," Lyons growled.

"We can cross it off our list," Schwarz pointed out and slid into the taxi.

Lyons climbed into the taxi after him and gave the driver an address while Blancanales took the front seat.

The ride across the city took a while. Even with the rioting now tamped down, the driver had to take a surreptitious route to avoid police checkpoints as his passengers requested.

Lyons was convinced that the driver was taking them sightseeing in an attempt to run up the fare on top of everything else. He didn't protest as he felt the erratic driving and random street changes would help with any possible tails.

He paid the driver too much when he got out at the train station simply because he didn't want to wait around while the guy tried working him for a better tip. Blancanales leaned back as he climbed out of the cab and popped his back. Schwarz used his CPDA to update Stony Man.

Lyons stuffed his hands inside the pockets of his jacket and headed into the train station with Blancanales and Schwarz flanking him. The three men didn't need to speak; they'd worked together for so long they each knew the way the other would think, react and process information.

The very last of the workday commuters was going home and the old building was clearing out quickly as Able Team entered. They wove their way through the thinning crowd, pushing away from the passenger areas and toward the freight docks.

Wire crates stuffed with chickens were set against one wall. The smell of animal was strong here. Lyons noted the hardy determination of people in a poverty zone to continue stubbornly on with their lives. He had seen it across the globe but it never failed to give him hope for the human condition.

Lyons nodded once and the three men split up, got lost in the crowd and then turned back the way they'd come, exiting the building. Lyons and Blancanales cut through piss-smelling alleys and dodged across busy streets until they made it about two blocks over from the central train station. Schwarz took a longer looping route, cutting their back trail for tails.

Lyons stopped in front of a window display filled with pictures of Asian girls in school uniforms being spanked or tied up. His eyes scanned the window, attempting to survey the street behind him in the reflection. The light was bad for that and eventually he went ahead and entered the porn shop.

Blancanales drifted away from the big ex-cop once they entered the store, feigning interest in a variety of garish and often distasteful items.

The inside of the shop was illuminated with starkly colored light from neon tubes. Skin magazines and the box covers for movies were stuffed into cheap racks. A section on the far wall was filled with various kinky devices and sexual toys. The main room was filled with furtive men who avoided any eye contact with each other.

Lyons walked through the store, ignoring the other patrons. He entered the gloomy mouth to the hall where the peep shows were located.

He could hear gasps and moans coming from behind the closed doors to the video monitor booths. He heard the slap of a hand on flesh. He heard the sound of women's cries—some in faux pleasure, many in pain. He moved past the doors. The layout for the coin-operated theaters was in a T-shaped hallway. He walked down the long leg of the T past the video booths.

Blancanales positioned himself just down an aisle from the hall opening, surreptitiously watching the opening to see if anyone followed Lyons inside the dark corridor.

Lyons turned left at the juncture and went to the second-to-last door. An out-of-style techno beat was hammering out through a crappy stereo system. A light above the booth door showed red, indicating it was occupied.

He cursed under his breath with impatience before stepping back to wait. After a few moments the song changed and a disheveled-looking middle-aged man in a suit scurried out. He almost ran into Lyons and squeaked guiltily. He looked up, eyes appearing enormous behind thick glasses.

Lyons snarled down at him and the man hurried out of the hall. Lyons stepped forward and entered the filthy booth.

"Jesus Christ, Smith," he muttered to himself in disgust. "You picked a perfect place for a dead drop."

Lyons looked around him, disgust on his face now that he was alone. He shoved the bolt on the door home and then fed a few coins into the wall slot to change the light outside the booth to red.

A narrow opening slid back and, through smeary glass, Lyons caught a glimpse of a bored woman dancing listlessly in a room surrounded by coin-operated windows. Lyons reached into his pocket and pulled a credit card from his wallet. He turned away from the window and squatted. He saw glory holes had been bored through the wood paneling of the booth dividers.

Using the edge of the credit card to spare his fingers any unpleasant contact, Lyons reached up under the seat mounted in the wall. According to the stringer they'd interrogated, the booth was Smith's blind drop. He was running stringers in his surveillance operation against the government and he'd been picking up hard-copy materials from them here.

Lyons paused as he felt his card touch something other than the wooden underside of the filthy little bench. He sighed and put the credit card away. He reached under the seat and immediately frowned. Smith had attached a thin metal sleeve to hold items and the drop was stuffed full of papers.

Drops were made in public places to explain movement patterns to unfriendly surveillance. They weren't meant to be cache points. There was seldom longer than an hour between delivery and retrieval at such points. Nor was one site usually meant for more than a single stringer.

Lyons slid out five manila envelopes of varying thickness. This was a bad sign for Smith. Operational security was dissolving all around the FBI counterintelligence agent. Lyons stood and slid the envelopes into the waist of his pants at the small of his back and flipped his shirt over to conceal the envelope. He needed to get out and away from the drop site. He had to assume Smith had been made. That didn't necessarily mean the operation was over. If Able Team needed to do open-source or interview-based investigations it would inevitably make them targets of the opposition. It was an old situation for Able Team.

Lyons was counting on it.

Kyrgyzstan

"WE'VE GOT TO GET ready to move," McCarter said.

Smith smiled up at him with a wry expression, and McCarter realized how much he didn't want this man to die. He wasn't used to failure and the contractor had shown real courage. But it didn't matter what he wanted and he knew that. War, politics and the eternal struggle of one man to exert his will on another, for good or for ill, made his feelings irrelevant.

He looked back toward the stair landing, almost willing a IMU terrorist to appear so that he could haunt his frustration in violent action. He had seen the man's wound with his own eyes. McCarter may have been no physician, but he had a lifetime of experience with bullet wounds. It was bad. He moved to one side and called James over to give him a situation report. The brutal truth was that Phoenix Force needed to leave.

"He's taken the round low and the intestines have been damaged," James whispered. "The intestine serves as the tailpipe of the human system, carrying biological impurities in the form of fecal matter out of the body. The round has spilled that dirty matter into the blood and healthy tissue. The medical term is sepsis, which means death is guaranteed." James paused, cutting his eyes back toward the man. "He needs a hospital now. With our com jammed, he's sitting on a death sentence."

"Who are you guys?" Smith asked again. "Pentagon? The Agency?"

His voice was weak and the pain ran through it in a dark current. McCarter wasn't an espionage agent: lying was not part of his job description. He was a soldier and he saw things through a soldier's eyes. It took everything he had not to simply kill Smith. Death was his gift. The man lay there suffering with no hope of salvation or relief, yet he witnessed Smith's strength and courage for himself.

McCarter shook his head, steeling himself. He had dedicated himself to a truth larger than personal vengeance, even if that had been the crucible that had spawned him. He had dedicated himself to a fragile ideology. One of immense potential but still fragile in the face of determined and violent opposition.

The ideology, the belief system, was larger than any one individual and, for the moment, a secret that could bolster that ideology in its time of need lay buried in Smith's mind. Smith did not deserve to be lied to in the last moments of his life. But McCarter's ideology deserved champions strong enough to lie.

"Who are you?" Smith repeated.

His words were so weak they sounded like a sigh in McCarter's ears.

"My name isn't important," McCarter said. "I was here to rescue you. But I'm unofficial."

"You're a mercenary?"

McCarter looked away from the dying man and back out into the hallway. Outside more gunfire erupted. The Ze contractors were fighting to get to their team; the IMU was fighting everybody. Only moments had passed since they'd entered the room but time was a strange sensation and McCarter felt as if he'd kept Phoenix Force in place for hours.

"Smith, there is no time. Ze wants to kill you because you know something. You found it out. You need to tell me what it was."

"Am I going to die?" McCarter was stunned by the naked strength of the acceptance in his voice.

He turned his head away from the hall and looked straight into Smith's eyes. "Yes," he said.

Out in the hallway Encizo caught the flash of movement and spun on reflexes so honed by experience that they were nearly preternatural. The weapon bucked as he pulled the trigger. From the stairs the man charged upward, a Chinese Type 56 assault rifle screaming staccato shrieks in his hands.

The 7.62 mm rounds poured into the compound room as the man cleared the landing edge and bounded onto the second-floor of the compound. Bullets lanced up and through the open doorway, one striking James in his body armor and sending him spinning. He fell into McCarter and the two men tumbled to the floor.

Manning shifted naturally, like a dancer responding to a cue, his own weapon firing in response. The machine gun's burst clawed up the floor, chewing through it as the stream of fire bore straight down onto Manning. The big Canadian tightened his own burst and put it on target and directly into his attacker. The IMU terrorist soaked up the rounds and stopped short at their impact.

Manning's heavy rounds tore into the Chinese assault rifle, smashing the wooden grips and frame before ricocheting off the metal barrel and receiver in a spray of sparks. Other rounds punctured the terrorist's limbs, and geysers of blood spouted as the bones of the man's forearms were shattered under the impact of the high-velocity rounds.

Above Manning, Encizo let the muzzle climb as he kept the trigger down. Three rounds arced over the assault rifle and slammed into the skinny man's chest, smashing bones and ripping into the pectoral and intercostal muscles. Immediately the triggerman's lungs collapsed and blood gushed out of his mouth.

The terrorist shook with the impact of Manning's, then Encizo's rounds. The Chinese assault rifle fell to the floor and the man collapsed. Manning saw the man's mouth work as he tried to speak around the spilling blood, then his eyes rolled up, showing the whites, and he plunged to the floor.

Manning threw the RPK, sure that its drum, his last, was almost spent. He dropped his right hand to his hip and claimed the pistol grip of the AKS-74 slung over his shoulder. He lifted it up as his left hand dropped to find a handhold on the front stock.

He pushed the weapon out to the edge of its strap to steady it and squared his shoulder against the pull. His finger found the smooth metal curve of the trigger and he swept the muzzle toward the stair, tensed.

Nothing moved.

"Clear?" Encizo asked, voice soft.

Manning blinked the sweat out of his eyes and looked again. Nothing moved. The terrorist Manning had just stopped coughed wetly then sighed with a sound like air escaping from a tire.

James grunted from the pain of the blunt impact and pushed himself off the Phoenix Force team leader. Reasonably reassured that the attack was over, McCarter risked a glance back toward Smith.

More than one of the bullets from the gunman had caught the man in the legs. McCarter saw the bullet wound in his thigh and saw another in the American contractor's shin where the white fragments of his crushed bones showed up in vivid relief against the pink of his torn flesh and the scarlet of his spilling blood.

McCarter looked up at Smith's face. It was white as chalk.

He realized Smith was so far gone he hadn't cried out at the impact of the new wounds. McCarter steeled himself the way he had a thousand times before and steadied his voice.

"Smith," he said. "Smith, tell me. What did you learn?"

Smith lifted his hand and pointed weakly across the room past the leaking corpses of IMU terrorists and Ze mercenaries. He opened his mouth to speak and McCarter realized he was so weak he couldn't hear him. He shifted closer and bent until his ear was almost touching the bloodless lips.

"What?" he asked.

"My cell phone," he said. "I wrote it down then took a picture with my cell phone. The grid coordinates and a summary of the record files. Short, but it will…tell you."

His voice trailed off and McCarter sat up and looked down at him. Smith looked up at the ex–SAS commando and McCarter watched his eyes become fixed. Just as suddenly they relaxed in a blank stare. McCarter saw the light fade from them and the chalky gray of his skin spread to the brown of his irises and he knew the man was gone.

McCarter reached out a hand and touched his fingertips to the man's eyelids, closing them. He looked up at the doorway, then back down at the dead man's face.

"He's gone," James sighed. "We'll be, too, if we don't get the hell out of here."

Outside the window McCarter heard the sound of vehicle engines running, then car doors slamming. Then he heard French and McCarter knew the mercenaries had arrived.

CHAPTER FOURTEEN

McCarter moved quickly over to where Smith's gear had been strewed around by his kidnappers. His duffel lay open with its contents spread in a pile on the floor. McCarter shifted his hand through the clothes and personal items, hunting for the cell phone Smith had mentioned.

Another burst of fire entered the room through the window and McCarter sank to one knee as he discovered and opened the phone.

He worked the buttons on the control pad furiously, looking up to the door every several seconds. It would be no good for the team to escape the compound room only to find Smith had kept more than one cell phone. He needed to verify he possessed the information before Phoenix Force began the run for home.

He opened up the menu and went to the camera option. He tapped his thumb against the button and scrolled down through a multitude of touristy pictures obviously designed as cover. Then he found the photograph of a yellow legal page of handwritten notes sandwiched between a picture of the mosque across the street and two smiling Muslim boys using Acacia tree branches as switches to drive sheep.

Satisfied, McCarter snapped the phone shut and secured it away.

"Got it," he told James. "All right, boys, we are leaving!"

He took up his Kalashnikov and started for the door to the room. Outside the broken window he heard what sounded like thunder in the distance. He knew it wasn't thunder. It sounded like 60 mm mortar rounds to him. With the break in the rain the European team had begun its assault again.

Dominican Republic

LYONS UNLOCKED THE DOOR to the booth and stepped out into the gloomy hallway. He sensed movement at the intersection of the theater hall and looked up. The broad-shouldered man with the dreadlocks from the casino rounded the corner. Their eyes met, locked in recognition.

In the hallway out of sight behind the man he heard Blancanales cursing in Spanish and the slap of fists hitting flesh as he fought a second man in the hall.

Lyons launched himself instantly, driving hard straight at the man, using his momentum to rise off the ground, swinging up his right knee. He drove his knee hard into the man's ribs. The guy grunted and staggered backward from the impact.

Lyons landed and swept his hands up to grip the back of the man's head in a maneuver designed to control and crowd him. The man's reflexes were lightning quick and he struck the inside of Lyons's right arm at the nerve cluster just behind the elbow. Pain flashed up Lyons's arm and it was knocked aside, leaving an opening.

The dreadlocked man stepped forward and struck Lyons with a fist in his now exposed ribs. Lyons stumbled backward, bruised and hurt and surprised. Lyons brought his arms up in front of him and instinctively turned to the side and raised a leg to ward off further blows.

Instead of pushing his advantage physically, the man shuffled backward and his right hand went for the small of his back. Lyons saw the movement and moved forward. The man's hands reappeared holding a black automatic pistol.

Lyons stepped forward, moving to the outside of the muscled killer's arm. The tight space of the hallway hampered his movements, slowing him down. He twisted so that he was facing the man at a nearly ninety-degree angle. Lyons's left hand caught the man's wrist just behind the pistol and, using the man's own forward motion, Lyons pulled him off balance. Lyons used his right hand to snap a straight punch into his opponent's temple.

The impact was loud in the confined space and the man sagged under the sharp force. Lyons stepped away, twisting at the hips. The hand that had just delivered the brutal punch now twisted to became a claw, sweeping the man's head backward while Lyons pulled the gun hand back and thrust his chest out against the trapped arm, overextending the elbow.

The gun clattered to the floor and the man dropped, as well. Without thinking, operating on a blind killer's instinct, Lyons lifted his foot up and drove his heel straight down into the man's throat. The killer's startled eyes opened wide, then rolled upward into his head.

Lyons moved quickly. He glanced around him and saw no one. The altercation had lasted only heartbeats and the computerized bee-bop music system still blared out the same song. Lyons knelt and slid the man's pistol into the small of his back before expertly patting the dead man down.

He stepped forward and looked around the corner of the hallway to where Blancanales stood over another dead man. The Puerco Rican looked at the ex–LAPD detective. "We get what we came for?"

"Let me shake this body down, then we better get the hell out of here," Lyons answered.

Bending, he pulled out a wallet, a cell phone and a balisong butterfly knife. Lyons pocketed the items and stood. He adjusted his shirt over the bulge made by the envelopes from Smith's drop point. He held his head up and coolly walked out of the dark hallway. Blancanales fell into step silently.

Lyons's nerves were on fire as he made his way for the door. He had no intention of being in the building when the bodies were found. He pushed through the door and on out into the street. He looked around carefully, as hitters seldom worked alone. The two-man team should have an overwatch backup.

Lyons started walking, looking for a taxi. It was possible the men had been assigned surveillance and had decided to take Lyons out on his own. If they were criminal stringers, then it was even possible they had been working alone on a zone defense surveillance. Lyons had no intention of taking that possibility for granted, however.

He needed to get to his safehouse and take stock of what he'd learned since hitting the ground in Santo Domingo. Lyons pushed his way through a lively crowd as he looked for a taxi. Blancanales scanned the crowd as they made their way toward Schwarz's position.

Lyons didn't see a cab and he decided to head back toward the central bus station. He'd have his choice of taxis there and the walk would give him a chance to shake out anyone shadowing him.

He crossed the busy strip, ignoring angry shouts and beeping horns. Such things were commonplace here. This section of the city stank and the cold, seasonal damp made him feel as if his skin was covered in a greasy film. Reaching the other side of the street, Lyons ducked into the alley he'd used to reach the street the porn shop was on.

Lyons stepped passed an unconscious man sprawled in the mouth of the alley. The man reeked of strong, cheap booze. Lyons entered alley, his nostrils flaring at the stench of rotting garbage.

Lyons was halfway down the alley when he turned to look over his shoulder. No preternatural combat sense had warned him, just good tradecraft. A simple matter of being careful. He saw the silhouette enter the alley and he spun, dropping to one knee. If there was any lesson he had learned over the years, it was that bullets traveled down walls. He pulled his appropriated pistol free and assumed a modified Weaver grip.

"There's two of 'em!" Blancanales warned.

The figure at the end of the alley already had his pistol out and it barked twice. Two rounds buzzed through the air above Lyons's head, just where his heart would have been were he still standing. He answered with a triple burst of 9 mm rounds.

Just in front of him Blancanales had taken a knee and returned fire, as well.

Instantly his vision was blurred by the blinding flash of the weapon and his ears buzzed from the sudden, sharp reports. At the end of the alley he had a sense of the figure spinning away. He heard the sleeping man shout in surprise and saw him sit up.

Realizing that the figure was going for the cover of the building edge, Lyons popped up into a crouch and shuffled quickly backward. The figure came around the edge of the alley and got off a hasty shot that sang wide. Lyons and Blancanales each answered with a single shot designed to impact the wall near the figure's head and spray chips.

Their rounds drove the gunman back behind cover, and Lyons took his opportunity to escape out of the alley.

"Let's go!" he shouted.

Lyons hit the street running with Blancanales right behind him. He shouldered his way through the crowd like a running back pushing for open field. He knocked several pedestrians to the ground, ignoring their cries of outrage. Half a second later the slightly slower Blancanales repeated the maneuver.

He reached the front of the train station and jogged over to the line of waiting taxis. He leaned forward and pushed some folded bills into the driver's waiting hand as Blancanales jumped into the vehicle after him.

Lyons rattled off an address to get the man moving and leaned back into the ratty seat as the driver pulled out into traffic.

The pistol was warm against the small of his back and its weight was reassuring. Finally the taxi driver made his way into the heavy traffic and Lyons allowed himself to relax. He pulled his cell phone out and flipped it open.

"Brognola isn't going to be happy about this."

"Tell 'em we'll fix it, no problem," Blancanales huffed. "We always do."

Kyrgyzstan

MCCARTER CAME OUT into the hallway, held the Kalashnikov up and risked a glance down the staircase as he reached the landing. He saw only corpses on the stair but heard movement from the lobby below. He triggered a 5-round burst of harassing fire downward to temper any enthusiasm on the terrorists' part.

Suddenly he heard Jack Grimaldi's voice through his ear-jack and he sighed in relief.

"Phoenix, do you copy?"

"Phoenix here," McCarter answered.

"I'm flying low altitude with counterintrusive measures. We need to speed up the timetable."

"Copy that. I'm sending data transmission to you. Relay it the mission controller."

"Understood. Go ahead and send."

Instantly, McCarter quickly manipulated his communications devices and sent the transmission.

"Received and pushed forward," Grimaldi replied after a moment. "I'm keeping this bird near the RZ."

"Copy that. We're en route," McCarter signed off.

McCarter pulled his weapon back and began to move quickly toward the end of the second-story hallway. Outside he heard a shell detonate somewhere close by in the village. He knew there would be a hell of a lot more fire after the Kyrgyzstan artillery spotters noted where the reconnaissance rounds landed.

McCarter shouldered through the last door at the rear of the hallway. The room was empty and identical to Smith's. The single window overlooked the alley Phoenix Force had used to approach the compound. McCarter let the Kalashnikov hang from its strap and used both hands to slam open the unbroken window.

James came up beside him, attempting to establish contact with Hawkins.

"Hawk here," the Phoenix Force sniper replied.

"Good to hear your voice again," James said with relief. "We're unassing the AO. Bring it in to the RZ."

"Copy. I heard J.G. and I'm rolling out. But look alive—the place is crazy with locals fighting it out with the strike team."

"Will do." James signed off.

James stepped back from the window and moved to one side. He pressed up against the wall next to the window frame and looked out over the rooftops and alley in one direction. McCarter maneuvered to the opposite side and repeated the process. He could see nothing, which only meant troops weren't standing in the open or moving through his field of vision.

Behind him the rest of Phoenix Force had clustered together in preparation for exfiltration. Gunfire poured up the stairs and more hammered into the building through the shot-out windows. Manning opened up with his machine gun while Encizo and James worked the stairs using grenades and long bursts from their assault rifles.

Two more shells struck near the compound and exploded, though McCarter couldn't see where they impacted. From outside in the street he heard machine-gun fire coming from downstairs rip up into the hall as the troops down there prepared to assault the second floor.

McCarter made his decision.

"Fall out, Phoenix!"

He sat on the window ledge and swung his legs through the opening. He took the Kalashnikov in his right hand and grasped the bottom of the sill with his left. He bounced himself off the lip and pushed away from the wall with his left hand.

He dropped the two stories like a stone. He struck the muddy ground with his feet together and his knees bent to absorb the force of landing. As soon as the soles of his boots struck the muck of the alley McCarter rolled down along his side, transferring the force of the impact along the length of his body the way he had been taught countless years ago as a paratrooper.

He rolled over his shoulder and came up to one knee, bringing the Kalashnikov to bear. James grunted softly behind him as he landed, followed quickly by Encizo. Manning came last, landing with agile grace for such a big man.

McCarter spun in a tight circle and scanned the opposite area. He saw nothing and leaped to his feet. He heard artillery shells detonating behind him, on the other side of the compound, and he crossed the alley, skirting the thatched animal pen where he had killed the IMU armed with the Dragunov sniper rifle.

He ducked under the cover of the tin roof and heard more automatic weapons fire from inside the compound. He heard a shout in what sounded like French and knew the mercenaries were behind him. He risked a glance as he rolled over the rails and into the sheep pen behind the compound building.

Two white men, one armed with a Remington 870 pump-action shotgun and the other with an H&K

MP-5, were in the mouth of the narrow alley that ran between the compound and the garage McCarter had cleared earlier. They wore black fatigues, balaclavas and boonie hats. The merc with the H&K was yelling something down the alley toward the main square while the one handling the Remington 870 leveled it toward McCarter.

"Shooter!" McCarter snarled, and rolled, bringing his carbine around.

McCarter flopped to the ground on his belly as .12-gauge shot tore into the wooden rails of the sheep pen. The stink of sheep feces made soupy by the heavy rains rankled his nose. He lifted the AKS-74 with one hand and leveled the barrel across the lowest rung of the fence. He triggered a wild burst and scattered the two men, sending them scrambling for cover.

Buckshot tore into James, catching him in the thigh with terrific force. He crumpled immediately. Encizo leaped to help him even as Manning spun and brought the machine gun to bear.

A third mercenary threw a hand grenade underhand with almost casual indifference. It struck the ground in front of the clustered men, bounced once and rolled toward them.

Encizo reacted without thinking. He dived forward and slapped the grenade back around the corner of the building, where it almost immediately detonated. Exposed, sprawled out on the ground, he caught a burst in the back and lay still.

"Hawk!" McCarter screamed into his throat mike. "We have contact!"

"Up!" Hawkins answered. "I'm moving toward your twenty."

Manning cut loose with the machine gun, firing one-handed as he pulled the unconscious Encizo back into the lee of the compound building. Mercenaries were crawling across one side of the alley and only the presence of IMU fighters on their flank kept them from overwhelming Phoenix Force.

For six minutes that seemed to stretch for an eternity McCarter and Manning held the enemy combatants at bay. The incoming fire was so intense it was impossible to perform first aid on the bleeding and unconscious men.

"Rolling up the stockyards behind you," Hawkins warned over the radio.

"Understood," McCarter replied.

Moments later Hawkins rushed in, threw himself down between the two men and began performing first aid. Hot shell casings littered the torn-up ground in front of the team's makeshift position.

"They patched up?" McCarter asked as he swapped out a spent magazine.

"Good as it's going to get at the moment," Hawkins shouted back. He picked up his sniper rifle and shot an IMU terrorist in the head. His weapon cycled as he shifted the barrel and he put a round into a balaclava-covered mercenary.

"There's more of them coming," Manning warned. "We've got to get to Jack at the RZ!"

McCarter knew what had to happen. He surveyed the scene but couldn't come up with another plan. He lifted his voice to be heard over the clatter of weapons.

"Listen up. I'm going to cover your withdrawal. You two will get Encizo and James to the rendezvous zone while I draw off these forces."

"We're going," Manning replied. "You make your way to the edge of this village, and we'll get Jack back as soon as we get James and Encizo across the border. That's a forty-minute turn and burn." The burly Canadian locked eyes with McCarter. "You be ready to go when I get back."

Despite the seriousness, McCarter felt himself smile. "Will do, big man. Now get the hell out of here."

Not giving them a chance to reply, McCarter jumped to his feet and took the Kalashnikov assault rifle in both hands before firing a second burst from the hip. The merc with the H&K subgun dived for cover behind the same oil barrels McCarter had used earlier. The other man threw himself down on the ground, hugging the side of the compound wall in the narrow alleyway.

Manning and Hawkins lifted their wounded comrades as McCarter recklessly made a target of himself to draw fire. His attention fully focused on his attack, he didn't see them leave.

CHAPTER FIFTEEN

McCarter lifted the AKS-74 to shoulder level and began to dance backward as he fired. Beyond the two men he saw movement at the public square end of the alley. He blinked in surprise but continued firing. A fire team of mercenaries cut two IMU gunmen down.

At the moment McCarter had no way of knowing it, but Phoenix Force had just interrupted Michael Klaus's operation. The puppet master's chief henchman in the region, Haight, was the leader of the mercenary team. The ruthless, amoral professional now moved forward to take command of his forces.

Haight came around the front of the mercenary vehicle. He began directing his men with short, sharp commands.

The merc behind the oil barrels popped up and sprayed the stockyard with his H&K MP-5.

McCarter ducked down and sprinted across the sheep pen to the far side. He dived over the fence and stayed down when he hit the ground. Cradling the Kalashnikov in the crooks of his arms, McCarter crawled away from the animal pen and over toward a round silo used to store crops.

More high-explosive rounds began to fall from IMU mortars. This time they hit much closer to the center of the village. McCarter knew the cluster of buildings around the main square would be a priority target for the Kyrgyzstan mortar crews, which was part of the reason he was trying to make it back out to the edge of the Kyrgyzstan village. Two streets over from his position a shanty house exploded when a artillery shell detonated after punching through its thin roof.

A white Land Rover gunned up the narrow alley. Mercs armed with AKM assault rifles hung out the front and rear passenger windows. The vehicle slid to a stop in front of the wool-shearing pen and the two troopers opened fire.

McCarter rolled over onto his back as rounds chewed through the humid air above him. He brought his AKS to bear and fired back at the men. His rounds dented and pockmarked the vehicle. The light-skinned doors dimpled and crumpled under the 7.62 mm rounds.

The man in the backseat screamed as he was struck through the door by the high-velocity, heavy-caliber rounds. His weapon dropped out of his hands and clattered to the ground as he fell back into the vehicle. McCarter pulled the muzzle of his weapon up toward his chin as he fired, directing his rounds toward the front of the vehicle.

The rounds climbed as he swept them to the side. Bullets burrowed into the front mercenary's shoulder and neck after shattering the man's elbow. His rifle fell into the mud, as well, and he slumped forward heavily. A torrent of blood spilled from the neck wound and rushed down the white door of the Land Rover.

McCarter rolled back over onto his stomach. He pushed up with one hand and came to his knees. He popped up to his feet into a crouch and dived toward the cover of the one-story grain silo.

He heard men scream behind him, then their voices

were drowned out by the shriek of an incoming mortar round. McCarter reached the curved wall of the silo and skirted around it. The 82 mm struck the empty sheep pen and went off.

McCarter felt the concussion slam his back as he slid around the edge of the building. He heard shrapnel strike the silo in a steel rain and his ears rang from the blast. The mortar crews had found their range now, he knew. One or two clicks on the sighting mechanism and the shells would begin raining down on the compound.

He thought of Smith lying dead in the shitty compound room, flies driven indoors by the rain feasting on his remains, crawling in a thick black carpet across his face. He hoped a mortar round blew the room to hell and gave the warrior a burial by fire.

He quickly risked a look around the edge of the silo and saw the mercenaries with the Remington 870 run up to the rail of the sheep pen. Miraculously the stockyard side of the fence was still intact.

The man took up a defensive position on one knee and lifted the pump-action shotgun to his shoulder. He scanned through the smoke and haze left by the mortar round, searching for McCarter. The muzzle of the sweeping shotgun froze as the man spotted McCarter peeking around the corner of the silo, Kalashnikov up.

The mercenary's eyes widened in shock at seeing McCarter draw down on him.

Switzerland

MICHAEL KLAUS REGARDED his board of directors with a solemn and authoritative gaze that emanated from eyes as flat and unreflective as a snake's. Mr. Skell stood in a quiet corner away from the conference table, quietly watching the proceedings.

"Gentlemen," Klaus began. "We are faced with a situation of grave severity." He stood, head bowed, and clasped his hands behind his back. "Several hours ago one of our field operations in Southwest Asia began to manifest…complications. This coincides with the difficulties we've seen in the Caribbean division."

The powerful man turned to regard his floor-to-ceiling black-lighted aquarium as gasps of outrage filled the room. He allowed the outburst to continue for several moments before turning back and leaning forward to rest his well-manicured hands on the black oak conference table.

"The operation in question was labeled Project Aristotle in your eyes-only quarterly reports." In Michael Klaus's corporations there was more than one set of quarterly reports. Those the shareholders got, those the board of directors got and those he got. "This project represents two years and several billion dollars in corporate funds on the deployment of an artificial intelligence enhancement formula."

One of the senior vice presidents spoke up. "I was under the impression that this project was unstable due to our researchers in Nigeria experiencing terminal hemorrhaging of the cerebral nexus due to chemical-induced burnout after only two exposures to the drug."

Klaus watched his king barracuda glide through the artificially lit waters of his aquarium. When he answered, his voice was soft.

"That is correct," he said. "But five weeks ago our biochemists were able to narrow the effects of the

Aristotle component down to sensory and informational procession, effectively increasing the chemical burnout to almost six months. This reduced volunteer mortality by fifty-one percent. With cycling this was reduced by a further thirty-three percent. We are very close to an acceptable threshold. We believe we have a highly viable product."

"Not mentioning illicit sales," a second vice president added. "If we can duplicate the American tobacco companies' framework for controlling regulated sales and black-market access, the profit margin becomes staggering."

Klaus merely nodded before resuming his seat. "At 7:00 p.m. yesterday evening a paramilitary strike force from the American CIA struck our Nigerian laboratory. Our private military corporation Ze had a platoon of security operators there. Seventeen were kil—"

"What about the drug?" a chief financial officer seated in front of Skell called out.

Klaus regarded him with an impersonal gaze that bore a remarkable resemblance to the look his barracuda was now giving a grouper. The CFO swallowed heavily and eased back into his leather chair as if trying to be absorbed by it.

"Seventeen of our security personnel were killed," Klaus continued. "All physical specimens were destroyed."

"Computer records?" a hesitant voice asked from the far end of the table.

Klaus shook his head slowly. Skell poured himself a drink, very neat.

"At 3:15 a.m. this morning a hostile predator virus was introduced into our system through our credit-card payment accounts. It was powered by what our IT people think was a supercomputer. The ninja virus wiped out four percent of our records, including the Aristotle Project, which was hidden in a communal equities account."

"Our informant on the Senate Intelligence Committee confirmed it was an American NSA operation," Skell broke in.

"Jesus Christ!" the first senior vice president moaned. "Moscow is going to have our asses." A wave of murmuring panic began to surge through the executive briefing room.

"Quiet." Klaus did not condone the public mention of the corporate ties to the criminal oligarchs of modern capitalist Russia. His tone was flat, without inflection, and he did not raise his voice, but the effect was immediate. Silence ruled the conference room. "We have the leaks identified and our own tactical operators are presently working on the problem. It appears to have been an accidental exposure by two low-ranking employees who've now left one of our umbrella companies. Brothers named Smith, as happenstance would have it. Most especially one of whom became an FBI agent currently working in Santo Domingo.

"However, if all goes well, the formula should be in our possession before the day is out. Making a report to the Moscow director completely unnecessary."

Sighs of relief echoed around the table as the board realized their jobs, and perhaps their lives, were still safe. Klaus, who had a lot more than his employment at stake, smiled at their petty insignificance.

Skell's cell phone, the only one allowed on during such meetings, buzzed and he answered it.

A VP from the middle of the table turned toward Klaus. "And the leak?"

This inquiry brought the attention of the board onto the head of the table again. Behind Klaus the barracuda struck, severing the grouper in two so that scarlet ribbons of blood hung in the water. Klaus smiled and bowed his head.

"That is why I called this meeting, now that the immediate threat has been identified," he lied with a smile. "This tasking is now international and crosses over into direct conflict with the interests of a superpower. As such a full committee vote should be taken before action can be initiated."

"Extract the son of a bitch," the CFO said without hesitation.

His suggestion was met with loud and vigorous approval by the rest of the committee. Behind Klaus the barracuda began gulping down chunks of the weakly struggling fish. Klaus spread his hands open.

"The board has spoken. Let the record show that extraction seven thirty-one has been officially authorized."

Skell closed the phone as the board members began filing out. He began to sweat. He knew Klaus's favorite procurement agency had sent over a new gigolo. The young man was now waiting in Klaus's inner office dressed like an investment banker. But he was going to have to wait, Skell knew. Haight and Lemis had each reported in to his operation control.

Things were going very wrong in both Kyrgyzstan and the Dominican Republic.

Dominican Republic

ONCE INSIDE the two-story house Able Team locked the door behind them and reengaged the alarm system. Lyons went into the Western-style kitchen and pulled open the fridge door. It was well stocked and he pulled out a bright red Coca-Cola can. He leaned against the counter and guzzled the soda. After finishing it in a few quick gulps he belched loudly and tossed the empty can into the sink.

"That was a bunch of bullshit," he murmured.

Blancanales reached for a soda in the refrigerator. He took the can and set it down on the kitchen table. He watched as Lyons pulled the envelopes free and threw them down on the table.

"Let's see what we have," Schwarz said.

Lyons sighed and leaned forward, putting his head in his hands and closing his eyes for a moment. His knuckles were still slightly sore from where they'd struck the man in the porn shop. Blancanales watched Schwarz open the material.

He pulled the first of the five manila envelopes over to him. Inside Schwarz found computer printouts. He shifted them around, studying details. It was a schematic diagram. He frowned. He had the technical expertise to tell what these were blueprints to, but they made no sense.

"I've got to send these to the Farm," Schwarz said. "I don't think they are electronics. I think they're using electronic schematics to hide information, maybe biological from the construction, but I can't tell without a good analytical program."

"What else we got?" Lyons asked, growing restless.

Schwarz pushed the schematic photocopy aside and opened the next envelope. More of the same. The third one showed a text list of numbers running down a spreadsheet. He knew he was looking at an accounting ledger. The numbers showed transactions, dates, amounts and specific account numbers.

"You were getting some good stuff," Schwarz murmured to the absent Smith.

He threw the papers on top of the pile of information and rubbed his eyes. Blancanales picked them up to look them over, then picked up his soda can and drank it off quickly.

Schwarz pulled the next-to-the-last envelope over to him and opened it with his knife. Several photos spilled out across the table. He sat up, suddenly alert, completely surprised by what he was seeing.

"What do we have here?"

In the photos two men were locked together, naked, on a bed. Schwarz held them up. It showed a younger Asian passionately kissing an older European male.

"Jesus." Blancanales frowned. "What the hell?"

He looked at the rest of the pictures. The men, already naked, progressed quickly beyond the kissing stage.

"What's this all about, Smith?" Lyons wondered out loud. "You don't work for J. Edgar Hoover," Lyons said, referencing the famous head of the FBI and his predilection for dirt and smut.

Schwarz pulled two photos out of the pile and set them in front of him. He slid the rest back into the envelope so they wouldn't distract him. The two photos each showed good frontal shots of the men's faces. Lyons studied them intently over his shoulder, memorizing every detail of their faces. When he was satisfied, he put them away and watched Schwarz open the final envelope.

Inside the envelope was a folded piece of stationery. Schwarz unfolded it and looked at what was written there. It was a simple series of numbers written in what he would guess was a feminine hand, though it was hard to tell with numerals.

5-3-20-9-1 13-2-10-17-22 5-19 1 12-8-15-22-4 3-19-7-3-24 5-6-4-9-4-22 2-23-8-11 1-9-3

"Spy shit."

Schwarz frowned.

"Can you bust it?" Blancanales asked. "Here, I mean, with the safehouse computer?"

"Maybe," Schwarz admitted. "If the drop was a fast turnover situation, then it was possible the code was a simple system meant for Smith to decipher quickly and then destroy, rather than sophisticated encryption."

The Able Team electronics genius got up and stretched. He went out into the living area where he had seen the desk with the computer. It might help with research, but this house had been set up as a hidey-hole, not a field operations center, and communications were not secure. There were the cyberequivalents of blind drops, but he had no intention of using them from this location unless he absolutely had to.

He got a pen and paper out of the desk and went back to the kitchen table, recalling cryptography and field procedure seminars run by blacksuits tasked with supplementing Kurtzman's cybernetic team. Schwarz needed a good down-and-dirty field code Smith might have used to instruct a stringer. From the numbers it was obviously a replacement code of some sort. While Lyons and Blancanales paced, he got to work with pen and paper. He was in operational theater 4. He needed to add that to the last digit of the day of the date of the drop and then transpose the numbers with letters of the alphabet.

He tried the day Smith had made his call. Got a jumble of alphabet letters, then tried switching the letters out with the next letter in the alphabet. Got nothing. Tried it with the letter prior and came up empty. He snarled and thrust the sheets of paper away.

Lyons went to the refrigerator, where he reached in and pulled out a can of soda. He idly wondered what poor schmuck had gone all the way through college CIA recruitment only to find himself putting his security clearance to use stocking the fridge in some rarely used safehouse in a shithole country.

Schwarz's mind worked furiously, cluttered with images, snapshot memories of a hundred different events and a thousand different days from his past. He got up, walked over to the doorway and reached up to grab the lip of the jamb at the top. He dug his fingers in tightly and began to pull himself up in slow, deliberate movements. The exercise was an old rock climber's movement designed to strengthen the hands and forearms as much as the biceps and back muscles.

After an easy fifteen chin-ups to get his blood moving, Schwarz lowered himself and walked back over to the table. He clenched and unclenched his fists, loosening the muscles of his grip. He shrugged his shoulders back to stretch and looked down at the table.

Shaking random thoughts away, he sat, pulling his notes back toward him. He looked at the numbers. They sat there, stubbornly refusing to give up their secrets. A slow smile slid across his face.

"Just maybe," he murmured.

He popped up and crossed over to the computer, where he immediately logged on. He set his notes beside him at the desk and signed on to the internet. He pulled up a Spanish/English dictionary and typed a word from his notes into the computer. The word came back unknown. Lyons threw that sheet down and picked up the sheet where he had transposed the letter corresponding with the number abstraction and the letter directly following it.

He hurriedly typed the series of letters into the computer. He got a match. He wrote the match down and then typed each word in until he translated the note in its entirety. When he was done he leaned back, feeling satisfied despite himself.

"Gentlemen, it must feel so lucky to be on a team with a genius like me." He grinned.

"Oh, God." Blancanales frowned. "You're going to be murder to live with."

"Just read the goddamn note," Lyons growled.

Schwarz read the note: "'Lemis works for Klaus. Break all contact.'"

CHAPTER SIXTEEN

Stony Man Farm

Hal Brognola hurried away from the helicopter while the blades were still turning. Beside the helipad Barbara Price was waiting for him in a Chevy Blazer. The big Fed in the rumpled suit got in and slammed the door.

"Good morning," Price said. It was now 2:00 a.m.

"Morning," Brognola agreed. Price turned the Blazer around and drove toward the farmhouse as the helicopter took off. "Give me the news."

"Let me give you the rundown as it unfolded from the start," Price said. "We roll Phoenix and Able for what we ostensibly thought were two separate ops. Then mission creep arrives when Bear's whiz kids figure out that both our kidnapped contractor and missing FBI agent are the brothers Smith."

"Both of whom worked at one time for Ze," Brognola agreed.

"Correct. And they found something out," Price continued. "Something big. Something about the mother corp, Ze. Which is run by Michael Klaus."

"Who's been on our radar for some time and who sold his soul to the Russian syndicates."

"Correct. The CIA and the NSA were pulling some kind of snatch-and-grab op in both the physical and virtual arenas. Both of them using information provided by Smith in the Dominican, who followed up on his personal leads."

"Serendipity is a bitch," Brognola grunted. "Okay. The CIA, NSA task force has the big problem under control. What are we doing?"

"Number one, we're putting the pieces together into the final picture for our friends in the alphabet-soup agencies. Number two, we're trying to save two patriots who've gotten themselves into a world of trouble. Able is hot on the case in Santo Domingo. Only Kyrgyzstan has gone wrong, thanks to the intervention of Klaus's bully boys, Ze. With the information Phoenix gave us via the uplink with Grimaldi, we've cracked the big mystery."

"And I got the directive from the President to dismantle Ze's field operation and sanction Klaus."

"Phoenix Force's part in this is over," Price said, her voice going tense. "Both James and Encizo are in medical facility, but in stable condition. Unfortunately things went FUBAR during extraction and McCarter is still in the field. Once he's home, that end is wrapped up."

"That's a big 'once,'" Brognola sighed. The Blazer stopped in front of the farmhouse, where Kurtzman was waiting for them.

"Don't I know it," Price muttered.

Kyrgyzstan

McCARTER SQUEEZED the trigger of the AKS-74.

His 5.45 mm round drilled the mercenary in the broad sweep of his jutting forehead. McCarter felt a flash of grim satisfaction as he saw the red mist explode out behind the man's head in the familiar scarlet halo.

McCarter rolled back around the side of the silo and began to run down the alley. Behind him he heard mortar rounds dropping into the square like bolts of thunder. He ran hard, cutting down dirt lanes and through filthy alleyways. He passed mud-brick hovels and shanties built from corrugated pieces of sheet metal. He cut through hard-packed courtyards strung with empty clotheslines left and chicken coops built right up against the side of houses.

Several times he was forced to step over corpses lying in the mud as he ran. He turned a corner and saw a mongrel tearing at the limp arm of one such corpse. The dog lifted its bloody muzzle and snarled a warning at McCarter.

McCarter came to a stop and faced the dog. The sight turned his stomach. He lowered the AKS and took it in his left hand. With his right hand he reached across and drew the silenced pistol. The dog was too experienced and knew what a gun was. It barked once, twice, and then took off running.

McCarter spat in disgust and holstered the pistol. He took up the AKS and turned to go. From the break between two rows of shanty houses an IMU "technical" drove out. The vehicle was a white Toyota pickup with a Soviet PKB machine gun mounted on a tripod in the back. Three terrorists rode in the front compartment, while two manned the crew-served weapon in the rear flatbed.

McCarter spun on his heel and darted back into the alley mouth from which he had just emerged. Behind him he heard men jabbering and the sound of the

Toyota's engine revving. A curt blast from the machine gun fired behind him as the vehicle driver gunned the engine.

McCarter turned left and knocked open the door to a little hovel. The technical turned the corner behind him and the machine gunner saw him enter the house. Immediately the terrorist opened fire.

McCarter hit the dirt floor inside the hut. The 7.62 mm bullets made pinging sounds as they punched through tin sheets and buzzed into the house. Wherever the family was, they had vacated at the first sign of fighting.

McCarter rolled farther into the building as the wood of the front door literally disintegrated under the impact of the PKB's rounds. Like flashlight beams, gray bars of light shot through holes left by the machine-gun fire and cut the gloom inside the hovel.

McCarter saw the impact of the rounds on the interior wall behind him, then they began to strike the floor as the technical's machine gunner lowered the aim of his weapon, anticipating McCarter's movement to the floor to find cover.

Bullets tore into the building around him. The hovel was a single room with a hot plate for cooking positioned within reach of a filthy mattress. There was a Kyrgyzstan flag on the wall and the PKB fire slashed into it, riddling the icon with bullet holes.

A cooking pan was knocked into the air and a filthy blanket torn to shreds as McCarter huddled against the relentless onslaught. Two windows facing the street, covered with grease paper, were vaporized under the barrage. Craters exploded out of the mud brick, and gritty material lifted a haze in the air.

McCarter huddled, waiting for the fire to stop. The front door he'd knocked open was shredded under the relentless machine-gun fire and hung in splintered chunks off one rusted hinge. Gouts of dirt spouted up like geysers from the blow holes of whales where rounds struck the earth floor. The din was deafening.

McCarter ejected his magazine and slid his only fresh replacement into the well. He hit the slide release and chambered a round into the breech. He knew that for an assault to work, right before the gangsters rushed the door, the technical's machine gunner would cease firing. He tensed in preparation for the moment.

As he expected, the lull came.

Without hesitation McCarter lifted his weapon and sighted in on the front door. The first terrorist filled the frame, kicking the wooden shambles out of his way. McCarter dropped him with a tight burst under the man's jaw. The gunman staggered back and collapsed in the threshold.

McCarter rolled over his back and laid his rifle across the still warm corpse of the gunman. What happened next unfolded too quickly for McCarter to decipher clearly. He had an impression of a second gunman coming toward the door from off to one side of the house and he swiveled the AKS around and triggered a burst.

The rounds tore into the man's thighs from point-blank range. The terrorist was scythed to the ground screaming. McCarter could see the technical parked directly in front of the house. The man in the back of the truck worked the slide on the PKB and lowered his weapon's muzzle in response to McCarter's action.

The man McCarter had shot in the legs lay within

arm's reach, still screaming. The man clawed for the pistol grip of the AK-47 he had dropped as he'd gone down. McCarter snarled like a cornered animal and jammed the still smoking muzzle of his AKS into the man's face. The man choked on his own scream a heartbeat before the 5.45 mm hardball rounds blew a cavity into his head.

Even before he had finished firing, McCarter was rolling back out of the doorway. As he twisted over he saw the bodies lying in the threshold shudder under the impact of the PKB rounds, splattering hot blood and chunks of flesh across the dirt floor and mud walls of the little hovel.

McCarter kept rolling until he had passed under the one of the room's two windows and up against the far interior wall. The technical outside was less than twenty yards away and McCarter heard the PKB jam.

McCarter didn't hesitate. He popped up like a demented jack-in-the-box and thrust the muzzle off his AKS-74 out the remnants of the ruined hovel window. He saw the machine gunner open the feed cover on the PKB and start yanking on the cocking handle, trying to clear a double feed. The technical driver opened the door to the Toyota pickup and lifted his AKM in an attempt to provide cover.

McCarter shot him first, splattering blood across the dirty white exterior of the Toyota. He lifted the pressure on his trigger and shifted aim. The machine gunner looked up at the blast that had killed his driver. McCarter put six rounds into his rail-thin body and knocked him clear of the pickup bed.

For one long moment it was still and silent. McCarter heard the mortar rounds dropping across the village. A frightened dog started barking. Time seemed to slow and stretch out with the peculiar elasticity specific to combat and tragedies. McCarter pulled the muzzle of his AKS-74 back inside the window and lowered his rifle. He twisted his head sharply and popped a kink out of his neck with a sound like knuckles cracking.

Outside the window the sky opened up without warning and the rains simply started pouring out from the heavens like some biblical downpour. The roar was significant and the sudden release of atmospheric humidity was so strong McCarter was immediately aware of the white vapor his body heat made as it rose off him, like smoke lifting from a fire.

Then his perception hit the fast-forward button and the last terrorist came through the door of the hovel with his assault rifle blazing.

HAIGHT DUCKED as exploding shells landed close by, and it seemed obvious the Kyrgyzstan mortar teams were walking their rounds directly toward the village mosque. The entire operation inside of Kyrgyzstan was a complete cluster fuck circus, he thought.

His forward operating teams had helped Haight coordinate the presence of the IMU terrorists regarding the issue of Smith, but almost as soon as the men had informed the mercenaries of the man holed up in the corner room of the compound, they had reported the presence of another team of outside operators. He had automatically forwarded that information to Skell.

Infuriated, Haight had deployed his men to encircle the building and then secure it. At about that time the rains had let up and the Kyrgyzstan mortar teams had begun their harassing fire. Then the sons of bitches had shot their way out of the hotel like Jesse James and he'd found himself face to face with the bastards.

Haight's first sergeant, an ex-Legionnaire named Glask, had run into the building first, seeking shelter from the mortar rounds. When Haight entered he found the man looking at a pile of corpses bunched up at the bottom of the stairs leading to the second level of the compound. It stank like cordite in the room.

One of Haight's men, a burly red-headed mercenary named Johnston, entered the compound lobby armed with an AK-104 submachine gun and followed by two black killers carrying AKM assault rifles.

"Take those two upstairs," Haight ordered. "Search the room those idiot terrorists were firing on, see if Smith is here."

Skell wasn't going to be happy, Haight realized.

CHAPTER SEVENTEEN

Dominican Republic

Lyons got out of the taxi on a secondary street in Santo Domingo's renovated financial district. The gigantic, gutted structure of the old oil ministry building cast long shadows over the consulate. The diplomatic station house was a tasteful, discreet building with darkened lead-lined windows and subdued walls.

Lyons surveyed the building with a distasteful eye. He'd tried to avoid making contact with the Dominican station only because Smith himself had avoided using the place when making contact with higher authority. He would much prefer it if he could have slipped in and out of this operations region without officially entering the fiefdom of the local station principal.

Working with the very Dominican Smith was most suspicious of was a risky proposition. It was also the fastest distance between two points: Lyons tended to like working in a straight line, stepping over corpses as he went.

Smith's failure to show for the meet and subsequent events had made such an approach unworkable. Nevertheless, Lyons had no intention of leaving Smith's drop envelopes with them. He'd put them in a safe at the secure house last night before taking a shower and going to bed.

The team had decided that they were too conspicuous moving through the city in a trio. They divided operational tasks among themselves and had set out in the morning after having made breakfast and dressing in clean clothes taken from the house closet.

Lyons entered the austere offices and approached a pretty receptionist behind a massive desk. A plaque on her desk read Ms. Pavarotti and her face seemed locked in a mask of perpetual boredom. She regarded Lyons with a disinterested stare. He smiled his good morning.

"I'm here to see Mr. Lemis," he said. "The Dominican attaché." He identified himself as an American security agent. It was only a small stretch on the truth.

The receptionist indicated a door set discreetly in the wall toward the back of the lobby, away from the elevator banks and half hidden by a potted rubber tree plant. Ms. Pavarotti reached out with a well-manicured hand under her desktop and a muted buzzer sounded.

Lyons crossed the room quickly and went through the door. He heard an electronically controlled dead bolt slide into place as the door swung closed behind him. He looked around him.

He was in a short, well-lit hallway. A line of comfortable chairs sat against a wall decorated in muted tones. Lyons sat, looking for the security cameras. Unable to spot them, he decided they were using telescopic fiber optics.

A door in the hallway opened and a man walked out. Lyons sized him up and decided he didn't like him. Lyons took in the man as he approached down the hall. He was Dominican and big. The man stood almost a full head taller than Lyons and must have weighed in at around 270 pounds. He looked like a bear in autumn, right before hibernation—powerful muscles covered by copious amounts of fat.

The man wore a mustache and beard, shot through with gray, and his hairline receded prodigiously. His suit was expensive, as was the gold watch on his wrist. His skin was that color of ebony so black it shone like polished onyx. He strode up and in front of Lyons, who had risen to his feet at the man's approach.

"You are from the States," the man said. It wasn't a question and he didn't offer to shake hands.

"I already know that. Now, who the hell are you?" Lyons snapped. "I'm here to talk to Lemis. If you're Lemis, speak up or go and get him."

Lyons was always ready to play alpha-male games.

The man stepped forward, into Lyons's space, a maneuver designed to intimidate the shorter man. It was the kind of bluster that occurred every day in boardrooms, but the disrespectful move could get you killed in a prison yard or the wrong kind of tavern.

Lyons stepped into the looming approach and both men stopped within a hairbreadth of butting chests. The man's gut was considerable, but up close he looked strong enough to wrestle tigers. Lyons didn't give a crap. The pair locked fierce gazes, neither man blinking.

"I see you've met Case Officer Lemis," said a cultured voice from behind them.

Lyons's eyes flickered away and he took in the second man who had just emerged from one of the office doorways. A mousy Caucasian woman stood behind him, arms hugging a massive pile of folders and paperwork.

"You're here about the Smith situation, correct?" the new arrival asked.

"Yes," Lyons replied.

Lyons turned and put his shoulder into that of the man identified as Lemis. He stepped forward, dipping slightly at the knees as he did so. As Lyons stepped past Lemis he rose up and caught the heavier man in the ribs with his shoulder, where he had a leverage advantage. Lyons brushed past the larger man, unbalancing him so that he stumbled as Lyons moved past.

Lemis swore and Lyons suppressed a smirk as the second man addressed him.

"I am Clarence Rumford, station principal. That is my director of operations for cooperation with Dominican authority, Robert Lemis. He's been running the Smith case." Rumford met Lyons's eyes with his own unaffected gaze. "He'll be your liaison in this manner. Lemis?"

"Yes, Mr. Rumford?"

Lemis stepped forward, brushing down the front of his suit where Lyons's nudge had left him disheveled.

"Please show our friend every courtesy. Bring him up to speed and then provide him with whatever help we can offer."

Rumford turned and ushered the tepid little woman into his open office door ahead of him. He turned back before he followed her in. He looked at Lyons like a lab tech trying to classify a distasteful but possibly deadly new strain of virus.

Rumford nodded at Lyons.

Lyons nodded back. Fuck you, too, he thought.

As if psychic, Rumford gave Lyons a freezing smile before disappearing into his office. Rumford never looked toward Lemis again after giving his instructions. Lyons pursed his lips reflectively as he watched the station principal's door bang shut. He turned and looked at Lemis.

"Well, Robert, we going to get this done?"

"Call me Lemis, asshole. Follow me."

Lemis turned and walked back toward the end of the hall Lyons had entered from. He moved fast for such a big man and he didn't look back to see if Lyons was following him.

Lyons looked on impassively at the man's retreating back before relenting and following after him. Someone had tried to kill him, and Lyons wasn't going to let macho posturing or turf wars keep him from his payback. Something was wrong here in Santo Domingo and he meant to find out what.

"HOLD MY CALLS," Lemis said into his cell phone. "Tell them I have a breakfast meeting at La Rue Cocotte. I shouldn't be gone long." Lemis hung up.

"Where are we going?" Lyons asked.

"I'm hungry. I know a place where we won't be interrupted and the help knows how to mind their own business."

"I imagine you know quite a bit about the restaurant scene."

"Screw you."

Lemis navigated the city streets efficiently, using diplomatic credentials to process quickly through security checkpoints. The riots had, for the most part, been pushed into the outskirts and the bulk of paramilitary police operations now took place along the city border.

Lyons looked out the tinted windows of Lemis's Mercedes. He watched landmarks slide by as Lemis made his way across the busy, modern streets of the city center. He had a feeling Lemis didn't spend too much time in the slums or out in the bush. He wouldn't like getting that Livingston-Kline suit dirty.

He and Lemis were like two bulls in a field and butting heads came naturally to them. Lyons was an interloper on Lemis's turf, and Rumford's, for that matter. Lyons had done his homework last night at the safehouse and he was nominally well versed in the history of both men.

Rumford had come up through the ranks old school. He been a logistics officer for FBI operations in the Asian theater during the seventies and then been assigned to Berlin, running counterintelligence operations against Communist incursions on all levels. He'd made his bones working the Iron Curtain and he'd stayed there.

Other than that cursory background, Brognola hadn't been able to swing a clearance high enough to read Rumford's Agency file. A fact the Fed had found very troubling. Rumford had enough pull with the old-boy network that Lyons, through Brognola, had been frozen out.

Lemis was a different story. Lemis was a classic Agency success story. He'd combined adequate fieldwork with a talent for playing the sycophant. He'd started out as a street informant for Dominican security services, then simply worked his way up using a lot of muscle and a certain reptilian savvy.

He bounced around from district duty station to district duty station, playing the role as Rumford's number two for past decade. He fed the Americans easy busts and they wrote nice reports to his superiors. Like Rumford, he was rumored to have a considerable financial portfolio he had built using information gleaned during classified operations. The pair of them were known as down-and-dirty operators who brushed the line often—but as of yet no one had suggested that the duo had actually crossed it.

But Smith had jeopardized his operational security to place that call from outside of station control, Lyons knew. That meant something. As did the last encrypted message Schwarz had broken.

Lyons mulled it over while Lemis drove. After about fifteen minutes they pulled up to a valet parking lot in front of a moderately expensive-looking restaurant in the international district. Such a place was a veritable Four Seasons in a city like Santo Domingo. A smiling employee in a red suit vest and a bulbous alcoholic's nose took the keys from the massive Lemis and gave him a paper ticket.

"This is on your expense account, not mine," Lyons said as they entered the restaurant.

Inside Lyons ordered an American breakfast and an entire pot of coffee. He noted that Lemis was eating enough for three normal "natives" given their average height and weight profiles. It was a lot of sausage.

"What do you know?" Lemis suddenly demanded.

Kyrgyzstan

HAIGHT LOOKED DOWN at Smith's dead body.

The muscles of the corpse had relaxed in death. It was too soon for rigor mortis to have set in, and the skin had begun to sag and puddle into lax shapes. In addition to the mushy elasticity, the skin had started to display a grayish-white tone on the top while the dark bruise color of liver mortis was already starting to show where blood was pooling in the lower portions of the body.

Flies crawled across the body and Haight noticed that Smith's left arm was swollen up to almost twice the size of the right one. Two red marks stood out prominently on the doughy flesh of his hand.

"This is too bad? No?" the first sergeant, Glask, asked.

The mercenary grunt stood beside Haight in the cramped compound room among the bloody corpses. For once Haight was grateful for the thin man's cigar. The stench of the stogie helped keep the death stink and putrefaction from gagging the gathered people.

"Yes, since I was supposed to get him out of here and to an interrogation center, this *is* too goddamn bad," Haight replied.

Outside a mortar round landed inside the walled courtyard of the mosque near the building housing the *madrassa*. Haight frowned. He figured the building would be the third target of opportunity for Kyrgyzstan forces. Important only after the compound offices and the mosque, but it had to be one of the major targets in Kyrgyzstan. The little border town only boasted a population of less than fifteen hundred; there simply weren't that many targets other than shanties and animal pens.

"What's wrong with his hand?" Haight asked.

"Looks like infection, possibly broke when the IMU took him," Glask offered.

"He was tortured *and* gut shot? Tough bastard."

"Not tough enough," the first sergeant pointed out.

"See if there is anything in his gear that might be valuable," Haight ordered Johnston. "Then we fall back onto the road out of the city and make contact with the home office in Geneva."

"With the rain stopped, the IMU forces stationed in the training compound to the north should begin to move down toward us," Glask said.

"Is that going to be a problem?" Haight asked.

"We've lost the element of surprise. We're outnumbered with more troops coming. The villagers we've driven off show up in other towns, then the Kyrgyzstan border forces could start showing up. This op is blown—we should go."

"You crapping out on me?" Haight demanded.

The first sergeant snorted his reply derisively.

"I need to see how the home office wants to proceed." Haight turned away from Glask and addressed Johnston. "Give the orders. I want us split into two teams. Heavy weapons are to be used to hold up IMU forces. Second team runs down the man they left behind. Some of them may have got out in that helicopter but we've still got a chance to make our bonuses for this op."

The thought of making their bonus put an urgency into the mercenaries responses and they leaped to obey Haight.

The principals weren't going to be happy with the way things turned out, he realized. The operation had been a long shot anyway. What troubled him most was the role the mystery unit had played.

He owed that team for the death of his men, soldiers sent on a relatively easy mission and brutally ambushed for their trouble. Those were the breaks in the mercenary game, but it still left a vicious taste in Haight's mouth.

The real question, he reflected, was what the man's true objective had been. Had he come to kill Smith to prevent him from getting some information out, or had he come to get something he had?

Outside it began to rain again.

CHAPTER EIGHTEEN

McCarter threw himself to the side as he tried to bring his own weapon around. He came up hard against the front inside wall of the hovel. He felt the sting of bullets as rounds clipped him in the shoulder, his forearm, the ribs and his waist. A bullet hit the hydration pouch on his back, splashing tepid water across the room.

The bullets grazed him, skipping off his body in superficial wounds the way flat stones skip off a lake. The skinny IMU teenager behind the AK-47 screeched, his face twisted with murderous emotion as he fired wildly from the hip.

McCarter swung the AKS up and thrust the folding-stock carbine out to the end of his extended arms. He pulled the trigger from a distance of less than twelve feet and saw his rounds hammer into the gunman's torso, slicing the teenager's sternum in two.

The gunman gasped and staggered back. McCarter pulled the trigger again, knocking the IMU triggerman farther back. The teenage killer hit the edge of the door and spun halfway around. His feet, clothed in filthy New Balance running shoes, tripped up on the corpse in the threshold and he fell.

McCarter skipped forward and pointed the muzzle of the AKS downward. He fired a short burst into the downed killer's head to finish him off, then snapped the rifle up to cover the doorway. Nothing happened.

Outside, through the frame of the doorjamb, the heavy rain poured down.

McCarter stepped up to the edge of the door and looked out. The Toyota pickup sat idling. Exhaust fumes poured out the tailpipe into the air. The rain had diluted the spilling blood in the bed of the pickup and rivers of watery red washed over the lip of the missing tailgate and dribbled onto the ground. McCarter set aside his 5.45mm AKS-74. He bent, picked up an AKM and then scavenged magazines from the corpses. He was thirsty but now had no water. The rain plastered his hair to his skull like a cap.

McCarter jogged out into the rain and crossed the dirt yard to where the still running Toyota truck was parked. His bullets had shattered the driver side window of the open door. He looked inside the cab where the keys hung in the ignition. McCarter threw the AKM onto the passenger side of the seat and knocked some loose glass splinters onto the floor of the cab.

He slid in behind the wheel. The vehicle had an automatic transmission and McCarter shifted it out of Park and into Drive. He checked his rearview mirror and could barely see anything through the driving rain. He figured that meant he would be hard to see, as well.

McCarter pulled away from the house and began driving down the narrow dirt alley. The Toyota sputtered a little as the transmission worked. He'd studied maps and satellite photos of Kyrgyzstan prior to insertion and he knew the rough layout of the village. Using the main highway out of town to the north and mosque as central points, he felt confident he could navigate it well enough despite not having memorized the streets, which was an impossibility given the ramshackle nature of the structures and alleyways.

McCarter knew he wanted to exit Kyrgyzstan to the east. The southern and western portions of the village contained IMU pockets and the highway entering from the north would carry reinforcements or authorities moving into place. To the east he would certainly run out of road, but it would allow him to escape the confines of the village quickly. Once free, Grimaldi could easily feed him a GPS coordinate for a rendezvous.

He just had to stay alive.

McCarter turned the Toyota around a corner and pulled out into the mouth of another dirt alley. A wide, unpaved avenue running east to west cut across the village through the houses in front of him. He stepped on the gas and turned the truck to the east. His windshield wipers worked furiously at full speed to keep up with the falling rain.

The rain came in through the broken driver's-door window and soaked him further. It kept his shirt wet, which was a blessing because the blood from his grazing wounds had begun to clot and it kept the fabric from being knotted up into the wound by coagulation. When he found a safe place he would treat the bullet scrapes, but for now he had no medical supplies available. McCarter pulled the truck out into the center of the muddy street and accelerated to a speed he felt was prudent under the conditions.

Dominican Republic

"I'M HERE TO LEARN," Lyons prompted. "Just start at the beginning. Walk me through it like I was a child."

"Not much of a stretch," Lemis grunted.

"Then it should be easy."

Lemis stared at Lyons for a moment over his plate. His eyes glittered and Lemis looked as venomous as a pit viper. Lyons bit into a piece of toast and smiled into Lemis's glare. Lemis relented.

"Smith claims he's working an investigation with ties to a private military contractor he worked for after the army. That the corruption reaches into the Dominican Republican government. He says he's got an informant, a woman on the inside named Felicity. I think it's bullshit."

At the mention of the name of the woman he had met at Smith's safehouse, Lyons kept his face carefully neutral.

"I think she's playing that puppy. I've worked counterops against Felicity for years now. I was the one who caught her penetration of the penetration of the government—Smith was my stringer. I have more experience with this agent than anyone in the American. Yet when Mr. Cowboy-FBI-Agent-Smith gets a lead in the case, he fails to contact me. I find that troubling...and so should you, frankly."

"Maybe he doesn't trust you. Maybe Smith thinks you've gone bad," Lyons said.

He kept his voice deliberate, completely dropping the baiting tone he'd used up until then. He was walking dangerous ground. He watched Lemis carefully for a reaction. He was disappointed.

"That's the point, Lyons. I thought you troubleshooters were supposed to be savvy operators. If Smith doesn't trust me, that means Felicity is playing him. It means he may think she is coming over, but the truth is she's probably working him for everything she can get. She's good, Lyons. She's good."

"How about Michael Klaus? He any good?" Lyons sipped his coffee.

Lemis's tradecraft went right out the window. His dark face grew ashen and he dropped his fork back onto the table with a disgusted look. He picked up his napkin and dabbed at his mouth where food had caught in his beard.

"How do you know about Klaus?" Lemis demanded.

Lyons shrugged. "Guys talk—you hear things."

"Klaus is a bogeyman," Lemis said finally. "Smith saw that Klaus was working here in the Dominican, that he had an institute for biological studies. That set him off. But it's all personal, understand? Smith's got a hard-on for his old boss. Klaus is like two hundred other international business men who set up shop in the Caribbean."

"You saying Klaus isn't dirty?"

"I'm saying if he's dirty it's the usual tax-haven, white-collar BS. Smith is sure it's a doomsday scenario." Lemis sat back. "Complete science fiction," he said.

The waiter came with the bill and discreetly set it in the exact middle of the table. Lyons smiled fully at the blushing young girl and pushed the little red attaché folder over towards the burly Dominican liaison.

"I know from Smith's case notes that Felicity got a job at this research institute," Lyons prompted. "How does Smith fit in?"

"I gave the Felicity surveillance to Smith as a way to get his feet wet. He surprised me. He got Durmstrange, the director at the institute, to put him on as a security consultant in addition to his liaison role from the agency. He began to cultivate Felicity. I think she's the one who led him to the Klaus connection originally."

"I'll need to see the files on Durmstrange, Felicity and the institute."

"Fine. You can have them back at the office. I'll call ahead to Ms. Pavarotti and arrange it."

"You're not coming back?"

"No. I have other matters. Matters that are none of your business."

"Great. You springing for cab fare?" Lyons goaded.

"Look, asshole," Lemis snapped, rising to the bait, "I don't like you American cowboys, and I don't like outside interference in my operations, and I don't like *you*."

"You don't have to like me, fat man," Lyons answered back. "You just have to make sure I have everything I need to get this job done."

Lemis rose and his face was so angry Lyons thought he'd finally pushed the case officer too hard. He tensed the muscle of his legs to rise up and meet Lemis's attack. A small, immature voice deep inside Lyons was laughing despite the potential seriousness of the situation.

Lemis made a visible effort to control himself. He reached into the pocket of his suit jacket and removed his cell phone. "Keep pushing me," he warned, "and the intergovernmental cooperation you managed to swing will dry up—" he snapped his thick fingers "—just like *that*."

Lemis turned and stalked out of the restaurant before Lyons could reply. Lyons watched him go, face impassive. He reached over and picked up the valet ticket. He contemplated it thoughtfully before also rising and making his way out of the restaurant. Felicity. Klaus. Lemis. This research institute run by Durmstrange. They were all breadcrumbs leading him to Smith.

He just hoped the agent was still alive when he finally found him.

LYONS SLID BEHIND the wheel of the idling vehicle after tipping the valet and pulled the car out into traffic. He wasn't an idiot and Lyons knew, given the attempt on his life, that if Smith had avoided clueing Lemis in on the op because of fears his supervisors were dirty, then Lyons had every reason to suspect that Lemis was setting him up now.

Lyons eyed his mirrors, reflexively looking for a tail. Lemis's hostility was hardly a clue by itself. Turf battles were a fact of life.

Lyons gunned the automobile through traffic. He didn't think Lemis, if he was crooked, would do anything so obvious as to plan a hit so soon after talking to him. But the tension from the recent riots made the possibility of street violence a very good cover for such things.

Lyons tried to order his thoughts. He'd been hit with a lot of information in a very short time. Each bit of information opened up a multitude of possibilities. He needed to itemize and then prioritize that information. He found a station on the radio, turned up the volume. The sound system in the car wasn't great but it'd do. His eyes flicked to his rearview mirror.

Lyons surveyed the traffic through his mirror. He didn't try to concentrate too closely on any one thing or automobile but instead let his eyes flit across the view, getting a feel for what was behind him. He tried to match up what Lemis had told him with the briefing he'd been given.

Smith had been running a flip operation for a free-lance agent who, unbeknownst to him, was already working not with American law enforcement but with American intelligence. The Department of Homeland Security should have caught the connection but hadn't. He'd been working the Dominican station under Rumford, in the field as Lemis's stringer for the Dominican security forces. He'd managed to somehow bunny hop Lemis's interference and get to Felicity herself. A feat Lemis hadn't been able to manage in over eight years of covert fencing. Felicity turned him on to Klaus, and Smith realized it was the same man he once worked for after getting out of the military.

Then, when it was time to bring the prize into the boat, Smith disappeared. He circumvented his normal chain of command and used unsecured lines to activate the turnover. A turnover he failed to show for. A check of his blind drop revealed an accumulation of sensitive material that Lemis should have known about and provided for. Then someone tried to kill Lyons when he came nosing around.

Lyons snapped out of his revere. Ahead of him a light at an intersection suddenly turned yellow. He was too close to the light now to stop, short of slamming on his brakes. Instead he shot through the light and across the avenue. Automatically his eyes found his rearview mirror.

A gunmetal-gray Audi cut out from behind a battered old Toyota delivery truck. It slipped around the larger vehicle and shot across the intersection, running a red light and triggering a chorus of angry horn blasts. The car cut its speed on the other side and fell into traffic about three cars behind Lyons's vehicle.

"Oh, it is on." Lyons grinned.

Kyrgyzstan

McCARTER DROVE like a bat out of hell.

"Jack, you up on this channel?" he asked.

"Copy," Grimaldi acknowledged. "We had a slight problem on our end. This has turned into a bit of an international incident. The flight officer wasn't going to let us take off. Manning almost killed the prick, but then I got Hal on the line and he was able to relay some codes to establish priority of authority. We're rolling toward you now."

"Cal and Rafe?"

"They're going to need a vacation," Grimaldi admitted. "But they're in good hands and stable condition. They'll be fine—your gambit worked. We need to worry about you right now."

"I'm headed east and the sooner I see you the better," the Briton said and signed off.

He passed a four-way intersection moving fast. From off the adjoining street two pickups pulled in behind McCarter and began to follow him. The first was a technical with a RPK machine gun mounted in the back, the gunner wearing an olive-drab Russian army rain poncho with a hood. The second truck contained a squad of men wearing the same wet-weather gear.

McCarter increased his speed.

Behind him the Daihatsu pickup increased its speed, as well. The ad hoc convoy stretched out like an accordion as McCarter increased his vehicle's speed and the others copied him to catch up. The RPK gunner held his fire though the muzzle of his weapon was leveled directly over the roof of the cab.

"What the hell?" McCarter muttered.

McCarter flicked his gaze to his rearview mirror. If they had made him, then why the hell weren't they opening fire? he wondered. Barely thirty yards separated his vehicle from the lead pickup. At that range the RPK would easily dismantle the thin-skinned Toyota McCarter drove. He wondered if it was possible they hadn't realized he was a Caucasian. That seemed impossible.

Up ahead the road split around a building built up on the street like the Five Points area in New York. McCarter guided his truck to the left. Behind him the convoy rushed up to the Y-intersection and at the last moment veered right. The vehicle behind the Daihatsu technical followed their leader.

McCarter sighed with relief. For the first time in this whole goddamn mission he'd caught a break.

Up ahead the road twisted in a lazy S-turn and McCarter steered the Toyota through the first turn. He sat up and slammed on the brakes as he rounded the corner. Two ancient deuce-and-a-half trucks sat parked nose to nose across the street, forming a roadblock.

McCarter slowed his Toyota as the gunmen controlling the checkpoint ran out of shanties on either side of the street waving at him to stop the truck. The man got a good look at McCarter and his eyes suddenly bulged.

The Phoenix Force leader tapped his brakes hard, then smoothly threw his transmission into reverse and hit the gas pedal. Mud flew as his rear tires spun, digging for purchase. Finally they caught and his truck lurched backward.

He threw his left arm across the back of the seat and twisted around to steer out his back window as he gunned the pickup. A white man driving a technical with the corpse of an IMU terrorist in the back was hardly incognito.

So much for my quick getaway, McCarter cursed. I might as well be displaying a flashing neon sign. It had been a gamble for time and the gamble hadn't paid off.

McCarter peered out his back window through the gray curtain of rain. He guided the truck back through the S-curve, hunting for a spot wide enough to allow him to perform a bootlegger maneuver and turn the nose of the truck around. He couldn't hear the terrorist gunmen shouting over the rain but he heard the clash of their automatic weapons fire and then his windshield was bursting apart.

CHAPTER NINETEEN

Glass shards exploded inward, spraying McCarter's exposed neck and cheek. More rain lashed through the broken windshield and instantly the cab was drenched with the torrential rainfall.

Steel-jacketed rounds struck the seat, jolting it under his arm. Bullets smashed into the rear windshield right in front of McCarter's face. He instinctively jerked his head away as the windshield cracked and spiderwebbed under the impact. Another round struck the damaged glass and punched a fist-size hole through the rear window.

McCarter was blind; there was no way to guide the vehicle through such a downpour with a cracked or blown-out windshield. Rounds tore into the cab and through the front grille of the Toyota. The vehicle frame reverberated with the impact of heavy-caliber bullets, shaking the steering wheel under his hand. It was only a matter of time before a bullet found his radiator, or his skull for that matter.

"Goddamn it!" he snarled.

He whipped the wheel hard to the side, sliding the truck around until it was perpendicular to the road. Bullets struck the vehicle along the length of the truck as McCarter threw open the driver's door and dropped to the ground. He popped back up and grabbed the AKM off the seat, dragging it to him. He rolled under the door and came up behind the front tire with the Toyota's engine block between him and the firing gunmen.

He looked over to the side across the street and saw a big building of some sort, made out of concrete blocks. The door had been ripped off its frame for an unknown reason and the entrance was an open, black mouth. McCarter coiled his legs under him as more automatic weapons fire rocked the truck. A bullet finally struck the radiator and it began to hiss madly as compressed steam billowed out.

McCarter exploded upward and sprinted for the side of the road. Five steps into his run McCarter stretched out like a great cat and dived forward. He cut through the falling rain like a six-foot missile. He saw the muddy earth rushing up to meet him and he struck the ground with his rifle. He folded along one arm and rolled over his shoulder.

Completing the somersault, McCarter rose out of the crouch and threw himself toward the concrete steps leading up to the open door. Bullets tore chunks out of the stairs as he scrambled up them. McCarter's face was bloody from shattering glass and now the exploding concrete.

His foot caught on the top step and McCarter sprawled out across the threshold, landing on his belly. McCarter grunted with the impact, then dug in with elbows and knees to scramble inside the doorway. Bullets struck the walls around him as he crawled into the building. He blessed the rain as he entered the sanctuary, then promptly rolled to his right out of the open doorway.

He quickly took stock of his surroundings. The interior of the building had been gutted some time ago from the look of it. The room was twenty yards by about twenty yards of empty concrete floor. Oil stains marred the ground every few feet and dust lay thick everywhere McCarter looked.

Bullets struck the front of the building outside as McCarter rose. The front wall of the building had no windows and ran unbroken except for the front door. McCarter had no idea what the place had been designed or used for. Off to his left he saw a door and, other than that, the entire first floor of the structure was wide open and empty.

McCarter caught a whiff of something ugly and turned his head. He saw a pile of moldy fur and realized a dog had been killed in here. Ants swarmed over the decomposing carcass in a black frenzy. Disgusted, McCarter turned away.

The building had windows that were still intact and ran along both the back and sides of those walls. The rain beat at them mercilessly and the interior was bathed in murky shadows. From outside the wild, random firing stopped and McCarter heard men shout as they tried to organize themselves.

McCarter knew it would only be moments before the men structured themselves into some semblance of order.

The windows set into the walls were too high for McCarter to access. The empty floor of the building would offer him no cover when the terrorists stormed the door. He was being driven like a wild animal into a corner.

McCarter turned and looked at the door. He had no choice. He ran to the interior door, tried the handle and found it locked. He stepped back and curled his leg up until his kneecap was even with his chin. He snapped his leg out and kicked the door hard, striking it parallel to the handle with the heel of his combat boot.

The door popped open and swung wide, revealing a dark pit and an old ramshackle set of stairs leading down into the darkness. A dank stench rolled up and assaulted McCarter's nose. He turned his head in disgust.

He stepped down onto the first rickety stair. It groaned in protest under his weight. He took another step. The staircase seemed to be holding. McCarter held no overwhelming desire to be caught in the dark hole in the earth, but his options were running out.

He walked down several stairs, then turned and sank to his knees. He lowered himself to his belly and stretched out, resting the muzzle of the AKM across the top stair. He commanded the only entrance to the building now.

McCarter felt adrenaline twist his guts. He needed medical attention, needed people to stop shooting at him and needed to get the hell out of this village. Most of all he needed to *not* be trapped like an animal in a hole.

He felt the stairs settle under his weight and heard them groan in protest. There'd been no way to determine how unsound the staircase was when he'd first entered the basement door and now McCarter began to rethink his plan. Perhaps it would be wiser for him relocate to a spot on the main floor at an angle to the front entrance.

Machine-gun fire riddled the frame around the front door even as the thought flashed through McCarter's mind. Green-and-white tracer fire arced into the room. He nestled in behind the buttstock of the AKM and drew down on the front door. He saw more streaks of green tracer fire fly through the doorway and the gray slashes as bullets cut through the dusty air.

McCarter tightened his finger on the trigger, taking in the slack. He narrowed his eyes and looked down the barrel of his weapon.

A baseball-size sphere arced into the room. McCarter cursed as the hand grenade bounced off the floor, landed and then rolled toward the center of the room. He put his head down and ducked underneath the lip of the stair.

Through his closed eyelids McCarter had an impression of a bright flash then the explosion deafened him. He heard shrapnel strike the walls around the basement door and he opened his eyes and lifted his head. Dark smoke filled the room. The wooden staircase under his body shook with the concussive impact.

From the entrance McCarter heard more weapons fire and saw muzzle-flashes. After the initial bursts men screamed back and forth at each other and the first terrorist entered the room firing his weapon from the hip.

Dominican Republic

LYONS FELT THE SURGE of adrenaline as he confirmed he was being tailed. For the Audi to take a risk on such an obvious play as running the red light, he could safely assume that he was dealing with a single shadow and not a team.

Was it a legit stringer for Lemis checking up on the new kid in town? Was it a part of some corruption on Lemis's or Rumford's part? Was it a third-party player, perhaps the ones who had taken a shot at him near the railway station? Lyons had questions, but he didn't have answers.

With Blancanales and Schwarz each working his own angle, he also had no backup.

At this moment, Lyons realized, the only people with the answers to those questions were in the Audi behind him. Lyons kept his speed down to match the flow of traffic as he crossed the bridge over the river and into one of Santo Domingo's refugee-filled ghettos and one of the largest open-air markets in the Caribbean.

Lyons had intended to head directly back to the liaison office to look over the files, but now he debated the merits of a new, bolder plan. This Felicity op was not an intelligence operation; it was a counter intelligence situation. He was not conducting a survey on a known article, but rather was attempting to ferret out an unknown. An unknown to which Lyons might already be a very well-established entity.

There was a method of operation used to jump-start investigations where there were either no leads or too many. Dubbed the Judas-goat scenario, it was risky and dismissed as cowboy antics by more cautious operators. Named after the practice of Indian or Kashmiri hunters, it was a metaphor for their strategy of using a staked goat to draw whatever tigers were in the area into an ambush.

The operator simply placed himself in the contested environment and announced his presence and intentions. Whoever went after the bait tipped his hand and revealed himself. Lyons needed answers and he was fortunate enough to know of someone readily available who could answer them.

The driver of the Audi.

Lyons took half an hour to get into position. He drove carefully, keeping in deep pockets of traffic, stopping for streetlights, driving carefully and defensively. He made every decision contrary to the way a person trying to lose a tail would act. His hope was to lull the Audi into complacency. It was imperative that the hunted think they remained the hunter.

Lyons chose his trap as best he could with his limited knowledge of the foreign urban environment. He stayed away from malls or shopping complexes. Those kinds of settings would encourage the shadow to get out of his car and follow Lyons inside, in hopes of observing whom the mark met with. Lyons needed something like a restaurant or apartment building where the tail would feel it too risky to do more than survey Lyons's entrance and exit times.

Finally, on the edge of a market district, Lyons found a suitable location. High-rise apartments, modern but obviously built for lower socioeconomic classes during previous leftist administrations, lined several streets between the market and the river. They were relatively unmarked by bullets or artillery fire.

Again Lyons took a chance. For this kind of play it was better to avoid both ends of the social spectrums. High-end communities came with paid security and subsidized social housing came with youth gangs, both of which could prove bothersome to someone wishing to move anonymously.

Lyons pulled his vehicle over. He took a moment before stepping out and checking the street. Groups of pedestrians loitered in the open. An alleyway between two buildings was strung with ropes of drying laundry.

The traffic on the street wasn't as thick as that of the market district, but was still busy.

Lyons approached a group of teenage boys with sullen looks on their faces. He walked up to them, smiling. He wasn't about to play the tough guy with a group of kids who could strip his car in seconds and then disappear into the urban topography like ghosts. The interest of the group perked up immediately when Lyons pulled a tight little bundle of U.S. dollars out of the pocket of his leather jacket.

Using a gutter patois he'd picked up after years of running ops in Central America and the Caribbean, Lyons promised to match the amount of money if the vehicle was fine when he came back from doing his business.

Arrangements made, Lyons loitered long enough for the Audi to move slowly past his position on the street. Lyons entered the apartment building through the front door in full view of the vehicle's driver.

Lyons stepped into a stark hallway lined with the apartment doorways. A staircase off to his left led up to the other floors. The hall bisected the building in a straight line and Lyons could see the rear door easily, blocked open by an old, stained cinder block to let in gray sunlight. Lyons turned and took up a safe vantage just inside the door to view the Audi's actions.

In textbook manner the Audi went up the street past the mark and parked on the opposite side of the street where the occupant of the vehicle could sit and watch his target using the rearview mirrors.

Lyons scoped out the street, figuring his approaches from the best possible angles. He memorized the license-plate number though he had little hope that it would provide a tangible clue. Turning, Lyons moved down the hallway and out the back of the building. He moved fast, avoiding any kind of contact with the people he passed. He stepped out of the rear door of the apartment building and turned in the direction away from where the Audi was parked.

Coming out of the alley, Lyons mixed in as best he could with the flow and rhythm of the street. He crossed with a knot of pedestrians to the side of the street opposite the apartment building he had cut through and moved past the first buildings on that block to the alley running behind them. He traversed a U-shaped pattern in an attempt to flank his shadow. A few burned-out hulks of cars set fire during the riots were scattered along the pavement.

All around him the life of the city went on with raucous noise. Unfettered by city ordinances, the refugee inhabitants kept livestock in the form of dogs, chickens and even the occasional pig. People milled about or called down from open windows and out of doorways. Children played boisterous games, and loud music from a wide mixture of cultures played and echoed down the crowded streets and alleys.

Lyons moved quickly to the mouth of the alleyway, heading for the building opposite where the Audi was parked. He'd have to move fast, and Lyons was positive that in the case of foreigners, the locals wouldn't hesitate to notify local police. When the time came to act, Lyons had every intention of abandoning subterfuge and engaging with speed and aggression.

Lyons cut down a smaller, narrower alley running off the main one behind the buildings. He picked his way through noxious piles of refuse and stinking garbage.

This was a far cry from the cleaner, more tourist-minded sections of Santo Domingo, and the sharp stench of urine and excrement was present in a nearly overpowering miasma.

At the lip of the tiny alley Lyons halted, getting his bearings for his final approach. The Audi was parked barely twenty meters away. Lyons frowned; the engine was running, which was in the driver's favor. The Audi was not boxed in by other parked cars, but the driver's room to maneuver was severely limited. Lyons called that a draw.

Without the element of complete surprise Lyons doubted he would have risked what he was planning. Then again, he'd always thought chutzpah an underutilized element in intelligence planning and operations. Barbara Price claimed it gave her ulcers.

Lyons looked up and down the street. There were pedestrians present but the throng of people was not immense. He reached around behind his back and pulled out the Glock 17. He had to neither chamber a round nor click his fire selector off safety. When Lyons carried a weapon, he carried it ready to roll. He put the hand with the pistol into the pocket of his jacket, keeping his finger on the trigger, but with the weapon safely concealed from sight.

Lyons decided the odds were heavily in favor of the guy having his doors locked. It would be stupid to plan any move based on any other assumption.

Lyons stepped out of the alley and began walking briskly toward the car. The guy had grown lax. Instead of constantly checking his three points of vision, he'd settled into a long surveillance mode with his eyes fixed

on his angled rearview mirror. Lyons used his free hand
to remove his cell phone from his jacket pocket.

As he came even with the car Lyons flipped his cell
phone open and his thumb rapidly clicked his acces-
sory options, bringing up the camera setting. He kicked
the car door of the Audi once, holding the phone up.
The driver, a thin black man with a gold tooth and a
tight, close-cropped afro, jumped, startled, and whirled
around.

Lyons clicked a picture.

"Smile, asshole."

CHAPTER TWENTY

Kyrgyzstan

McCarter scythed the men down with a short burst then shifted his weight and pointed his captured AKM back to the door. A second IMU gunman entered the building, and McCarter put a 3-round burst into his chest, knocking him straight back out the door. A gunman on the outside stuck his weapon into the room from around the doorjamb and began spraying wildly, trying to provide cover fire for a second entry team.

Screaming like a madman, another terrorist burst into the room firing his weapon from the hip, as well. McCarter sighted in on him and pulled the AKM trigger. Two shots rang out and both struck the man in his torso, knocking him down but not killing him.

The AKM suddenly stopped firing despite McCarter's finger on the trigger. McCarter broke his cheek seal with the butt of the weapon and looked at the weapon ejection port. He didn't see a misfeed. Across the room the wounded IMU terrorist rolled over onto his side and looked around.

McCarter automatically began to perform an immediate action drill on his weapon the way he had practiced a thousand times. He slapped up on the bottom of the AKM magazine to ensure it was seated properly and then pulled the weapon charging handle all the way to the back, locking the bolt to the rear. No cartridge ejected.

The wounded gunman shouted something to others outside the door and lifted his own weapon, bringing it to bear on the doorway where McCarter had set up his hasty defensive position.

McCarter saw his chamber was clear and slid the charging handle forward and released the firing bolt from its locked position. He pointed his AKM up at the wounded terrorist and pulled the trigger on the AKM just as the other man began firing.

McCarter's weapon failed to fire and he ducked as 7.62 mm rounds began hammering in around his position. There was no time for him to perform a remedial action drill to try bringing the Kalashnikov back on line. He twisted onto his side and pulled his pistol out of his leg holster.

McCarter had the pistol ready to go but the fire coming into the doorway was too intense for him to lift his head up, much less bring the big autocannon to bear. He shifted to avoid a flurry of splinters kicked up by enemy rounds and he felt the staircase suddenly lurch under him.

"Shit!"

Then the staircase groaned like an old man in pain and McCarter felt it give way beneath him. As automatic-weapons fire sprayed in an unending fusillade through the open basement door McCarter fell into the dark.

"I UNDERSTAND," Haight said.

Haight broke the connection on the sat phone and

turned around calling out. Johnston walked into the room, his weapon casually slung over one shoulder.

Haight's group had taken over a house on the southern outskirts of the village, setting up a mobile command center from which he commanded his forces.

According to what Glask had been told by Haight's recon elements, a Kyrgyzstan advance force had entered the town and now held the mosque, compound and the primary road. Lackluster fighting had broken out between the IMU in control of the village and the national forces, but the regular army troops were obviously only holding out until reinforcements could arrive.

Skell had offered to pay the full amount of the contract again if the mysterious white commando who had apparently met with Smith before his death could be apprehended. A smaller but still generous sum was offered for his death.

"What is it, Johnston?" Haight asked.

"Sergeant's outside."

"What does that bastard want?"

"He says they caught a bleeding IMU runner and used the blowtorch on him. They say they have a white man cornered in a warehouse on the west side of the town, away from the main fighting."

Haight felt elation well up in him. A smile pulled at the corners of his mouth.

"Get the men ready," he ordered. "We may just make our bonuses after all."

MCCARTER FELL DOWN through the hole in the rotted stairs and plummeted into the black below. As he fell he curled into a ball, drawing the pistol in close to prevent losing it, and twisted around like a cat in an attempt to land on his back.

He struck something hard with the top half of his body and bounced, spinning so that his head was above his feet. He struck the floor hard with his buttocks and rolled backward. His teeth snapped together and he felt the hot, metallic tang of his own blood rush into his mouth as he bit the inside of his cheek.

He was thrown over onto his back and his head bounced cruelly off a dirt floor. McCarter opened his eyes as dust and debris rained down on his upturned face. The open door ten or twelve feet above him stood out like a box of pale light in the murk.

A figure appeared suddenly, silhouetted in the opening. The shape thrust out a rifle and began to spray rounds into the room. Still dizzy from the fall and impact, McCarter lifted his pistol. He pointed the muzzle upward and aimed center mass on his target.

The handgun went off with a boom loud enough to deafen McCarter in the confined space. The muzzle-flash caused spots to form on McCarter's eyes. The figure, now simply a blurry smear against the backdrop of light, staggered backward. The rifle fell out of his hands and bounced off the ruined staircase.

McCarter fired again and the man's hands flew up from the shock of the slug's brutal impact. McCarter twisted to the side and instinctively lifted his arm over his head to avoid the falling rifle.

The weapon struck him hard in the shoulder and bounced off. McCarter winched, hissing at the impact of the ten-pound assault rifle. It clattered as it struck the ground. McCarter rolled onto his back again. He slid his pistol back into its holster by feel and snatched up the dropped assault rifle, some model of the Kalashnikov.

A figure appeared in the door and McCarter just had time to bring the Kalashnikov to bear. Tracer fire ripped out of McCarter's weapon and shot through the dark pit he was trapped in. The rounds ventilated the second gunman and knocked him back out of sight.

McCarter scrambled to his feet and moved toward the wall directly under the open door. His heart hammered in his chest as his eyes began to dilate, giving him a better impression of the basement he had tumbled into like Alice falling down her rabbit hole.

He looked up and saw that the set of stairs he had fallen through ran against one wall of the room. Remnants of the stair hung from the door frame and dangled above him. On the other side of the hole he'd created when he'd fallen through, the staircase was intact and ran down to the dirt floor of the basement. McCarter figured he'd fallen about eight feet.

Before he could take in further details of the room he saw a familiar metal sphere fly through the door and drop down toward him. McCarter exploded into action without thinking. He leaped forward as the grenade struck the ground at his feet and scooped it up.

He prayed he had time.

Dominican Republic

THE DRIVER'S FACE went tight in fury and then gray. He reached for a paper set on the passenger seat beside him. Lyons tapped the barrel of his pistol against the glass of the driver's-side window. At the unmistakable tink of metal on glass the driver froze. He looked up;

Lyons smiled sadistically. He clicked another picture. The driver was a lean man in his late twenties.

Slowly the man sat up.

"Roll the window down," Lyons ordered.

"Go to hell."

Lyons lowered his phone and stepped forward against the door. He tapped the muzzle against the glass twice.

"Roll down your fucking window."

"Or what? You'll shoot? In the middle of a street like this?" The man's Caribbean English was concise but heavily accented. "No way."

"You didn't care last night when you tried to take me out."

The man's eyes narrowed slightly. That was all Lyons needed to attribute guilt.

"I don't know what you are talking about, I'm just here to meet my girlfriend."

"Your girlfriend pees standing up, just like your mom."

The man said nothing but he gripped the steering wheel until his knuckles showed white.

"Was that your boy I got last night?" Lyons asked, goading the man. "The one who screamed and cried like a sissy-bitch? You guys close?"

"I don't know what you're talking about," the man said, his voice tight with emotion.

Lyons's opinion of the man dropped. That he could get to him verbally spoke a lot less to Lyons's own interrogation skills than it did to the man's internal discipline. Lyons tired of baiting the driver. It was fast becoming pointless.

It was a stalemate, and Lyons knew it. He had taken

a chance and it wasn't playing out how he wanted it. He wasn't going to blaze away with his pistol on an open street like this unless the guy went for his own gun. Without that as a threat, the shadow didn't feel the need to cooperate. Lyons had disrupted the survey operation and had the means to identify the agent. He would take the situation as a win.

"Get the hell out of here," Lyons said. "I know your face. I see you again and I assume you're there to take me out. I don't care if it's Sunday Mass in a cathedral or two-for-one-night at the whorehouse, I'll come at you shooting. Now go."

The man didn't bother trying to argue. He simply put the Audi into gear and drove off. Out of a habit of thoroughness Lyons used his phone camera to snap a shot of the vehicle and its license plate. Quickly he emailed the pictures to a secure host source in his cellular network. The digital information would be threaded and sent to a site accessed from secure servers by Barbara Price or Aaron Kurtzman.

In the meantime Lyons had some homework to do. He crossed the street and paid off the youths loitering protectively around his vehicle. He pulled out into traffic and headed back across town toward the liaison station.

AT THE OFFICE the receptionist assigned him an assistant who seemed anxious to ensure that Lyons saw as little of the building's interior as possible. He brought Lyons the station files on both the Klaus Institute and Felicity. The assistant politely refused Lyons's request for the agency files on Smith's corruption investigation, stating that Lemis directed access to all of those files personally and, as he was out, the assistant could not provide them. Lyons didn't push the matter. Instead he bullied the assistant into getting him some takeout and providing an unending pot of black coffee.

Lyons started with Felicity.

A slow smile slid across the veteran's face when he opened the file and saw the picture of the pretty Dominican woman he'd met at the safehouse. Lyons quickly digested the contents of her file.

Twenty-nine, 5'1" tall, 116 lbs. Well educated in British-run private schools. Felicity Castillo had worked as a stringer agent for many years. He was surprised to see that part of her motivation was ideological. Corruption in the Dominican government hurt the people and despite her somewhat affluent upbringing she seemed concerned with her country's poor. Her work with the CIA had all been the acts of a patriot for her nation.

Apparently not realizing her intelligence community connections, first Lemis and then Smith had kept her under observation and it seemed Smith had somehow managed to make contact with Felicity through the head of Klaus's institute—Durmstrange.

This was an accomplishment that eclipsed Lemis's work on the case. But then Smith had made every attempt to remove Lemis from the loop. If it was simply personal animosity among the two agents, then why hadn't Smith gone to Rumford? Had Smith known Lemis was working for Klaus on the side, or had he never gotten the information Able Team had found at his drop site.

Lyons leaned back in his chair. He drank the dregs of the coffee in his cup and put it down. He felt like a bloodhound tracker, following traces to find the trail of his quarry. Instead of footprints and bent blades of grass, or tufts of fur, he was following conjecture, innuendo and rumor. The longer he took, the colder the trail got. He wondered briefly how Blancanales and Schwarz were making out. He had to brief them as soon as possible.

He pushed Felicity's file away and reached for the file on the institute itself. It was much thicker than Felicity's and the chronology went back over a decade. Lyons sighed. He'd been given a responsibility, a duty, and he fully intended to execute his warrant, no matter how damn boring it was. He opened up the thick package in front of him and began to read, quickly taking in huge swathes of information.

The Klaus Institute was run by Victor Durmstrange, a Dutch national from Aruba. Ostensibly the institute ran tests for making generic copies of name-brand drugs once patents ran out. It was a good cover for illicit biological research.

Further reports showed that, for the past several years, Durmstrange had struggled with a growing narcotics addiction. Lyons leafed through copies of local police and intelligence reports stating that Durmstrange had several times been seen in the company of heavyweight drug traffickers.

It was during this time Felicity first came under suspicion and survey by the Dominican. Lemis had made the decision to use her as a stalking horse to strike out at her foreign handlers.

Lyons sat back and rubbed his eyes.

How did that fit in with the information he had gained at Smith's drop?

Why would someone warn Smith that Lemis was working for Klaus? They knew Felicity was cooperating for adversarial intelligence, so how was Lemis handling it? By running interference on Smith's investigation.

Lyons closed the file. He knew it was time to go see Felicity. With the information from Phoenix Force's operation in Kyrgyzstan, Lemis was the number-one suspect now. He was Klaus's man in the Caribbean.

Lyons left the office without telling anyone that he was leaving, but he knew no move of his had gone unmonitored.

Blancanales was currently paying Felicity a visit at her home. The woman had resisted Lemis but had aligned herself with Smith. Now Smith was missing. As far as Lyons was concerned, the woman was a hostile agent who had been given too much rope and bitten the hand that fed her. Bad dog.

Bringing bad dogs back into line was one of the things Lyons did the very best. First the woman, then Lemis. Then Klaus. Simple.

CHAPTER TWENTY-ONE

Kyrgyzstan

McCarter spun out away from the wall and cocked his arm. He lobbed the cooking grenade up toward the door and then threw himself back against the wall. The grenade sailed through the open door and exploded.

The explosion detonated loudly over McCarter's head and he was grimly rewarded by the sound of screams. Their superior numbers had emboldened the IMU terrorists up to this point, but McCarter felt confident that they did not have the discipline or morale needed to commit to the kind of causalities it would take to pull him out of his hole. If they tried, then he would make them pay.

With the blast of the grenade still ringing in his ears, McCarter pushed himself off the wall. He scanned the area around him, trying to gain some sense of the size of the basement he found himself trapped in. He could see immediately that he was dealing with a cavernous structure easily as large as the open warehouse directly above him.

The wide, open storage area was filled with items; shapes covered in canvas, rusting machinery, oil drums and construction materials on plywood pallets. McCarter fired a burst of harassing fire into the open door above him and quickly scrambled in among the mess.

Finding a position that offered him some cover, McCarter squatted, turned, lined up the AKM sights on the door and closed his left eye to spare his night vision before firing a burst. The harassing fire sprayed the open doorway and shot out into the open floor beyond.

After the burst McCarter turned and forced his way farther into the basement. He moved toward the cellar wall and saw a series of metal pipes set in brackets running along the length of the basement and back into the darkness. He didn't allow himself to hope, but he felt a grim smile tug at the corners of his mouth. He thought it possible that he had just caught a break. About goddamn time, he thought.

He reached up and touched the largest of the metal pipes. He pulled his hand back and inspected his fingers. They were black with soot. This time he allowed the smile to linger. When it had been in use, the building had utilized a natural resource for energy that was in no short supply in the old Soviet Union—coal.

A coal furnace for an industrial site meant an industrial-size supply depot, as the coal would have arrived by the truckload. The coal chute for a furnace that size would be more than large enough for a man to crawl through.

McCarter began fighting his way toward the rear of the basement. It was hard going, made more arduous by the occasional terrorist brave enough to broach the basement door.

He didn't see any insects but his movement upset more than one nest of rats, and they squeaked at him angrily or hissed, their beady eyes reflecting red in the meager light.

Finally, McCarter reached the rear of the basement

and quickly began to search along the back wall of the basement. As he had suspected, the furnace was huge, as big as an SUV, made of cast iron and covered in thick, filthy soot. McCarter wormed his way through the debris around it and found the coal chute. It ran up into the wall at a forty-five-degree from a railroad coal truck. Coal so old it had turned gray spilled over the edges of the bin and across the cellar floor. It had been a long time since Communist bureaucrats had needed to worry about coal supplies for a village in Kyrgyzstan. Cobwebs clung in thick curtains at the corners of the chute.

McCarter stepped forward and waved the hot muzzle of his AKM through the mess. Spiderwebs clung to his barrel, wrapping around it like cotton candy. McCarter scraped the mess off on the edge of the coal bin.

McCarter bent and looked up the coal chute. He could see a sliver of gloomy gray daylight at the top of the short tunnel where the chute hatch hung imperfectly on its ancient hinges. The tunnel was clogged with dense spiderwebs. It was as unappealing an escape route as McCarter had ever used.

Behind him he heard the crack of metal striking concrete and instinctively he hunched against the blast. The grenade explosion shook dust loose from the ceiling and it rained down on McCarter's head, enforcing a feeling of claustrophobic tension. Shrapnel scattered out through the room, gouging chips out of the wall and cutting into the materials crammed into the basement.

An assault rifle opened up in the doorway and sprayed down into the darkness. McCarter squatted behind the furnace in case of a stray bullet or unlucky ricochet.

The IMU fighters were showing slightly more tenacity than he had given them credit for.

McCarter stepped around the corner of the furnace and lifted the AKM above his head, angling the barrel of the weapon so that its trajectory would fire over the massive piles of industrial relics filling the huge basement.

He triggered an exploratory burst. His bullets arched out over the mess and sailed into the far wall and staircase remnants. Satisfied, McCarter fired a second, longer burst designed to encourage caution on the part of the IMU fighters.

McCarter lowered his weapon and stepped back around the edge of the furnace. He eyed the choking mess of spiderwebs inside the old coal chute. "Who Dares Wins," he muttered.

The slogan was the motto of the British Special Air Service and McCarter had heard his fill of it as he had come up in that outfit as a trooper.

He got ready for his crawl to freedom.

Dominican Republic

OUTSIDE THE WINDOWS of Felicity Castillo's upscale apartment in the international district the nightlife of Santo Domingo began to stir. Streetlights clicked on and neon signs flickered. Brothels and trendy bistros began to see an upswing in business as citizens put the day's work behind them. Traffic first thickened, punctuated by the blare of horns, and then thinned as the main arterials bled off the human excess. At various points bored Russian soldiers manned security checkpoints.

A slight breeze brought the smell of the river with it

as it wafted in through Felicity's open apartment windows. The aroma was pungent but muted and in the background. The air hinted rain as the sun had slid down out of the sky.

Blancanales set his cell phone on the table beside his chair in the dark. He took out a Victor High Standard .22-caliber pistol and began methodically screwing a silencer into place. He looked up as he heard the sound of a key turning in the lock to the door of the apartment. He lowered the silenced pistol until the muzzle covered the doorway. He breathed out through his nose, releasing the pent-up tension inside him as the door swung open. He could see a female outline framed against the hallway light.

From deep shadow Blancanales watched, weapon ready, as the figure fumbled with the light switch just next to the inside of the door. He heard an exasperated sigh after the switch was flipped several times with no effect. Earlier, he had simply unscrewed all the light bulbs connected to the electrical switch.

The figure entered the room, switching both an attaché case and a woman's purse, as well as a ring of keys, from one arm to the other. As the figure moved farther into the room Blancanales could make out the femininity of her form more closely. He took in the sweep of brunette hair, the angle of a cheekbone. He was sure, before he moved, that this was Felicity Castillo.

He rose from the chair he had placed at an angle to the door. He kept the pistol steady and moved in to close the door. He swept in behind the Dominican freelancer, overpowering her easily. Their last meeting at Smith's safehouse had ended well enough but he could afford to take no chances until they were one hundred percent sure she wasn't working with Lemis in any fashion.

He moved rough, imposing his will upon her, tapping into psychological fears and overwhelming her mentally. The door closed with a bang, cutting off the source of light from the hallway. He spun the woman around and put her face up against the wall.

He pressed the fat muzzle of the pistol silencer against her skull, down low where it met the spine. The feeling was unmistakable. She gasped in surprise and then horror. Her bags and keys tumbled from her hands and fell to the floor.

"Move and I splatter your brains on this wall," Blancanales said, using vivid language to assault his quarry's psyche. It wasn't pretty, but it was brutally effective. From the very first days of his time at Stony Man, Blancanales had been concerned with results rather than methods.

"Are you armed?" he demanded, his lips pressed hard up against her ear.

"No, no." The woman shuddered but stayed calm.

The woman shivered under his touch as he quickly frisked her. Satisfied, Blancanales slid his rear foot back and changed his point of balance. He replaced the end of the silencer with the cruel grip of his free hand. He squeezed her neck hard enough to make her gasp, then jerked her off the wall and spun her off to the side, throwing her into the deep cushions of a large living-room chair almost the size of a small sofa.

"Stay," he snarled.

He trained his pistol on the woman and reached for the dead bolt with his free hand, never taking his eyes off of Felicity. He found the bolt and twisted it shut. He turned fully and regarded the still woman. The room was still dark and he stood in shadow. He had positioned the chair he put her into so that a bar of light from a streetlamp outside ran across her face.

She looked scared and confused, and deeper inside of her smoldered a growing anger.

"The last time we saw each other we seemed to be on better terms."

"Yes," Blancanales agreed. "But you weren't exactly completely forthcoming about certain aspects of Smith's investigation."

Felicity nodded, her pretty features now unreadable. "You suspect Lemis now."

"Good. No playing coy. This may turn out all right."

Her face set into a sullen affect.

"Have I impressed upon you that my intentions are serious?"

Her black eyes flickered up to where Blancanales sat, cloaked in shadow. Bright points of hate burned in her eyes.

"What is it you want to know?" she demanded.

Kyrgyzstan

GUNFIRE RANG OUT from the opposite end of the basement.

McCarter lifted his leg and stepped into the coal bin. The old coal shifted under his weight as he waded across the bin to the mouth of the chute. He changed his fire-selector switch to safe and hung the AKM around his neck by the sling, muzzle down so the barrel would drag between his legs as he crawled up the gutter.

McCarter eyed the run. It was large enough to accommodate him but narrow enough that he would be forced to scramble up it using his elbows and knees to dig into the corners. McCarter drew the Beretta 92-F from his shoulder holster and stuck his upper body into the opening.

The sides of the coal chute were narrow but McCarter shoved himself inside and began to inch his way up the enclosure. His pant leg caught on a jagged section of metal in the opening and he jerked his leg to clear it. He heard the ripping sound as his pants tore but his leg came free.

McCarter continued crawling upward, taking shallow breaths with his mouth. It was ugly and fetid, and McCarter could feel the urge to cough as he breathed in the ancient dust. He reached the end of the chute and twisted his body, pinning his hips and knees against the sides of the chute to acquire leverage.

He took his free hand and pushed against the chute door, which was the size of a large coffee table. It opened about a quarter of an inch, and McCarter realized that smoke must have billowed out of the opening during the brief fire. It could have easily attracted the attention of people outside the building.

He listened for a moment, acutely aware of how vulnerable his position had become. All he could hear was the sound of the rainfall with its monotonous hammering. He had gone too far now to go back, and he cocked his hand back and struck the chute door with all his strength.

There was a screech of metal on metal and the chute door sagged then opened about a foot. McCarter drew back his hand and thrust it forward again. A bottom hinge popped off like a gunshot and he scrambled out.

He slid through the gap headfirst and fell a few feet into the weeds and mud against the side of the building. He rolled immediately and lifted the Beretta, tracking for targets. He saw nothing and turned in a tight circle, covering all points.

The rain hammered into him and once again McCarter felt grateful for its incessant company. He looked at his surroundings and saw he was standing next to a concrete loading dock in the middle of knee-high weeds. A narrow alleyway ran between the warehouse he had just escaped from and an almost identical one set across from it. McCarter turned toward the front of the building where the alley met the street on which the IMU fighters had set up their roadblock.

Not wanting to risk exposure by elements coming in as reinforcements to the gunmen who'd trapped him in the warehouse, McCarter spun on his heel and sprinted up the alleyway in the opposite direction. He scooped up the dangling AKM in one hand and clicked it off safe as he holstered the Beretta 92-F.

He crossed the muddy alley and turned the corner of the second warehouse. He saw a large Quonset hut with a sliding door that had obviously served as a vehicle garage at one time. A random mortar shell had torn a hole in its side and blown out the windows. He heard automatic weapons firing almost continuously from several blocks over.

McCarter crawled under a loose section of chain-link fence and scrambled into the building through the blast hole. He scanned the interior of the building, tracking with the assault rifle. Nothing moved. A large Peterbilt tow truck showing obvious signs of damage from the 85 mm mortar round filled the hut, but other than that, McCarter was alone.

McCarter leaned back against the wall and closed his eyes. He was exhausted and so thirsty he was savage with cotton mouth. Dehydration was a critical factor and had sapped the strength of many strong, fit men. Water was becoming his top priority.

Just a little bit longer and he could link up with Jack Grimaldi. Just a little bit longer.

"THAT THE BUILDING?" Haight asked.

The mercenaries looked at the warehouse through the sweeping rhythm of the windshield wipers as the motorcade pulled onto the Kyrgyzstan street.

"That's what the prisoner said," Glask answered.

The team had caught the squad of IMU fighters focused on catching the foreigner. They had been easy enough to kill. Two wounded men hadn't resisted Johnston's interrogation methods long.

"Had they managed to get him before we ruined their party?"

"Apparently he's trapped in the basement and is resisting their efforts."

Haight snorted and got out of the vehicle. Johnston ran up to him, and Haight wasted no time in directing the other mercenary to take some men and reconnoiter the warehouse from all sides, as it was readily apparent that the IMU terrorists had succumbed to tunnel vision in their efforts and concentrated on the basement door to the exclusion of other possibilities.

He watched as a terrorist fighter conferred with the sergeant, who listened closely, unmindful of the rain, and then nodded vigorously when the man finished speaking. The prisoner had been shot in the leg and arm, then bound with cuffs and beaten half to death. He now seemed eager to give the mercenaries any information they asked for.

"What did he say?" Haight demanded.

"He says that they have stopped receiving answering fire to their grenades a little while ago. They believe him to be badly wounded or dead."

Haight frowned to himself. He watched Johnston direct some of the mercenaries down the street in front of the building before taking Glask and entering the alleyway directly in front of where the motorcade was parked.

"Let's go inside," Haight said.

"Fine," the sergeant answered. "The main floor is perfectly safe in any event as they have the entrance covered."

"We still ahead of the army?"

"Our communications specialist caught the troop broadcasts. Apparently someone ambushed a convoy of trucks on a narrow road in the mountains last night. It's blocking the way. Only small elements of light infantry have arrived, not numerous. The motorized units are backtracking and going around. We have time." He paused. "Not a lot," he added.

Haight nodded absently. Things moved quickly when neither side was particularly interested in continuing the fight.

Haight slammed the car door and began to stalk

toward the front of the building, his AK-104 gripped loosely in one hand.

"Look out, Mr. Superman," he muttered. "Here I come."

CHAPTER TWENTY-TWO

Dominican Republic

Blancanales moved slowly around until he was behind Felicity, who was sitting. He stood to her rear, where she was unable to see him, where she had no idea of his posture or intention. He waited for a moment, listening to the subdued sound of her breathing. When he spoke next, his voice was a soft monotone, absent of threat or innuendo.

"Lemis. Tell me what you know. Don't leave anything out. You were clever once and we let you go. As you can see, though, we always come back."

Felicity sat stiffly, her back ramrod-straight, her body quivering with the energy of her indignation.

"Smith was investigating Lemis," Blancanales demanded. "Why?"

"Wrong. Smith wasn't investigating Lemis. That came later. He was investigating Durmstrange at the institute. I was helping him with that. That was when he learned Lemis was dirty."

"Why the institute?"

"I never understood that part. I still don't know what he found really. He learned the institute was run by someone named Michael Klaus. All I really know is that he discovered the institute was working on some pharmacological agent other than the generic medicines they claimed. And that Lemis was on the payroll of the man Klaus. Then he disappeared. I waited. Then I tried to find him. Then I met you. End of story."

"Where is Smith? Is he still alive? Did Lemis take him?"

"I told you, I don't know! I don't know any of it!" She paused and caught her breath. "I think Lemis took Smith but I don't have proof. Nothing I can give you, nothing I could have given my handlers, either."

"Lemis suspect you know?"

"I think so, but even if he wasn't sure, I'm a loose end. Loose ends in the Dominican don't last long, Mr. American-Secret-Agent. That's how you found me, isn't it?" she accused. "My handler told you where to find me."

"There's an American FBI agent missing. We're going to move heaven and earth to try to find him. The clock is ticking and you didn't tell us about Lemis. What else aren't you saying?"

"There's nothing—you have to believe me," she said. "Lemis is your next link in the chain. Not me."

Blancanales left her and went outside. He called Lyons and got him on the first ring.

"Lemis is dirty," Lyons said without preamble.

"Jinx, you owe me a soda," Blancanales replied.

"Felicity said the same thing?"

"Yep. Hell, you just got done talking to the man. What's your take?"

"That Rumford will cover his link into the Dominican regime at any cost. He'll want evidence. Not the kind of evidence they use at the Pentagon or in the Agency. He'll want actual go-to-court evidence before he pulls back the no-touch order on Lemis."

"We don't do court."

"Exactly. It's time to go simple on this. But this means since Lemis is dirty, Klaus is dirty. Everything Phoenix gave to Barb has now been verified. We are green light."

"Schwarz still running down that address tied to Klaus?"

"Yep. I sent him the picture of the guy that tailed me, told him what had happened. He's going to see why Klaus's company has been paying the rent on the hotel room, then meet us back at Smith's safehouse."

"You know it doesn't look good for Smith."

"Nothing we're involved in ever looks good. It's why we're involved in it."

HERMANN SCHWARZ SAT in a rented Saab across the street from the address supplied by the digital copies of receipts in Smith's records.

He was in a poor neighborhood on the southeast side of the city, near the countryside where jungle hills crowded the urban areas. Smith's lead was a rundown motel set in an old industrial area. Built on the cheap, the place looked shabby. Made up of fifteen single-story units running from the office in an L-shape, the entire establishment looked dark and deserted. Three cars sat in the otherwise empty parking lot. The place was low rent but, despite this, the institute run by Michael Klaus's company had been paying the rent on Room 11 for the past three months.

Schwarz got out of the Saab, sliding the Glock 17 into the small of his back. He crossed the street, avoiding the sparse skeletal traffic. He could smell rain on the horizon and the moon hung obscured by thick, low clouds.

He could see his own breath in the crisp, damp air. Reaching the other side of the street, he turned left and began to circumvent the rental property. The business's neon sign sputtered in a blinking, staccato pattern.

Hugging the fence line, he circled around toward the rear of the property. On either side of the motel dilapidated warehouses sat empty. In the distance an overpass led deeper into the city. Behind the motel the countryside pushed right up next to the fence. Once at the rear of the property, he stopped in a patch of shadow, broken hills to his back, and surveyed the rundown old motel.

Just as in the front, all of the rooms of the motel had their window curtains tightly drawn. Away from the noises of the street, Schwarz could hear radios playing and more than one television set turned up loud. He spotted no hidden sentries.

Moving quietly, he pushed his way through a gap in the chain-link fence and entered the property. His eyes shifted to the motel office, saw no movement, and he pressed forward. He cut to his right now to finish circumventing the L-shaped building.

He passed room after room with curtains pulled closed and doors shut. There was none of the raucous feel of crowded urban life here. Out in the thick undergrowth beyond the fence he heard the calls of night birds. From around the front of the building the sounds of radios and televisions was less aggressive. Fat drops of rain began to fall on the broken pavement of the motel parking lot.

Reaching Room 11, he paused, head cocked to one side as he listened. He heard the sound of a television set turned up loud from inside the target room. The noise overrode any other sound that might have come from inside the motel room.

Squinting, he looked at the door with the burnished metal, twin numeral ones set into it. The door was cheap wood, the paint was peeling and no spy hole had been bored into it. However, the window next to the door would allow the occupants to peek through the curtains and look out to see who was at the door.

Lyons was at a disadvantage. The occupants of the room would be able to identify him before he had any inkling of who was on the other side of the door. He briefly considered retreating to the Saab and keeping the place under surveillance.

He rejected the idea and decided to act. He stepped over to the window and wrapped his knuckles against the dirty glass pane of the window beside the door, then stepped back so that he had an equal field of vision between anyone opening the room door or pulling back the window curtain to peek out.

He heard the volume on the television set in the room being turned down. A shape moved in front of the screen, casting a distorted shadow across the hanging curtain. Lyons heard a voice murmur something indistinct. A second voice, equally faint, answered. The shadow moved away from the curtain.

Schwarz swallowed. He felt the hairs on the back of his neck rise like the hackles of a dog in an old reaction as his body prepped for any possibility. Cold adrenaline flooded his body. His skin felt taut, stretched tight across a frame quivering with potential motion.

Slowly he relaxed the field of his vision to take in the full spectrum of his surroundings. At the slightest hint of danger he was prepared to explode into action.

The fear worked on him in that peculiar, uncommon reaction that so many others felt incomprehensible. He began to feel nearly giddy, euphoric. The corners of his mouth were pulled up into a tight smile.

He felt alive.

A dark-skinned, masculine hand grasped hold of the curtain hanging in the window. Time stretched out as the man pulled it back. Schwarz caught movement as the person inside the room shifted to peek around the curtain. A pair of black eyes set met Schwarz's own blue ones. Both sets of eyes widened in recognition.

It was the man from the picture Lyons had sent him of his encounter with the surveillance. Schwarz snarled at the driver of the Audi and the other man released the curtain.

Kyrgyzstan

McCARTER CROUCHED in the rain and watched the mercenaries team sweep around the warehouse. Four men entered the alley where the coal chute was located, moving in a loose overwatch formation. Two of the men took up positions in the alleyway while the second team swept around the back of the building.

McCarter faded around behind the Quonset hut where he had holed up. He circled it, then left the area through an open gate in the chain-link fence. He jogged over to the edge of the second warehouse and hugged the wall as he moved up to the mouth of the alley, completely out of sight of the team pulling security there.

McCarter caught a flash of movement up ahead of him through the driving rain and he stopped moving and sank to one knee against the lee of the building.

He narrowed his eyes and was able to make out the last man of the first team as he rounded the corner on the far side of the initial warehouse.

McCarter rose and continued to make his way toward the alley mouth. The Quonset hut where he had stopped momentarily now lay on his right side, surrounded by the dilapidated chain-link fence. He reached the corner of the second warehouse and stopped, back up against the wall.

Holding the AKM muzzle up, McCarter quickly looked around the corner and then snatched his head back. He internalized what he had seen, placing each of the mercenaries performing security on that side of the old warehouse. Beyond the mercs McCarter had caught a glimpse of a vehicle he recognized as the one Haight had pulled up in outside of the compound earlier.

A vehicle he could very much use if he hoped to break through IMU lines and meet Grimaldi.

As far as McCarter had been able to see across the distance and through the rain, no one had been in the Land Rover or on the main street. What he proposed to do was so obviously risky it was almost beyond the need of acknowledgment. McCarter acknowledged it, internalized it and then executed it.

He let the AKM hang around his neck and over his left shoulder. The muzzle pointed straight down by his leg with the pistol grip riding snuggly at his right hip. He pulled the Beretta 92-F out of his shoulder holster the way he had a thousand times before and took the deadly Italian pistol in both hands.

McCarter came around the corner and extended the silenced weapon in front of him. The mercenaries crouched on either side of the obviously broken coal chute hatch, facing each other. Sensing movement, the one facing in McCarter's direction looked up.

McCarter saw the mercenary's eyes narrow as he scrambled to lift his weapon, an AKS-74 with its stock folded down. The man's mouth opened to shout a warning as he lifted the assault carbine. McCarter shot him between the eyes at fifteen yards.

The man's head jolted back as if he'd been punched, and blood spilled over the bridge of his nose and ran down his cheek and into his beard as he slumped downward. The sound of the slide racking another round into the chamber on the Beretta was lost in the driving rain.

The mercenary with his back to McCarter saw his partner go down and tried to turn. He was too slow by a country mile. McCarter's shot struck the man in the temporal lobe of his skull, and the 9 mm Parabellum round cracked his head like an egg. The man slumped to the side, dropping his weapon and falling to the ground.

Still charging forward, McCarter holstered the Beretta. He reached the coal chute and grabbed the broken hatch with both hands. McCarter kicked one foot up against the warehouse wall and pulled with all his strength, bending the door back on its one good hinge.

Grabbing the corpses bodily, McCarter heaved the first one up and shoved him into the chute. Without waiting to see what happened, McCarter whirled and snatched up the second dead man. He turned and muscled the body up before shoving it headfirst down the coal run, as well.

Satisfied, McCarter removed the AKM and took it up in one hand. Now he just had to steal their car.

Dominican Republic

THE GLOCK 17 APPEARED in Schwarz's fist. He stroked the trigger, sending half a dozen rounds through the window as he skipped backward. Glass shattered under the impact of his 9 mm rounds. A burst of automatic gunfire erupted in answer from inside the motel room.

A brilliant flame of unsuppressed muzzle-flash splashed behind the curtain. Fired at such close range, the weapon ignited the ratty old fabric of the curtain. Bullets ripped through the air around Schwarz and sailed out across the parking lot. He went to one knee and fired a tight trio of bullets into the burning curtain. He heard the audible smacks as his rounds found a target, and then the flaming curtain was ripped aside as a falling body crashed through it and rebounded off the broken glass of the windowsill.

He shifted to the left, putting himself at an angle to both the window and the door. From his vantage he had a good view of a large segment of the room. Figures moved inside its confines and he shifted his posture into the familiar Weaver stance as he searched for some sort of substantial cover.

There was nothing. There was no cover for him to get behind. He was caught in the open by opponents who wielded superior firepower. In the shattered window, flames licked up as the burning curtain ignited the carpet inside the room. From behind the growing flames two men rushed forward, Tech-9 submachine guns held up at the ready.

Schwarz threw himself flat out on the pavement. He brought up his Glock 17 and sighted from the prone position. He squeezed his trigger coolly and an untidy third eye opened up on the forehead of one of the gunmen. A red mist appeared behind the man's head and he crumpled forward, his submachine gun tumbling from slack fingers. The falling man's corpse fell halfway out through the shattered window.

The second gunman flinched as his comrade's sticky, hot blood and brain matter splattered across his face. The man's triggered burst sailed wild as he jerked in surprise at the gore splatter. Schwarz shifted his pistol's aim to center mass and pulled the trigger on the Glock 17 twice.

The man staggered backward like a punch-drunk fighter, arms flailing wide. Schwarz brought the muzzle of the Glock down, sighted and put a final round through the man's throat and he was driven down by the kinetic force of the 9 mm round.

Unsure of how many others might be in the motel room, he threw himself up and rushed forward. Inside the room the carpet's acrylic fibers spread the fire rapidly. The nylon cover on the bed caught and then burst into flame. Thick black smoke began quickly filling the room.

He shuffled forward, weapon up as he moved. He heard shouts coming from around him. A woman screamed and doors were opened and then slammed shut again. In minutes Schwarz knew heavily armed special police units would be on their way.

The front door to the room next to the gunmen's popped open and a shirtless man with a sagging stomach and a walrus mustache looked out. A clear glass bottle was still clenched possessively in one fat, grubby fist. Lyons twisted at the hip, centering his Glock 17 on the man. The fat man's face dropped in surprise.

"Get back in the room!" Schwarz shouted.

The man staggered, throwing himself backward, and slammed his door shut. Schwarz shifted his attention back to Room 11. The inside of the room was fully engulfed in flames now, and he realized there was no way the motel would escape, as old as it was and built on the cheap with secondhand materials. People would have to get out of their rooms immediately or face the real chance of being burned alive.

Cursing, he began moving away from the room and toward where his car sat parked across the street. Black smoke poured out through the shattered window and billowed up into the sky. Flames licked at the edges of the window, completely unaffected by the slight rainfall. Schwarz turned sideways away from the room, still watching it, and began to move at a faster pace toward his vehicle.

The gunman came through the window screaming. His Tech-9 submachine gun fired wildly as he leaped over the sill. Schwarz again threw himself flat as a wild, ragged spray of rounds slapped out in his direction. He hit the pavement hard and grunted.

He thrust his arm out straight and rolled over onto his side as he tried to target the charging man. Still firing, the man shuffled toward the nominal protection of a nearby car. He went to one knee behind the bumper of the dark blue car and brought his weapon to his shoulder.

Schwarz didn't hesitate. He rolled back onto his stomach and took his Glock 17 in both hands. He released air out through his nose in a steady stream and used both hands to sight in on the automobile. His first shot hit wide of the gas hatch. His second punctured it. A jet of gasoline shot out of the hole in an arc and splashed out onto the pavement of the parking lot.

Working smoothly, Schwarz squeezed his trigger twice and put two more bullets through the bleeding gas tank. The second bullet ignited the flammable gases trapped inside the tank, and it went up with a whoosh. A ball of flame erupted and was followed hard by a wave of concussive force.

The gunman was knocked clear of the car by the force of the explosion. His hair ignited and he rose screaming, dropping his submachine gun and slapping at the flames licking around his head. Schwarz dropped him with a precise 9 mm slug to the head.

Bullets ricocheted off the pavement a yard to the front of where Schwarz lay prone on the parking lot asphalt. He pivoted his head back toward the building and saw a gunman standing in the doorway of the motel room. The man had been sighting in on Schwarz when the vehicle had gone up. His burst had been knocked wide in his surprise at the sudden force of the exploding automobile. He cringed away from the rolling heat, one arm thrown up protectively over his face.

Schwarz twisted, rolling onto his left shoulder and bringing his pistol up to bear on the target. He pulled the trigger once and the man's frame shuddered. Blood spurted from a hole in the man's upper thigh and he sagged against the door frame. The man swept up his weapon as Schwarz sighted in again.

The Able Team electronics genius fired again and hit the man in his stomach and then put a second 9 mm bullet into his sternum. The man's clothes billowed out under the twin impacts and he dropped, collapsing inward on himself. Blood began pumping out rapidly in a growing pool around his body. His weapon clattered against the concrete of the sidewalk running past the door to the motel room. His eyes fixed open, staring, and from where Schwarz lay they showed a glassy reflection of the flames burning around him.

Slowly, Schwarz rose. In the distance he heard the sound of sirens. He turned and sprinted for his car. He ran across the street and slid behind the wheel of his Saab. He threw the still smoking Glock 17 pistol on the passenger seat beside him and pulled his car keys from his front jacket pocket. He slid them into the ignition and started the car. The engine roared to life.

He heard the shriek of sirens and looked up in his rearview mirror. Red lights spun on the top of the compact police car that was arriving first on the chaotic scene. Slower moving, but more heavily armored, UN troop carriers would be following behind the lead cars. If the first officer on the scene decided the situation warranted it, Sikorsky gunships could be mobilized almost immediately from military bases around Santo Domingo.

Schwarz tensed then relaxed as the car shot past him and turned into the parking lot of the blazing motel structure. He stepped on the accelerator and turned his vehicle in a tight semicircle. Straightening, he smoothly powered his car down the street. He checked his mirror. An overweight woman in a loud housedress had run out from the motel office. She rushed up to the police car and began frantically pointing in his direction.

"Shit," he snarled.

He pushed the accelerator to the floor. He had to make his escape before the police behind him got a good look at his vehicle or its license plate.

He got his phone out as he sped away.

"Ironman?"

"Go ahead," Lyons said.

"I got good news and bad news. The good news is that that guy from today, the one in the Audi? He won't be bothering you anymore."

"That's nice, thank you, Gadgets. What about the bad news?"

"Bad news? I blew up our lead."

"I'm sorry. Did you say you 'blew it up'?"

"Yep. Blew it up. It's burning to the ground as we speak. Sorry."

"Screw it. Come back. We got enough to verify Lemis. He's on the menu now."

CHAPTER TWENTY-THREE

Kyrgyzstan

Caught in the alley, McCarter began fighting for his life.

He heard a car engine race and he looked up, bringing the AKM to the ready. Several foot soldiers shouted in anger and turned toward the British commando.

A Land Rover turned hard out of its parking spot and rushed into the alley. McCarter lifted the AKM and took aim. He wielded his Kalashnikov in a sloppy figure 8, bringing fire down on the gunmen closest to him. His rounds struck the men and punched through the light skin of the vehicle doors, driving them back into the Rover's cab. Shell casings spun out in an arc, bouncing off his biceps and tumbling like loose change to the dirt road.

He felt the jolt in his hands as the AK fired its last round and the bolt locked in the open position. McCarter threw his empty weapon to the ground, where it splashed into the mud. On the other side of the vehicle the driver's weapon jammed and the stricken man also threw his rifle to the ground. Unlike McCarter, he turned and ran.

The man firing from the rear corner of the car turned his head to watch his comrade flee. He turned back around and tried to trap McCarter in his weapon sights.

He saw the ghostly killer lift a handgun in a smooth draw from his shoulder holster.

The man felt a freezing terror as he saw the muzzle on the handgun. The pistol exploded in McCarter's hand and a blaze of flame flashed. The bullet punched through the door frame of the Land Rover as if it were paper and struck the man in his gut, shoving him back.

The man screamed in agony at the searing pain plunging through his abdomen. McCarter's pistol jumped in his hand again, and the round struck the wounded mercenary square in his screaming face with sledgehammer force, flipping him over backward. The man lay faceup in the grass with the falling rain filling up the bloody cavity where his face had been.

McCarter felt the sting of falling rain, then the dull throb of a wound high on the outside of his thigh. From behind him he heard a wounded man moaning and the hiss of escaping steam from a perforated radiator.

Time rushed back into McCarter like a tornado and everything he had just accomplished slammed into his consciousness in a whirlwind of images.

He ran forward and threw his arm across the still warm hood of the Land Rover. He sighted down the barrel of his weapon and planted his sights dead between the shoulder blades of a fleeing man. McCarter pulled the trigger on his pistol and the firearm bucked in his hands.

Cordite burned into McCarter's nostrils like an amphetamine. Out in the street the mercenary driver was thrown forward and landed facedown on the grass. The man lay on the ground as red soaked his fatigue shirt. His leg kicked once, then the body tensed up and finally relaxed.

McCarter stood. He dropped the magazine out of the pistol and slid a new one into place. He racked the slide and jacked a new round into the chamber. He looked over at the vehicle perched on its side in the middle of the road and took aim at the vehicle's exposed under-carriage. The gas tank seemed as big as a bathtub to McCarter's experienced gaze. His first round pierced the tank. Gas began to pour out in an amber stream. His second round penetrated the tank, the scrape of bullet on metal lighting a spark that ignited the gas fumes inside the tank.

The car went up like a Roman candle. McCarter turned his face away from the sudden flash of searing heat as burning pieces of wreckage came raining down into the mud. Black smoke roiled up in a column as flames engulfed the vehicle.

From the ditch on the other side of the first vehicle McCarter had shot up, a wounded man continued moan-ing in agony.

Some instinct made him look up then and he saw a line of vehicles racing out of the street beside the warehouse and toward him. Then a bullet hit his leg with crushing impact. McCarter's legs were swept out from under him and the muddy road flew up to meet him, slamming him hard in the face.

McCarter grunted at the impact and the world spun around him like a carnival ride. He heard the sound of a gunshot and looked up. He saw the mercenary he had wounded lying on the ground across from him at a distance of about fifteen yards. The man held a black pistol in his hand and was firing from underneath the vehicle. Mud splashed up into McCarter's face as a pistol rounds burrowed into the earth inches from his head.

McCarter rolled over once and swept the Beretta around. The wounded mercenary under the car was screaming as he pulled the trigger on his pistol. McCarter stroked the trigger on the Beretta, squeezing harder than was prudent for accuracy but too juiced on his adrenaline to prevent the response.

The Beretta jumped in his hand as he unloaded the rest of his clip at the already wounded mercenary. Bullets flew under the Land Rover as the two men shot at each other. McCarter saw blood geyser as his rounds struck the man in the chest and shoulders. The mercenary sagged to the earth, limp and silent.

Knowing he couldn't afford to hesitate, McCarter forced himself to his feet. He rose and looked up. The second convoy of mercenary vehicles were less than one hundred yards away. He hobbled toward the only vehicle undamaged enough to still drive. His leg bled freely and wouldn't work properly.

He looked down at the wound but couldn't tell how bad it was because of all the blood. McCarter fell forward into the open passenger door and crawled across the glass-littered seat and slid behind the wheel. The keys dangled from the ignition and the engine was still running.

McCarter heard the sound of gunfire from behind him. He threw the vehicle transmission into drive and used his left leg to stomp on the gas. The vehicle peeled out as it raced away and threw mud in a shower up behind it. With all four doors still hanging open, McCarter sped around the flaming wreck of the first Land Rover and back onto the road.

He lifted the Beretta pistol and hit the magazine release with his thumb, ejecting the spent clip onto the floor of the bloody cab. He stuck the gun in his lap and took the wheel with his right hand as he used his left to reach across his chest and pull a fresh magazine from his shoulder harness.

His leg felt as if it was on fire, and McCarter knew he had to stop the bleeding soon or everything was moot. He took the wheel in his left hand and grabbed the fresh magazine with his right. Like a crime-scene detective lancing a spent shell casing with a ballpoint pen, McCarter slid the magazine into the pistol butt. Grabbing the Beretta, he tapped the magazine into place on the dash and then hit the slide release, chambering a round.

The Land Rover jerked and bounced under his hand as he took the ruined and potted road too fast for safety. He heard more gunfire and he looked into his rearview mirror. The Land Rovers were gaining on him and he could clearly see the yellow flashes of weapons fire through the gray streaks of falling rain.

McCarter realized he wasn't going to make it.

As HAIGHT'S LAND ROVER swerved to avoid the burning vehicle in the middle of the road he turned his head to watch it. He'd seen the foreign operator commandeer the mercenary vehicle as his force had borne down on the battle scene.

"This is becoming a very real problem," Glask snarled. "We're running out of fucking guys!"

Haight turned his attention back to the furious mercenary. The sergeant held his burning cigar between two thick fingers and he jabbed it over the seat at Haight as he yelled.

The mercenary captain was unimpressed by the display of bluster, but he really didn't blame the man. The whole Kyrgyzstan situation had turned into a real cluster fuck and there was little use trying to deny it.

"I negotiated a flat fee based on the number of men under my command. Everyone is getting a little bit richer."

Glask's face relaxed as the implications of what Haight was saying hit home. He slowly put his cigar in his mouth and bit down on the butt. Sensing an advantage, Haight pushed ahead with that line of reasoning.

"We have to kill this son of a bitch first."

"Don't I fucking know it. Now let's just get him!"

Haight had lost all but three of his men as they'd pursued this bastard. The man had killed his team, humiliated him and was taking bread out of his family's mouth by screwing up Haight's operation. The grudge was fast becoming personal. "We'll get him," he promised.

The sergeant nodded from the front seat. "We better, my friend, or all the money in Skell's bank account won't buy us out of our trouble," he said.

"We'll get him," Haight repeated.

He looked out through the furiously working windshield wipers at the battered Land Rover racing over the ruined road just ahead of them. Three of the Toyota's doors still hung open and most of the vehicle's windows had been shattered by gunfire.

The driver, a badly frightened soldier almost two yards tall and all of 150 pounds, was pushing the chase but the rains had so rutted the road that he could barely keep his vehicle out of the ditch at the present speeds.

Haight forced himself to be patient. He longed to hang out his window and fire at the fleeing Land Rover but he knew under such conditions such action would be futile, a sign of weakness. He refused to give in to such base emotion. He was a professional and he would conduct himself as such.

Haight's hands massaged the weapon he held across his lap, squeezing and releasing, squeezing and releasing. His hate was like a bitter pill that he kept chewing but could not swallow.

"What's up ahead?" he asked the sergeant. "Anything that'll slow the bastard down?"

"The east road crosses the main railroad tracks," Glask shouted back. "After that the road simply gets worse."

"We'll get him."

"You keep saying that and it might even happen," Glask snorted.

The Land Rover hit a rut in the road and both Glask and Haight were thrown hard against their doors. The driver managed to straighten the vehicle out, but when he was through fighting the steering wheel they were no closer to their quarry than they had been. Haight fairly gnashed his teeth in frustration.

"We'll get him."

McCarter reached down and snatched up the AKM, pulling it over to himself. Once it was across his lap he bent and pulled his Gerber boot knife from the sheath in his boot. He looked up and swerved to avoid a gigantic pothole. The primitive condition of the road was killing him, tearing the vehicle frame apart at these speeds and jolting him around hard, which only increased the rate at which he was bleeding out.

He saw a line rising out of the grass and paralleling the road. It was the ballast dike of a railroad track and McCarter could barely make out where it crossed the road about a quarter mile ahead of his current position. He placed the rifle sling between his teeth and quickly used the Gerber to slice the nylon belt off at the muzzle and shoulder butt sling attachment points.

McCarter turned the boot knife point down and stabbed it into the seat. Gritting his teeth, McCarter lifted his wounded leg and slid the nylon strap under his leg. He pulled it up and then quickly tied a knot in it about four inches above his gunshot wound.

The wheel jolted hard under his hand and he looked up. He released his tourniquet, grabbed the steering wheel with both hands and fought the Land Rover back onto the road. He climbed the slight incline and used the emergency brake to swing the Land Rover onto the train track. The wheels immediately began to pound with a harsh, undulating rhythm as he raced over the wooden ties.

Though the shaking felt just as brutal as that of the washed-out road, McCarter's chances of losing control dramatically decreased. All he had to do was keep the SUV between the rails. McCarter forced himself to use his wounded right leg to work the gas and then propped his left knee against the steering wheel. With both hands free he worked frantically to finish tying the tourniquet into place before he bled to death. He laid the handle of the Gerber in the center of the knot he had secured above his wound and tied a second knot directly over the handle.

McCarter grabbed the blade by the center and began to twist the boot knife around, cranking the nylon belt wrapped around his leg tighter and tighter. When his wound stopped bleeding, McCarter tied off the flat of the blade against his leg with the extra length of sling.

The vibrations from the railroad ties shivered up through his body in a brutal staccato beat and the pain it caused made him dizzy. He would start to fade and the rubber of his SUV tires would chafe against the iron rail of the track and jerk his attention back to reality.

The rain was omnipresent. In his shell-shocked state McCarter couldn't remember a time without the rain. It seemed there had always been rain. McCarter could see the headlights in his rearview mirror and knew the two vehicles were still behind him. They are persistent, McCarter allowed.

"McCarter, this is J.G.," Grimaldi came up over his earjack.

"Please tell me you're here," McCarter said into his throat mike.

"I'm trying to follow your GPS signal but you're moving pretty damn fast. I'm five minutes out from the RZ point."

Christ, McCarter thought, five minutes was forever.

"Copy. Just haul ass. It's going to be hot when you land," he warned.

"We're coming," Grimaldi promised.

McCarter cursed as he broke off communication. So close, but maybe not close enough.

He couldn't stay on the track forever, had known that even before he'd mounted the rails. Desperate times called for desperate measures and McCarter had also known that fact for a long time, but that didn't really change the maneuver from being what it was: a simple stalling tactic.

The railroad was heading south and sooner or later, as close as he was to the RZ, McCarter knew he would have to turn off and swing east again. He was running out of options, may already have run out of options. He felt woozy, sleepy. He realized he must have lost more blood than he'd first thought. He tightened his grip on the steering wheel and forced himself to remain alert.

McCarter's mind raced, considering options then discarding them just as quickly.

McCarter was trapped, battered and bleeding in a war zone, and time was running out. He'd pushed his body to the very edge of its capabilities and he was living on borrowed time now.

McCarter made his decision. He looked to either side and saw the sheer grade of the ballast dike dropping away from the edges of the train track.

Any attempt to pull off the dike at too high a speed would lead to a rollover. McCarter checked his rearview mirror. The two Land Rovers behind him were pushing the chase and had closed to within fifty yards. That was point-blank range for a long rifle and only the incessant jarring of the vehicle wheels on the railroad ties had kept their shots wild so far.

McCarter shifted his foot off the gas and pinned the steering wheel with his left knee. He didn't touch the brakes, to avoid shining the rear lights, which could alert his pursuers to his intentions. Instead he flipped up the emergency brake and sent the Toyota Land Rover into a power slide.

The car tires butted up against the iron railroad tracks violently but the vehicle kept in its groove. McCarter snatched the AKM from the seat and twisted around, laying it across the seat rest. His rear windshield had already been blown out and he was sheltered from the falling rain by the roof of the SUV.

He laid his sights on the vehicle careening toward him.

"Good morning, assholes," McCarter whispered.

He began to fire with a systematic and precise carnage. The rifle recoil into his shoulder was like the reassuring hand of an old friend. In that moment on the track, trapped in the vehicle between the rails, the SAS trooper came alive.

McCarter blew the windshield out on the lead chase vehicle and place his second round into the driver of the speeding SUV. The driver's head jerked and he slumped forward and slid down against the steering wheel until the vehicle horn began to blare. The Land Rover continued rushing toward McCarter's now immobile vehicle.

McCarter shifted the AKM. At thirty yards the range was ridiculous for a man of McCarter's capabilities. He saw the front passenger scrambling for the steering wheel, desperate to bring the racing vehicle under control.

Be careful what you wish for, McCarter smiled, you just might get it. Here I am, you son of a bitch.

McCarter put a round through Glask's face. The man's head snapped like a whip popping and the top of his skull detached and flew into the back of the vehicle. McCarter shifted his weapon an almost imperceptible degree and fired another round through the sergeant's seat at twenty yards.

Haight was already scrambling. The 7.62 mm round punched through the center of the sergeant's seat and struck the man in his right arm as he threw himself down to the floor of the SUV.

McCarter turned and rolled out of his Land Rover just as the second vehicle struck it in the rear. He gasped in surprise at the intensity of the pain as his injured leg struck the ground. He gave in to the pull of gravity and rolled down the bank, spilling gravel wildly.

The Land Rover struck the back of McCarter's vehicle with a crash like thunder. Headlights turned on against the gloomy rain exploded in a shower of sparks. The front and back ends of each respective vehicle collapsed like matchboxes, crumpling inward under the appalling force. The dead mercenary driver catapulted out through the windshield to sprawl across the crumpled hood of his vehicle.

The final Land Rover remained unaware of the rapidly unfolding events and raced forward. As McCarter looked up from the bottom of the ballast dike he saw the driver, a bearded mercenary, twist the wheel in a desperate attempt to avoid the pileup.

The speeding SUV left the tracks going much too fast for the terrain. The front end of the vehicle popped up as it crashed over the railroad. The Land Rover bounced down hard and began to slide over the edge of the ballast dike. The driver gunned it and his vehicle began to slide farther out of control.

CHAPTER TWENTY-FOUR

The panicked driver overcorrected and the vehicle began to pitch. McCarter watched the Toyota begin its tip, his hyperstimulated senses making it seem as if the action was unfolding in slow motion. He saw the men in the vehicle cursing as they were thrown around inside the cab.

He thought of how the Smith had died and he felt good as he watched them suffer.

The second Land Rover rolled over in an awkward somersault of crunching metal and shattering glass. The vehicle rolled again and cleared the railroad bank, spinning out into the elephant grass. After rolling twice more, the vehicle came to a rest on its back with exploded tires spinning madly.

Merciless, McCarter lifted himself up on his good knee and pulled his salvaged rifle to him. He swept the AKM up and poured a long stream of gunfire into the wrecked SUV, spraying his bullets with lethal accuracy.

He tried and failed to ignite the second Land Rover's gas tank as he had back on the edge of the Kyrgyzstan village. He shot until his weapon came up empty and then cast it aside. He looked down; his tourniquet had come loose during his fall and his leg was bleeding again.

He picked up the AKM and jammed the muzzle into

the ground, using the assault rifle as a makeshift crutch. McCarter staggered to his feet. How much could he take? How far could he go? He wanted to lie down and sleep. He had suffered too much, faced too much, undergone too much. It would be easy to lie down. How many could have survived what he had already?

Overhead he heard the sound of Grimaldi's helicopter rushing toward him. It was just in time to be too late.

HAIGHT CAME OUT of the back of the Land Rover with his submachine gun blazing. The Kalashnikov filled his hands. McCarter's bullets had hurt him badly and as he died he wanted only one thing. A hope that Mc-Carter understood immediately—the insatiable need for vengeance.

In the early-morning dark and the rain, each with their ears abused by the cacophony of weapons fire, the two killers turned on each other. Haight owned the high ground and in that moment wielded both the advantage of aggressive momentum and the ace card of superior firepower.

The helicopter was in sight now, just over McCarter's shoulder. It grew larger with each passing moment.

Haight scrambled out of the back of the ruined Toyota Land Rover and unleashed the firepower of his AK-104. The 7.62 mm rounds stuttered out of his gun with mechanical intensity. Confused and hurt, bleeding and wounded, Haight had been reduced to his animal state, striking out in a blind rage at the adversary beast that had brought about his demise.

McCarter returned in kind.

Into the teeth of Haight's superior firepower and insane anger McCarter replied with cool accuracy. He swept up the Beretta 92-F and unleashed torrent after torrent of 3-round bursts across the distance.

The mercenary took the rounds, absorbing them like a sponge as he tumbled from the vehicle. He took a 9 mm Parabellum round in the belly and dropped to his knees, still firing. He felt bullets destroy the bones of his arm until it was impossible for him to hold his blazing weapon. Then McCarter's soft-nosed pistol bullets smashed through his throat, and Haight struggled for breath.

Haight went down hard. The Kalashnikov tumbled from fingers turned to liquid. The unforgiving rock of the railroad ballast reached up and slapped him. His head snapped forward and bounced off the rocks while his blood poured thick as mud across the gray-and-white stones of the ballast.

He rolled to his back and lifted his arms into the rain, but death was an elusive partner in Haight's final dance. He tried to gasp and inhaled only his own blood. Coughing, he rolled his eyes outward and saw his enemy sag into the tall grass, as exhausted as he was.

Haight's fingers scratched for the pistol grip of his weapon as he saw his enemy falter. He felt a cold black rushing in to smother his vision and he thought about nothing.

OUT IN THE GRASS McCarter forced himself up again. He felt the beat of rotor wash as Grimaldi brought the helicopter in. He couldn't hear anything over the spinning blades.

McCarter lifted the Beretta once again. He sighted down the barrel, seeing Haight scratching futilely at the ground, his weapon beyond reach.

Behind him the skids of the helicopter struck the earth.

McCarter pulled the trigger.

Dominican Republic

TWO BIG BLACK SUVs with heavily tinted windows pulled off the crowded Santo Domingo street into the alley. Inside the first one Lemis signaled the driver to stop. He looked up the flight of wooden stairs leading to the safehouse.

In the vehicle with him were several off-duty police officers, each man a longtime paid employee of Lemis. In the second SUV behind them were four members of a local gang that controlled cocaine distribution throughout the city.

The cops picked up their weapons, a combination of riot shotguns and assault carbines. Each man wore body armor and a balaclava hood. Before arriving at the target site Lemis had stopped at the local precinct house with an envelope of cash. It would be a long time before any responding police units were able to find the scene.

"That door is the only way in or out," Lemis told the corrupt cops. "There are three men inside. They will be armed and they are trained."

"Then we'll go in fast and hard." The driver shrugged. "Let this baby do its work." He smiled and patted the collapsed tube of an M-72 LAW rocket.

"Yeah." One of the others smiled. "And this," he said, and held up an M-57 antipersonnel grenade.

"Nothing to it but to do it." Lemis grinned.

ABLE TEAM SAT around the table in the safehouse.

Rosario Blancanales field-stripped the H&K MP-7

submachine gun and lightly oiled the parts after cleaning them thoroughly. Bolt, receiver, barrel, trigger mechanism. Then he reassembled the weapon and began pushing bullets into extra magazines.

Beside him Hermann Schwarz began inserting pencil timers into plastique shaped charges and geo-synching his CPDA to their new cell phones. He absently chewed a toothpick as he worked.

Carl Lyons walked back and forth in front of the table, setting up the final details for their operation and coordinating his activities with Stony Man.

"Once we pull the snatch," he said, "we need a location to take him to. We've been at this location too long as it is."

"I've got a new house set up for you, on the water," Price told him.

She gave him the coordinates and address, which he quickly relayed to a waiting Schwarz, who then plugged them into his CPDA.

"Got it." Schwarz nodded.

"Rumford isn't going to like us stealing a Dominican national right out from under his nose," Price pointed out. "He'll know it's you and without concrete proof about Smith he'll have nothing to give the State Department to lodge a complaint."

"Lemis knows where Smith is," Lyons said. "We pull him in officially and he won't talk. Then he'll use Klaus's big-money lawyers and all his own political connections to walk. If Smith is even still alive he wouldn't last the hour. We have to get Lemis, make him talk, then make him disappear. Nothing's changed."

"All right," Price allowed. "You are green as in go, I'm out."

"Out," Lyons replied.

The ex-cop slipped away his cell phone and drew his Glock. It would need cleaning before they rolled out to get Lemis.

The window in the front room broke with a crash.

As one Able Team turned their heads and looked. The grenade bounced once off the carpet, then rolled to a rest.

"Grenade!" Blancanales shouted.

Lyons spun and threw himself across the small counter and into the kitchen. Schwarz spun out of his chair and threw himself flat through the opening, his explosive charges and CPDA protected beneath him. Blancanales shoved the dining room table over and flung himself down behind it, hugging the floor.

The grenade went off.

The concussive force of the blast blew out the rest of the windows in the little covert apartment and muffled the hearing of the three men trapped inside. A curtain of razor-sharp shrapnel flung out in an arc. A portion of the fusillade was slowed as it passed through the couch and heavy wood of the table. The rest exploded in an arch above the prone men.

Lyons, safe behind the counter, popped up first. He looked immediately toward the front door, the only ingress point to the apartment. Thick smoke from the grenade and a haze of plaster dust obscured his vision. He sighted down the barrel of his pistol preparing for the entry team to breach the door.

Blancanales, his right leg bleeding from several light shrapnel wounds, rolled over and brought up his MP-7. Schwarz searched frantically for where his weapon had been blown out of his hands.

The door came straight off its hinges with a sound like a jet fighter going supersonic. A wall of flame pushed into the room like a freight train, sending the furniture tumbling like dice. The blast knocked the standing Lyons off his feet and shoved him hard into the refrigerator.

A wave of heat and force rolled over the still prone Schwarz and Blancanales with enough power to rattle their teeth in their heads. Schwarz, closer to the blast, felt his head jerk and then bounce off the wall hard enough to momentarily blind him.

Then the hit squad came in.

Kyrgyzstan

JACK GRIMALDI pulled up on the stick of the helicopter as soon as Manning and Hawkins pulled McCarter in. The bird lifted off the ground beside the railroad track and the nose swung around.

Tracer fire burned past the windshield. There was the ominous ping-ping-ping as bullets strafed the main compartment. Rounds arched in through the open door and burned through the cargo bay, forcing Hawkins down over the wounded McCarter.

A rocket struck the railroad track just under the helicopter, and a section of a steel beam flew up and went twisting end over end into the spinning blades of the helicopter.

With a horrendous screech Grimaldi heard the chopper blades sputter in their rotation. The yoke jerked in his hand like a bull bucking and he felt the tail start drifting of its own accord.

"We're going down!" he shouted.

The jerk tossed Gary Manning out of the door gun opening. The Canadian Special Forces veteran tumbled down fifteen feet and struck the ground.

Above him the helicopter drifted fifty yards on a skewed vector and Grimaldi just managed to belly flop it down right side up next to one of the burning vehicles. One blade dipped down from the centrifugal whiplash and bounced off the gravel ballast of the rail dike.

The blade chopped through dirt and ripped free from its moorings on the rotor housing. Six feet of helicopter blade spun off and buried itself in the ground. The nose of the helicopter smashed into the ground and crumpled like a soda can.

Grimaldi was thrust hard up against his seat restraints and his head snapped forward so hard his spine felt as if it had stretched an inch or two. He blinked away his dizziness and looked at his gauges out of habit. He saw the fuel meter dropping steadily and realized that could only mean there was a leak.

He unbuckled his restraints just as the windshield exploded around him. He threw himself down between the seats and slugs burrowed into the backrest where he'd been. He saw Hawkins untangling himself from McCarter, a cut open on his forehead and bleeding so profusely the soldier's face was a mask of blood.

"Get out!" Grimaldi shouted. "Fuel leak!"

McCarter forced himself up off the floor and Hawkins helped him up as Grimaldi crawled forward. Bullets continued to hammer into the aircraft superstructure forcing the three men to keep low as they scrambled to collect weapons and escape the cargo bay.

Outside on the ground Manning grunted like a wounded animal and pushed himself up. The fall had given him a flash knockout and his body ached but he could tell instantly that he hadn't broken or cracked any bones. He looked over and realized he'd landed just a few yards from the rail line and that if he'd hit there instead of the grass he might have been killed.

Bullets cut through the air above and he turned toward their source. An old Soviet army jeep filled with IMU terrorists had arrived. In the back of the jeep the thug was manning a .50-caliber machine gun while three other gunmen charged forward.

The attackers' entire attention seemed focused on the downed helicopter and the men struggling in the wreckage. Manning looked around, saw the burning and wrecked vehicles that McCarter had left in his wake. Several yards away a mercenary lay dead, torso perforated with rounds. The man's AK-74 lay on the ground just beyond his outstretched fingers.

Manning put his nose in the dirt and began low-crawling for it.

Behind him McCarter came out of the helicopter and saw the IMU foot squad racing toward him. He cast around to see where his weapon had fallen as Grimaldi followed him out of the downed helicopter.

Hawkins was already out and up. In preparation for McCarter's extraction he'd switched out his sniper rifle for a Squad Automatic Weapon. He lifted the 5.56 mm weapon, heavy with its 200-round drum, and opened fire.

He caught one of the running terrorists with the initial burst and drove the remaining three onto the ground. Behind them the .50-cal gunner opened up and pieces of the helicopter came loose and went flying. Hawkins threw himself to the ground.

"We got to get clear!" Grimaldi shouted. "Fuel line!"

"Go!" Hawkins shouted, and opened up with his SAW.

Ahead of them the battered Manning reached the fallen mercenary's rifle and snatched it up. He twisted it around and put a single bullet through the machine gunner. The man jerked under the impact and a loop of blood splashed out before he buckled and fell out of the jeep.

Hawkins jumped to his feet as soon as the machine gun quiet. He cursed in anger and ran forward, swinging the blazing SAW back and forth, pinning the final three terrorists down.

McCarter threw an arm around Grimaldi's shoulder and the pair shuffled off out of the line of fire and away from the helicopter. Manning, seeing the pinned-down terrorists, fired on the prone gunmen. His rounds found them easily at that range and soon the battlefield was silent except for the sound of burning vehicles.

"What do we do now?" Manning yelled.

"Steal a car," McCarter shouted back. "It's what I did."

"Yeah, well, no offense, brother," Hawkins said and laughed, "but you don't look so damn hot right now."

"Just get us that damn jeep and let's drive." McCarter grinned back. "You think flying with Jack's any better?"

"Uh, guys," the pilot said. "We've got company."

CHAPTER TWENTY-FIVE

Stony Man Farm

"What do you mean, you've lost contact!" Barbara Price barked into her satellite connection. The Pentagon official working liaison was unruffled.

"I mean our AWACS flying on the border lost the helicopter. The Kyrgyzstan national army is crawling all over the place. They're saying on the radio they shot a bird down. I've deviated a Blackbird from the Pakistan border to fly photo recon over the area and double-check, but we're pretty damn certain that whoever the hell those boys are, they've been shot down."

Price frowned. She turned around and saw Carmen Delahunt and Aaron Kurtzman looking at her, faces anxious. She released a stream of pent-up air through her nose and made a fist. She didn't have time to count to ten so she settled on three before she spoke again.

"All right," she said, voice calm. "I don't have assets for this, General. What are the chances of backup from any special operations troops? What about the Nightstalkers?" she added, referencing the Army's elite unit of helicopter pilots. "You have to have a wing or a squadron stationed at Bagram, right?"

"That's classified," he responded immediately. "And it's classified need-to-know. Doesn't matter anyway.

Those flyboys may be special operations but they're also in the Army. It'd take an act of Congress to get them across the border in Kyrgyzstan. We're not exactly at war with them at the moment." He paused. "The only one set up to cross an international border like that is the Agency. They can do it if the President signs an executive order."

Price knew Hal Brognola was already at the White House working just such an angle. She also couldn't be anywhere sure that it would happen in time.

"Will you keep your communications people on the tasking?" she asked.

"Ma'am, we've kinda got a shooting war of our own going on here," the general said. "But whoever your boys are, they've got balls, and I'll do what I can."

Price prayed that would be enough.

"Thank you, General." She signed off. Her voice was so calm it was icy.

The connection died and immediately Price whirled around and slapped her hand down so hard onto a desktop it sounded like a gunshot in the room. "Goddamn it!" she cursed. "This operation is supposed to be over. We have all we need from Phoenix. The NSA and CIA task force has already dealt with the repercussions of Klaus's operation."

"They'll get out," Kurtzman said. "That's Gary and T.J. and David. Jack's been downed before. He's always made it back. A bunch of B-team terrorists from a backwater sect aren't going to be the ones to end Phoenix Force." He held his hand out and made a definitive, chopping motion. "End of story."

"I hope you're right," Carmen Delahunt said.

Dominican Republic

THE HIT SQUAD rolled in, weapons up.

Blancanales sat up in a half crouch and fired a burst with his MP-7, putting the shotgun-wielding point man down. The second man tried to jump clear of the falling body and fire his submachine gun, but his foot caught on an outflung arm and his burst went wild.

Lyons shot him in the face.

The third man went to a knee and let loose with an American-made M-4 carbine, triggering successive 3-round bursts. High-velocity rounds slapped into the wall and chewed up the counter before ricocheting off the refrigerator. The fire forced Lyons down and sent Blancanales rolling for cover.

Schwarz swung his own pistol around but found his aim obstructed by tipped-over and smoldering furniture. Bullets whizzed over his head and he quickly pulled his bandolier of preset engineering charges to him.

The third man was pinned in the entrance, so intent on keeping Able Team down that he couldn't gain enough momentum to move forward and clear the doorway. A second gunman came up and shoved the barrel of his shotgun into the apartment and began indiscriminately firing.

Schwarz hurriedly thumbed the digital timer on a preset breeching charge all the way down to two seconds. "Fire in the hole!" he yelled, and tossed the wedge-shaped hunk of explosive.

Blancanales rolled away and curled up into a ball. Hearing Schwarz's warning, Lyons put his head in his arms and opened his mouth to keep pressure from building up in his eardrums and possibly rupturing them.

The charge flew through the air and landed on top of the corpse of the second assassin. The gunner in the door caught the motion and looked down. He saw the timer read 00:00:01. His eyes grew round and he opened his mouth to shout.

The explosion, designed to blow a steel-reinforced door off its hinges and snap several dead bolts, went off. The explosion knocked the two killers in the doorway back and hit the first man so hard his submachine gun went spinning up and caved in his face.

Lyons came up half a second later. He hurtled the kitchen counter and brought up his handgun. Off to one side Blancanales came up to one knee, swinging the muzzle of the MP-7 into position. Schwarz popped up off the floor and aimed his own handgun.

"Window!" Lyons yelled, and raced forward hurdling broken furniture like a track star.

"Door," Blancanales called, and shuffled forward, submachine gun.

Schwarz performed a maneuver known as slicing the pie as he moved.

His handgun went off six times as he moved from left to right in a tight semicircle sweep that moved him from a disadvantageous position on the breech point to a more defensible angle with a clearer field of fire.

His bullets burned through the empty space in the door providing cover as he maneuvered. Blancanales and Lyons used his suppressive fire to cross the room. Lyons came up next to the shattered window overlooking the alley while Blancanales threw his back to the wall right next to the door.

He looked down. The breeching charge Schwarz had thrown had ripped the two corpses into bloody pieces and spreading puddles. As soon as Schwarz stopped firing and raised the barrel of his smoking pistol toward the ceiling, the ex–Green Beret went into action.

"Lemis!" Lyons shouted from the window, and began firing.

Blancanales shoved the barrel of his subgun around the corner of the doorway and burned off a wild burst angled down the stairs. A line of men with assault rifles were filed up on the stairs and they returned a withering avalanche of fire.

Rounds buzzed through the entrance in a literal wall of lead forcing Blancanales to throw himself back and Schwarz to again hug carpet. In the window Lyons emptied an entire clip at the Dominican but only managed to shatter the windows of his black SUV.

"Blow the stairs!" Blancanales yelled at Schwarz. "They're wood! Blow 'em."

"We'll be trapped!"

"They won't be able to get to us!"

"Rocket!" Lyons yelled.

The 66 mm warhead of a second LAW rocket slammed into the apartment inches below the window sill where Lyons had stood a moment before. If Lemis's aim had been better, the ex–LAPD detective would never have made it.

As it was the interior wall exploded outward slightly and fire ignited the broken blinds on the window as Lyons jumped well clear.

"Throw it!" Blancanales yelled from where he had been tossed by the muffled explosion. "The assholes are bottle-necked."

Schwarz didn't bother to argue. He mashed two breeching charges together in a softball-size lump, set the timer and tossed the Semtex underhand out the door. Blancanales watched the plastique arc through the air, his eyes bulging wide.

"Too much!" he yelled, and threw himself forward.

The lump of explosives disappeared out the door. A half second later there was the sound of men cursing. Then the entire front of the apartment was blown clear of the building.

Switzerland

MICHAEL KLAUS LOOKED at himself in the mirror.

He took a half step and regarded the cut of his navy Brioni suit. It was impeccably tailored. He turned again on his Berluti shoes and straightened his Satya Paul Design Studio tie. He was wearing well over ten thousand dollars even before he slid his VISA Black Card into a Louis Vuitton wallet and shrugged on his black cashmere Ermenegildo Zegna coat.

"You have to admit I'm terribly handsome," Klaus said.

"Absolutely," the prostitute said.

The young man with the close-cropped red hair turned away and stuffed his feet into his loafers. His hand went to his eye where a bruise was beginning to form, as distinctive as a brand on the side of a longhorn steer.

He didn't complain, but took his envelope full of euros and left.

As soon as the prostitute had left, Skell hurried into the room. He took in Klaus's overcoat and saw his second-best attaché case, the one he took on planes, was lying on the rumpled silk sheets of the bed.

"You're leaving?" the lawyer said with surprise.

"It is for that razor wit I pay you so much?" Klaus remarked lightly.

His voice had taken on that light tone that meant he was at his most dangerous, but Skell was so upset he blundered on.

"But we have problems," he insisted. "I just got confirmation that Haight is dead. Lemis has dropped all pretenses and is using a frontal assault on the American agents in the Dominican."

"Skell, things are a lot worse than the outing of a crooked fixer in a Third World country and the death of a notorious mercenary killer," Klaus snapped. He crossed the room, picked up his Valextra Diplomatico briefcase. A vice president in the accounting wing of Ze had dropped almost ten thousand dollars U.S. to give it to him for his birthday two years ago. "We have the NSA hacking our mainframe, stealing data and freezing accounts. We have CIA agents tailing me and conducting snatch-and-grab operations of my research. I have U.S. State and Justice Department officials suing the Swiss for my extradition. Fuck Haight and fuck Lemis—I'm in trouble."

"Extradition?" Skell murmured. "How can that be? I'm not handling that—"

"I've put another legal cadre on that matter. You've become tainted. Apparently Interpol is investigating you for international irregularities with the hope of having you disbarred."

"What!"

"I don't know the details. I wasn't paying attention. But you can see why I decided to go another way on this."

"Where are you going?" Skell demanded.

"Venezuela."

"Venezuela?" Skell repeated.

"Yes. No extradition with the United States. I own controlling interest of several companies there. Including the arms manufacture for the state. Chavez will be happy to shelter me until this unpleasantness can be sorted out."

"Christ," Skell whispered. He felt as if he'd been punched in the gut. "Fucking Venezuela."

Klaus spun on him then, jabbing a finger into the defeated man's chest. "That reminds me. How could I have forgotten?" He smiled at Skell like a lizard. "Man does not live by bread alone." He waved his hand toward the messed-up bed in the presidential suite. "Take this card, contact my agent-procurer and arrange for them to see to my needs once the Lear sets down in Caracas. Tell them I want someone local, someone ethnic right off the bat but high end."

Skell took the offered card and placed it in the pocket of his suit coat. Klaus brushed past him into the lobby, where his chauffeur was waiting to carry his bags down to the lobby.

"Venezuela," Skell said to the empty room.

Kyrgyzstan

HAWKINS RAN UP on the ballast dike forming the platform for the railroad track. He turned his head toward the dirt road he'd seen while Grimaldi was bringing their helicopter in.

"Damn," he cursed.

He turned and slid back down the gravel bank. He

looked over to where Grimaldi was helping McCarter hobble toward the idling IMU jeep. He turned to Manning.

"I suggest we expedite our little excursion," he said. "Some local boys are coming and they look fast."

"Right." Manning nodded. "Sorry, David."

Without preamble the burly Canadian dipped down and pulled the injured McCarter over his broad shoulder and began running with him. Grimaldi, now out from under the Briton's arm, took off at a run toward the jeep, as well.

"I'll drive," he shouted.

Hawkins clambered into the back of the jeep and took up his position behind the .50-caliber gun. Blood from the dead IMU machine gunner had crusted black on the now cooling barrel.

Manning set McCarter down in the middle as Grimaldi slid behind the wheel. The Stony Man pilot threw the rig into gear and Manning forced his bulk into the open cab next to McCarter.

"How many?" McCarter demanded.

"Three Soviet jeeps just like this one and a half track!" Hawkins shouted.

Grimaldi put the vehicle in gear and it lurched forward, bumping over the ground in a jarring, unfocused rhythm. Manning jacked a round into his stolen rifle and shouted up at Hawkins.

"Half track? There ain't no IMU bastards with a half track. Those clowns have to be Kyrgyzstan national army."

"They're going to shoot us just the same!" Grimaldi shouted.

As if to punctuate his words the lead jeep's gunner

opened up with his machine gun. Red tracer fire arced out of the night as Grimaldi wove back and forth.

"Get on the road!" McCarter ordered. "It's one track. They'll have to line up so they can only use one .50 at a time."

"And we'll outrun that half track," Manning added.

As Grimaldi swerved to put the jeep back on the dirt road Hawkins began to return fire with the .50 caliber. Manning shoved his Kalashnikov into McCarter's hands, then clambered into the back beside Hawkins, where he began feeding the ex–Delta Force trooper his belts of ammunition, preventing any fouling.

Grasping the twin spade handles in both hands, Hawkins used his thumbs to depress the butterfly trigger of the massive gun. The sound of .50-caliber ammunition cutting past the racing jeep was terrifying.

Hawkins leaned down into the gun on its swivel tripod, trying to bring the wildly bouncing barrel under control as he triggered a blast. He kept his aim low and as the morning sky began to lighten he could actually make out his rounds tearing gouges out of the road.

Falling rain whipped into their faces as Grimaldi pushed the jeep wide open. McCarter's leg wound began to bleed again as he sat in the jeep, helpless to engage the enemy with only a carbine for a weapon. He concentrated on desperately trying to recall the terrain photos he'd pored over prior to insertion, but the team had drifted way off course by now.

"Border's south," Grimaldi shouted over the .50. "But that'll mean military outposts. We'd be better off lost in the woods."

"We need to get to the woods!" McCarter shouted back. "There is a base stationed nearby. The same one

Smith worked out of as a contractor. The army's got to have helicopters they'll put in the air. We're screwed."

"I've got an emergency GPS transponder sewn right into my flight suit," Grimaldi said. "When they come for us they'll have no trouble finding us. We just have to get as close to the southern border as we can."

"*If* they come for us," McCarter shouted.

Behind them Hawkins cut loose with another long burst from his machine gun.

"Yeah," Grimaldi muttered. "If…"

CHAPTER TWENTY-SIX

Dominican Republic

The blast echoed off the brick wall directly across the street from the safehouse. It rolled back across the narrow bridge of space and threatened to shake the rest of the apartment into the alley.

The front wall of the apartment was gone, leaving only open, yawning space and roiling smoke in its place.

"Did you use enough explosives?" Blancanales demanded.

"Semtex is powerful, I was in a hurry and you were yelling at me!" Schwarz shouted back.

Lyons rushed up to the edge to look, his pistol at the ready. He saw the building's old wooden staircase collapsed in a pile of splinters. The hit team that had been on the stair was nowhere to be seen.

Lyons saw movement in the dust and smoke and turned, pistol coming up. Below him Lemis fired, his burst going wild. Lyons dropped to his belly and returned fire, arms extended over the jagged edge of the apartment floor.

Seeing him take fire, Blancanales shuffled forward and sprayed a burst with his MP-7. Behind them Schwarz clambered to his feet to help his teammates.

"You want more Semtex?" he shouted.

"No!" Blancanales and Lyons barked in unison.

Lemis, now the last man standing, fired up with his M-4 carbine. Blancanales raked the SUV he was hidden behind with fire. The car was not armored for executive protection but was merely a commercial model. Blancanales's rounds shattered windows, shredded tires and tore through the hood, slamming into the V-8 engine block.

While the ex–Green Beret sprayed the area, Lyons used the cover fire to draw a more accurate bead on Lemis. Then he realized what he was doing and held his fire. He turned on his stomach and shoved Blancanales back.

"Stop! Stop firing!" Lyons ordered. "He's our only lead to Smith!"

"I'll wing him, like in the movies," Blancanales said, but stopped firing.

The two men rolled out of the Dominican criminal's line of fire. Below them Lemis fired off several more bursts.

"You fucked his ride up," Lyons told Blancanales. "He'll have to flee on foot. We can follow him, catch him, then hook his nasty ass up to a car battery until he gives us Smith."

"Boys, when the police get here—" Schwarz waved his hands at the missing front of the apartment "—and they *will* get here and soon, Lemis is the one with connections, not us. In fact our only connection is Rumford and he's going to be pissed."

"Good point," Blancanales admitted.

Outside Lemis had stopped firing. Lyons high-crawled over to the edge and took a look. He saw the big black man turn the corner on the alley and disappear at a dead run.

"Fuck all that," Lyons grunted. "You guys coming?"

The ex-cop shoved his pistol in his pants and rolled over the edge of the blown-out floor, dropping ten feet to the alley below using an airborne roll to prevent injury.

"Carl Lyons, man of action," Schwarz snorted.

"Come on," Blancanales growled. "Someone has to keep that knuckle-dragger out of trouble."

Washington, D.C.

HAL BROGNOLA SAT ACROSS the desk from the President of the United States of America. In his time he'd sat across from more presidents than he could count on one hand. In this town of partisan politics that was a monumental feat.

Next to him sat the director of the CIA. Next to that man sat the national-security advisor. No one in the cabal was currently happy. More than one of them, Brognola included, was fighting mad.

"It is out of the question, Hal," the NSA representative insisted, not for the first time. "We are not at war with Kyrgyzstan. We are in fact allied with Kyrgyzstan. The first helicopter we sent in faced IMU troops—that was one thing. The next is going to take fire from Kyrgyzstan national army troops. That is an international incident."

"Then call the Kyrgyzstan leader and cut a deal!" Brognola replied. "I guarantee you that if my boys are shot at by a bunch of wild-eyed rabble while trying to save their leader, then they will fire back. That'll mean dead Kyrgyzstan soldiers."

"You goddamn cowboys are going to cost us—"

"I have a troop slick waiting," the CIA director said quietly. He met the President's eye. "I'll need your go-ahead, of course. But I have a tactical insertion chopper sitting on the pad at a mountain base just across the border."

"And what if they get shot down?" the NSA demanded.

"Enough," the President said. He looked tired. He looked as if he didn't appreciate getting woken up to deal with a no-win situation. "I've had to write men off before," he said quietly. "Those men, just like yours, Hal, knew the odds going in. But it never sits right, it always…weighs on you. I have never had to pull the plug on men who've done as much for this country as your unit."

"Sir—" the NSA started to protest.

The President cut him off with a curt hand motion. "My mind is made up. I'll sign the order." He looked at the CIA director. "Make the call."

"Thank you, sir," Brognola said, voice grave.

"It's the right thing to do," the President said. He reached for the secure phone on the desk. "Now, if you gentlemen will excuse me, I have a call to make."

Kyrgyzstan

"HERE," Jack Grimaldi said.

McCarter looked over and saw the pilot was handing him a military geotransponder unit about the size of a cell phone. The leader of Phoenix Force recognized it immediately as part of the pilot survival gear Grimaldi wore on every mission.

"The fuel tanks?" McCarter asked.

"The fuel tanks," Grimaldi confirmed.

Once McCarter had taken the device, Grimaldi put both his hands back on the wheel of the wildly bouncing jeep, fighting it under control as Hawkins continued to send harassing fire at their pursuers.

"What's the code?"

"What else? Nine-one-one!"

"Cute."

McCarter quickly typed in the code and hit Send. A second later the downed American helicopter, along with all of its classified electronic and communications systems, went up like a star going supernova.

"Jesus!" Hawkins shouted. "Was that you?" he demanded.

"Tee-hee," McCarter said dryly, and waved the device at him. "Operational security."

"Look!" Manning shouted suddenly. "They're slowing and turning off!"

"They must think we have artillery or airpower!" Grimaldi said, his voice excited.

"Oh, man," McCarter said and laughed, "the State Department is going to be so pissed."

"That's Hal's problem, not ours," Grimaldi said.

Suddenly the Stony Man pilot's enhanced GPS transponder began to blink, then vibrate.

"That's Barb," Grimaldi said, looking at the device in McCarter's hands. "Looks like coordinates. I think the cavalry redux has arrived."

"Just in time to be too late...again," McCarter muttered, voice rueful.

Stony Man Farm

"I'VE GOT bad news," Kurtzman greeted Price.

The honey-blonde mission controller, bags heavy under her blue eyes, grimaced. She crossed the floor of the communications center room and sat heavily in a padded office chair. She let out a long sigh and nodded to the director of her cybernetics team.

"Shoot," she said.

"I was in midconversation with Schwarz. We were going over some technical details after you gave them the address to the new safehouse. Midconversation he cut out."

"You were talking to him directly?"

"No, I was texting him on CPDA while sending him some explosives specs for breaching doors. The CIA had stocked that house with Semtex, which is powerful, and he wanted to double-check some engineering details before possibly using them in a crowded urban setting."

"Then?"

"Then nothing. I waited, attempted to reestablish contact and couldn't. Since they were supposed to be in between active operations I attempted to follow up with their handhelds and then headsets. Nothing."

"Not good," Price admitted. "But not totally out of character for Ironman and crew, either."

"True. Able's used to a loose leash but it was midconversation."

"Could be anything. Let's hold off. If we can't establish contact in two hours go to CIA, not FBI—that station chief Rumford is pissed at us for trampling his rose garden—and have someone do a pass on the safehouse."

"Will do. How are we looking for Phoenix?"

Just as Price was about to answer him, Carmen Delahunt came into the room. She carried herself with a brusque, all-business attitude that spoke volumes to her capabilities and professional demeanor.

"We've lost track of Klaus," she informed Price without preamble. "He fled Switzerland in a private jet. We suspect South America but it could be Ireland or South Africa."

"Great," Price muttered. "More bad news. When it rains, it pisses."

"Maybe not," Delahunt said.

"Oh, yeah?" Kurtzman asked. He leaned forward in his wheelchair. "How's that?"

"The second primary, the lawyer, Skell, also ran," replied Delahunt. "Only he's not got Klaus's resources."

"We know where he's at?" Price asked, eyes bright.

"Amsterdam."

"Great." Price jumped up. "Get me Phoenix on the line. What's left of the team is going to Amsterdam and we are going to start sewing up loose ends."

CHAPTER TWENTY-SEVEN

Dominican Republic

Carl Lyons was running flat-out.

The early-morning street was only just starting to stir with people. In the middle distance he could hear the whooping wail of European model police sirens as emergency responders began descending on the scene.

His chest was heaving with exertion as he sprinted. His nostrils flared as he sucked in lungfuls of air. His feet pounded into the pavement and he ran with his pistol out in the open.

Just ahead of him Lemis was slowing, unable to maintain the pace. He darted off the street and down a narrow alley between two ramshackle buildings. Wet clothes had been strung out to dry overnight and he plunged through them, gasping for breath.

Lyons ran up to the mouth of the alley and quickly ducked his head around to check Lemis's position. The Dominican criminal was waiting with his M-4 and triggered a 3-round burst. Lyons jerked his head back around the corner and the burst went wide.

The ex-cop dropped to a knee, changing levels, and swung around the corner with his pistol up in both hands. He saw the hulking figure of Lemis claw a line of wet sheets out of his way as he tried to run farther. Lyons drew a careful bead and fired a single round.

The pistol jumped in his hands, the barrel lifting slightly as the 9 mm round exploded from the muzzle. There was a sharp, flat crack that Lyons barely registered after the repetitive trauma of weapons fire and explosions he had just endured. The round struck the man low, clipping him in the calf.

The Dominican's pants blossomed out and blood spurted like paint onto the pink-and-white sheets. Lemis cursed and dropped, twisting as he fell, and brought the carbine up with one hand by the pistol grip. He snapped the trigger back twice, but his aim was hasty and wild and all the rounds burrowed into the building wall.

Lyons fought the urge to jerk back behind cover. He stayed in the pocket and completed his aim. His second round smashed Lemis in the left biceps, gouging out a chunk of flesh and forcing a cry of agony from the man's lips.

He turned over on his stomach and began to crawl away, almost sobbing with the pain.

Behind Lyons a dark SUV screeched to a stop. Startled, the ex-cop spun and flung his gun up. The window was down and Blancanales, MP-7 in hand leaned out, teeth flashing.

"You like my new ride, Ironman?" Blancanales asked from behind the steering wheel of the hit team's second SUV.

From the other side of the vehicle Schwarz jumped out, pistol up. Lyons snorted and turned back to watch the wounded Lemis crawling pitifully away.

"Put it down!" Schwarz barked. Lemis, as if delirious with panic and pain, continued to crawl. "I said, put it down!" Schwarz ordered again.

"Fuck this," Lyons muttered.

He hopped up to his feet and strode into the alley, lifting his arm. He sighted down the barrel and fired several times. Each of his rounds smacked home into the receiver of the American-built carbine just above the pistol grip.

The weapon virtually exploded in Lemis's hand. Schwarz shoved the barrel of his own pistol into the back of his jeans and jogged forward to assist Lyons. The two men jerked the wounded criminal to his feet, unmindful of his wounds, and quickly shuffled him down the alley and into the waiting vehicle.

Blancanales put the SUV in gear and drove off.

Amsterdam

LARGE GREEN GARBAGE bins were set against the alley walls.

Hawkins kept his gaze roving as he moved closer to the back door of the centuries-old brownstone style building. He and Manning had utilized a flat punt with a commercially available trolling motor to navigate into position using Amsterdam's canals.

Moving carefully, the ex–Delta Force commando stepped out of the punt and onto the dirty canal-front sidewalk.

A couple of empty beer bottles were littered among wads of crumpled newspapers. It was too cold for there to be any significant smell. Slush clung to the lee of brick walls in greater mounds than out on the open street. Several patches of slush were stained sickly yellow. Halfway down the alley Hawkins drew even with the building housing Skell's town house.

Dark, polluted water in the channel lapped the edges

of the canal. Gary Manning stayed in the boat, huddled in a low profile as he scanned the area for unwanted attention.

An accordion-style metal gate was locked into place over a featureless wooden door. A Master lock gleamed gold in the dim light, obviously new. Hawkins shuffled closer to the security gate and drew a lock-pick gun from his jacket pocket.

He inserted the prong-blades into the lock mechanism and squeezed the lever, springing the dead bolt. Hawkins reached up with his free hand and yanked the accordion gate open. The scissor gate slid closed with a clatter that echoed in the silent, cold alley. Hawkins quickly inserted the lock-pick gun into the doorknob and worked the tool.

He heard the lock disengage with a greasy click and put the lock-pick gun back into his jacket pocket. He grasped the cold, smooth metal of the doorknob and it turned easily under his hand. He made to push the door inward but it refused to budge. Dead bolts.

Hawkins swore under his breath. He placed his left hand on the door and pressed inward. From the points of resistance he estimated there were at least three independent locks securing the inside door.

His mind instantly ran the calculations for an explosive entry. He factored in the metal of the bolt shafts, their attachment points on the door frame and the density of the door itself. He estimated how much plastique he would need and ascertained the most efficient placement on the structure.

However, Hawkins also calculated the risks of blowing the door of a building in downtown Amsterdam. He was not exactly sure of what he would find inside. He was well versed in various forms of surreptitious entry and had been thoroughly schooled in the techniques of urban climbing, or buildering as it was sometimes called, during his time in the Army.

The fire escape was directly above the back door and ended in an enclosed metal cage around the ladder on the second floor.

"Change of plans," Hawkins whispered into his throat mike. "I'm going up."

"Your call, Hawk," Manning answered. "Everything is good at the moment."

Hawkins looked around the alley. He thought briefly of pushing one of the large green city garbage bins over and climbing on top of it to reach the fire escape. He rejected the idea as potentially attracting too much attention.

He looked around, evaluating the building like a rock climber sizing up a cliff face. Above the first floor the squat building was constructed with five uniform windows running the width of the building along each floor.

Hawkins made his decision and zipped up his jacket. It would keep him from getting to his concealed weapons quickly but it was a necessary risk if he was going to attempt this climb. He opened the scissor gate again and grasped it at the top. He stuck the toe of one boot into a diamond-shaped opening and lifted himself up off the ground. He placed his other hand against the edge of the building, using the strength of his legs to support him as he released one handhold on the gate and reached for a gutter drain set into the wall.

He grabbed hold firmly there and held on before moving his other hand over. The drain was so chill it

almost seemed to burn the flesh on the palm of his hand
and fingers. He pulled himself up despite the great strain
of the awkward position and grasped the vertically running drain with both hands. He moved his right leg and
stuck his toe between the drainpipe and the brick wall,
jamming it in as tightly as he could.

Once he was braced Hawkins pulled his boot from
the scissor gate and set it on top of the door frame. It was
slick along the top and he was forced to knock aside a
minor buildup of slush along the narrow lip. Confident
with the placement of that foot, Hawkins pushed down
hard against the lip at the top of the door frame and
shimmed himself farther up the drainpipe.

Hawkins's muscles burned and he forced himself
to breathe in through his nose. Idly he wondered what
his antics must look like to Manning down in the punt.
Hawkins squeezed the frigid, slick pipe tightly as he
inched his way up it. He lifted himself up until only the
toe of the boot on the door frame was in contact with
the narrow edge. The muscles of his calf flexed hard
under the strain, and he released his left hand from the
drainpipe and reached out and grasped the ledge of the
second-story window closest to him.

He set himself, then knocked a ridge of slush off the
window edge. He pushed down against the ledge and
inched his right hand farther up the drainpipe. One of
his legs found a metal bracket securing the gutter drain
to the wall, and Hawkins wormed his boot toe hard
into it. He shoved down with his left arm and lifted his
free leg until his knee was resting on the second-story
window ledge.

His body stretched into a lopsided X, Hawkins carefully pressed his hands against the window pane and

pushed upward, testing to see if the window was open. He met resistance and realized it was locked. Hawkins eased his head back and looked up. A light was on in the window on the floor directly above his position. Above that the fourth floor was as dark as the second. Directly above that was the building roof.

From his careful study of the architect's blueprints Hawkins knew the internal staircase rose up to a roof-access doorway. He debated breaking the glass on the window and working the lock mechanism from inside. He decided the risk was simply too great and made a decision to keep climbing.

"This is a no-go," he muttered. "I'm going all the way up."

"Copy," Manning answered.

He chose this route for the same reason he had decided not to use the fire escape. The metal structure was as dated as the building and ran directly next to the softly lit third-floor window; he feared the occupants in the lighted room would be aware of the rattle as he climbed and be alerted to his presence.

Decision made, he shimmed his way up to the third floor despite the toll the physical exertion was taking on him. Hawkins was in exceptional physical shape, but the task of urban climbing was extremely arduous. Hand over hand and toehold to toehold, Hawkins ascended the outside of the building. He worked himself into position by the third-floor window where the light burned from behind a thin blind, causing butter-yellow light to seep into the cold Amsterdam night.

Hawkins paused. He could hear the murmur of voices and sensed shadowed movements beyond the blind, but not enough for him to gather any intelligence. Moving carefully to diminish any sound of his passing, Hawkins climbed the rest of the way up the building.

Hawkins rolled over the building edge and dropped over the low rampart onto the tar-patched roof. He rose swiftly, unzipping his jacket, and freeing the MP-7 submachine gun. Exhaust conductors for the building's central air formed a low fence of dull aluminum around the freestanding hutch housing the door to the fire stairs.

Out across the rooftop the spectacular vista of one of the oldest cities in Europe beckoned. With single-minded determination Hawkins ignored it, concentrating solely on the matter at hand.

Hawkins crossed the roof to the side opposite his ascent, icy slush crunching under his boots, and reached the door. He tried the knob, found it locked and quickly worked his lock-pick gun on the simple mechanism.

"All right," Hawkins said into the throat mike. "I'm going inside."

"Be careful," Manning's voice said across the distance.

Hawkins glanced quickly around to see if the occupants of any of the other rundown buildings surrounding the roof had witnessed his climb. He saw no evidence of either them or Manning in his overwatch position and ducked into the building, leaving the door open behind him.

Hawkins descended into darkness.

CHAPTER TWENTY-EIGHT

Dominican Republic

Lyons got out of the taxi and paid the driver.

Behind him Blancanales smoothly pulled the black SUV into position. Lemis had given them everything they needed. It was as simple as it was tragic. Smith was dead. He always had been. Michael Klaus had a lot to answer for, as did his man Lemis.

But they weren't the only ones. There still remained the matter of the physician who had used the kidnapped FBI agent as a human lab rat, injecting him with the formula Klaus's company had been working so hard to perfect, despite the cost.

With the information taken and Lemis in a hood and manacles and on his way to a black-site prison, there was one last chess piece to eliminate from the Dominican board before moving on to settle with the mastermind.

As Blancanales and Schwarz watched him, Lyons surveyed the building and grounds of the Klaus Institute as the taxi drove away. The building was made of sturdy, respectable old brick and obviously dated from before the Second World War. L-shaped, it was surrounded by a high chain-link fence with a single security-manned entrance that allowed access off the main street.

Two Dominicans in private security uniforms and

boasting side arms, directed traffic in and out of the electronically controlled front gate.

Lyons lifted his knapsack to his shoulder and checked traffic before crossing the street. He felt time, like the slow burning fuse of a detonator, burning down on him. At any moment opposition could come screaming in like dive-bombers. Able Team was wanted by not only local police but also by national-security services.

So far they had stayed one step ahead, but they remained on a tightrope.

Government advice and subsidies, due to the delicate nature of the Klaus Institute's work, had provided for expensive, if unspectacular, security upgrades. The security booth in front of the electronic gate was bulletproof and camera-monitored. The two guards were checking IDs before opening the remote-control gate.

One of the guards looked over at Lyons as he approached the booth. The man made no attempt to open the door as Lyons came up to him. He was built thickly but flabby, with a pockmarked face and a light dusting of dandruff on his navy-colored uniform shirt. His partner was a younger and thinner version of the first man.

"Hello. My name is Smith." Lyons smirked. "I do not have an appointment. Please alert the receptionist that I am from the Klaus home office."

The pockmarked guard stared at him with flat, muddy eyes. He blinked once, reptilian in composure.

"You understand my words?" Lyons asked.

"I understand," the man answered.

"Great. Now, will you alert the receptionist?"

"I'm sorry, sir, but our protocols are very strict."

"I'm not asking you to let me through the gate without

an appointment. I'm asking you to check me in with Durmstrange's receptionist."

Lyons kept his face impassive, though at any moment he expected carloads of local assets to roar around the corner and gun him down where he stood.

"*Dr.* Durmstrange is a very busy man, sir."

"That's why I'm asking you to contact his receptionist first."

"This is highly irregular. Perhaps if you had some sort of paperwork for me…" The man's voice trailed off, thick with innuendo.

The younger guard behind him snickered, and Lyons realized he was being shaken down for a bribe. He sighed and then reached reluctantly inside his jacket. The older guard allowed a little smile to play on his rubbery lips and he slid open the metal door to the security booth.

"I think I have a few 'papers' here that might persuade you," Lyons said. "You don't mind American papers, do you?"

"Depends."

The man grunted the last noncommittally, but betrayed himself by leaning forward, avarice gleaming in his eyes. The kid behind him was grinning openly now. He idly picked his nose while he watched the transaction unfold.

"Nice," Lyons muttered. "You're making your country a real shithole, you know that?"

The guard grunted, uninterested.

Lyons pulled his wallet out, held it open while the older guard's eyes went to it. He dropped it and watched the man's eyes follow the money. Lyons struck like a snake uncoiling.

Reaching out with one bear trap of a hand, Lyons snatched the guard around his wrist. Lyons yanked hard as the man leaned in, pulling the man off his stool. As the man fell forward, Lyons's left hand struck him hard in the shoulder. Lyons smoothly stepped inside and spun the man around, locking his arm up behind his back.

The guard squawked as Lyons shoved him roughly up against the metal-edged doorjamb of the booth. The other guard, mouth gaping, leaped to his feet in protest. Lyons smoothly unholstered the guard's Smith & Wesson .38-caliber pistol. The younger man froze, eyes bulging.

"Sit!" Lyons snarled.

The guard sat.

Lyons threw the pistol onto the ground inside the guard station. He shoved the older guard in after his weapon. The man sprawled into the arms of his comrade, who struggled to keep the man from falling to the ground.

"If I have to get on the phone and call the receptionist myself and tell her that the fucking gate guards prevented a representative of the home office from solidifying a contract, there will be hell to play. Now, how are my papers?"

The younger guard scrambled to pick up the phone in the booth. He turned his back on Lyons while the older man retrieved his weapon, a sullen look on his face. As the pock-faced guard stood, the other man hung up the phone and turned to Lyons, his face flushed.

"You may report to the receptionist."

Lyons did not thank him.

Amsterdam

HAWKINS MOVED DOWN the stairs and deeper into the building. Just inside the doorway he reached up and pulled the edge of his watch cap down, revealing a bala- clava mask. He moved past the landing door leading to the fourth-floor apartments and down toward the two levels housing the hole-in-the-wall Amsterdam apart- ment building.

The MP-7 was up and at the ready in his grip as he ghosted down the staircase toward the third-floor landing. Hawkins stepped softly off the staircase and stopped by the interior door on the narrow landing. From his check of the blueprints Hawkins knew the third floor housed offices and a small kitchen-and-bedroom apartments while the second floor was a real-estate law firm.

Hawkins tried the knob to the fire door. It turned easily under his hand and he pulled it open, keeping the MP-7 submachine gun up and at the ready. The door swung open smoothly, revealing a dark stretch of empty hall. Hawkins stepped into the hallway and let the fire door swing shut behind him. He caught it with the heel of his boot just before it made contact with the jamb and gently eased it back into place.

Down the hallway, in the last room, a bar of light shone from underneath a closed door. Hawkins heard indistinct voices coming from behind it, too muffled to make out clearly. Occasionally a bark of laughter punctuated the murmurs as Hawkins stalked down the hall.

He eased into position beside the final closed door and went down to a knee. Keeping his finger on the trigger of the H&K submachine gun, Hawkins pulled a preassembled fiber-optic camera with a tactical display from his inside jacket pocket. He unwound and placed the coiled bore scope cable on the floor.

It was awkward working with only his left hand, but the voices on the other side of the door were clearly audible and speaking in what he thought was Dutch, though Hawkins's own linguistic skills were low enough that it might have been German. Hawkins turned on the display with an impatient tap of his thumb and then slid the thin cable slowly through the slight gap under the door.

The display began to reflect the shifting view as Hawkins pushed fiber-optic camera into position. A brilliant light filled the screen and the display self-adjusted to compensate for the brightness. A motionless ceiling fan came into focus and Hawkins twisted the fiber-optic cable so that the camera no longer pointed directly up at the ceiling.

He saw the antechamber to a flight of private stairs used by employees servicing the presidential suite that Skell currently occupied.

"We're clear on the outside," Manning whispered. "I'm beginning my ascent."

"Copy," Hawkins acknowledged. "I'm on the final approach. Let me know when you're in the elevator."

"Roger."

Hawkins moved through the door in a sudden, fluid movement, pulling it quickly shut behind him and stepping to one side as he entered the antechamber. His pistol was out to the front of him, tracking. He moved up a short flight of stairs and entered the bottom level of Skell's town house suite through the service entrance.

The big room was dark, a jumble of hulking, shadow-cloaked shapes. Going to one knee, pistol held ready, Hawkins waited for his eyes to adjust after having his night vision blown by the house lights outside.

"I'm inside," he murmured into his throat mike.

"Copy," Manning replied. "I'm through the lobby and rolling up the elevator."

"See you on the other side."

Quickly, Hawkins's pupils expanded and he began picking out details around him. He was in a game room. To the side there was two billiards tables and a massive, even ostentatious home entertainment system. There was expensive, comfortable furniture scattered around. Across the massive room from the outside door a short flight of stairs led up to the main floor of the town house.

Hawkins stood, shifting his knapsack off his back as he did so. With it in hand Hawkins crossed the room to the stairs. He could clearly hear music from the stereo system playing upstairs. He was banking on it to cover any normal noise he made while moving. To his possible detriment, however, it helped increase his chances of being surprised going through transition points in the structure: doorways, stairs, halls and arches.

Reaching a flight of internal stairs, Hawkins looked up. The door to the next level was tightly closed, a bar of light showing through at the bottom. Hawkins mounted the steps and knelt in front of the door. A light sheen of perspiration coated his forehead, part concentration, part apprehension. The time he spent implementing his close-quarters observation equipment was time when he was at his most vulnerable. He set down his pistol.

Hawkins dug the fiber-optic camera system out once

again. He slid the cable under the doorway and then turned on the handheld video display screen. An image of the room on the other side of the door popped up, and Hawkins smoothly panned the camera across the room.

The great room stretched from the front to the back of the house, encompassing a wet bar along one wall over to a sunken leisure area containing costly pieces of furniture and objets d'art. The floor was dark hardwood and a spiral staircase ran downward from the third level next to the bar. The room appeared empty.

Hawkins frowned. Then Skell stepped around a corner on the same wall as Hawkins's door, coming around the end of the wet bar with a drink in his hand. Bile rose in the back of Hawkins's throat. Skell sure didn't look like a man run to ground, in danger for his life. He looked pretty at ease in his surroundings.

Hawkins set his mouth in a hard, straight line. Through the bore scope he watched Skell walk across the area and step down into the entranceway. The front door opened and a beautiful woman walked into informal entertaining area. Skell trailed her, standing close at her side.

A massive man in a dark trench coat followed them in. When he moved, his coat flared out and Hawkins could see the pistol in the shoulder holster.

They crossed to the bar and Skell watched the woman pour both of them a drink. While they did this Hawkins quickly broke down his surveillance device and secured it in his backpack. Steeling himself, Hawkins bent and picked up his stun grenade. Slowly he released his breath, like a pressure valve bleeding steam. He focused himself, mentally imagined each step he was about to execute as clearly and precisely as he could picture. He was like a dancer choreographing a particularly difficult routine. Each step had to be perfect.

He lifted his hand up and reached for the door. His fingers found the knob and rested there lightly. Come on, Gary, he thought, let's do this.

CHAPTER TWENTY-NINE

Dominican Republic

Lyons presented himself in front of the camera overlooking the front entrance to the institute. He waited a second while he heard someone controlling the camera lens from a remote, then there was a buzz as the locks to the dead bolts were disengaged. Lyons reached out and pulled one of the heavy doors open.

He stepped into the Klaus Institute. Lyons felt a strange sense of arrival. What had gone on in this place had resulted in the deaths of two brothers. The secrets conducted here had stolen lives. Lyons had picked up the disparate pieces of information, broken lives, bloody handprints and followed them all back here, to this quiet, efficient building.

Lyons looked down the hallway past rows of office doors on either side. At the far end of the hall a skylight had been placed above a solarium and in the center, behind a formidable desk, sat a sharp-eyed receptionist. She glanced up as the door swung closed behind Lyons then returned to typing busily on a PC workstation.

Realizing that he currently looked nothing like either a research scientist or an executive, Lyons began walking calmly toward the woman. If he could keep her from alerting the local police units or sending a security detachment down on him, he thought he'd be doing pretty well.

He stopped in front of the desk, taking in the plethora of potted plants arrayed around the otherwise rather clinical room. The nameplate read K. Celeste. The woman stopped typing and looked up at him. Her looks were classically Caribbean and pretty in the no-nonsense sort of a way Lyons associated with blue-collar workers and technicians. She seemed to be slipping into late middle age with dignity and poise.

"Hello," Lyons said.

Looking over pince-nez glasses, Ms. Celeste took in Lyons's casual dress and the black knapsack slung casually over one shoulder. Lyons could fairly see her deducting points behind her cool exterior. He tried to prevent himself from smiling.

"You are from the home office?"

"Please inform Durmstrange that a representative of Mr. Lemis is here to speak with him."

"That's *Dr.* Durmstrange."

Ms. Celeste arched a questioning eyebrow at him. Lyons continued to smile back at her. He was acutely aware of the sinister black eyes of multiple cameras focused on him. Lyons was fairly certain that Durmstrange had been alerted to his presence upon arrival and was even now looking at him through a CCTV screen inside his office.

"One moment, please," Ms. Celeste said, relenting.

She picked up a telephone and punched the numeral 1 on the pad. Her voice dropped to a discreet murmur. Lyons waited patiently as she listened to the response. She murmured an answer into the phone before placing the handset carefully back into its cradle. She looked up at Lyons over her glasses.

"Dr. Durmstrange will see you. Please follow me."

Lyons stepped back to give the woman some room as she stepped out from behind her desk. The woman smiled perfunctorily and stepped aside as she pushed open a door of dark blond wood and ushered Lyons into Durmstrange's office. Lyons nodded agreeably and walked past her. He rather hoped he wouldn't have to frighten Ms. Celeste by beating her supervisor half to death to get what he needed.

The office was a large corner model with blinds drawn across floor-to-ceiling windows. The room was done in mahogany and leather, with a dark chocolate carpet Lyons was sure would seem more at home in Durmstrange's native Netherlands than in the more relaxed style popular in the Dominican Republic.

The room looked more like the office of a D.C. corporate lawyer than that of a man who had spent over a decade leading cutting-edge biological research. Research apparently modeled on that of Josef Mengele.

Lyons stepped fully into the corner office and heard the receptionist close the door firmly behind him. Durmstrange looked up at Lyons from across a desk cluttered with papers, files and computer printouts of schematics and graph charts. Three phones and two separate computer stations sat on the desk in front of the man.

Durmstrange blinked blue eyes behind thick glasses. He stood, rising to an impressive height, and extended a big hand at the end of a long skinny arm toward Lyons. He wore a white lab coat, complete with a full pocket protector, over a stylish business suit of austere brown and a matching tie. His fingers were blunt, the nails cut short, and his blond-silver mustache was thick but carefully trimmed.

Lyons met the firm, dry handshake with one of his own. The man wore a Rolex Executive wristwatch and a heavy signet ring of thick gold. Durmstrange appeared cosmopolitan and stylish without crossing over into effeminate. He seemed a man unlikely to bend under threats of blackmail, but heavy cocaine habits had made stronger men than him weak in the face of ruthless pressure.

"You are from Lemis?" His voice was curt, the tones clipped. "Excuse me for being blunt—I hope you appreciate that I am a busy man."

Lyons nodded and settled into one of the big, comfortable chairs across from the man's desk. When he sat Lyons saw that one of the computer screens showed four separate views from a CCTV security feed, just as he had suspected.

"In a manner of speaking," Lyons answered, waiting for a reaction.

"What does that mean?" Durmstrange snapped. "I do not have time for games, as I have said. Are you from other than Lemis?"

"Let's say I'm from the overseas holding company behind Lemis."

"Do you delight in being obtuse?"

"Not as much as you do in screwing teenage hookers and snorting coke."

"I've never—! What—!"

Durmstrange's voice was fairly strangled with his outrage, and his face had blossomed red in anger.

"Asshole, if you'd 'never,' then you wouldn't have sold

out any vestige of honor you had and gone to work for Michael Klaus. Now cut the crap and start answering my questions, *Doctor*."

"You have identification?"

"That won't be necessary."

"How can you expect me to speak—?"

"Shut up," Lyons snapped. "I'm not here as a courier. I'm not here to give you security tips or to try to strongarm information out of you because the last hooker you were with took pictures of you snorting coke on her camera phone. Understand?"

Lyons rose out of his chair and leaned forward, placing both of his hands on the heavy desk. Durmstrange, despite his physical size, cringed from the more aggressive Lyons. His eyes blinked like a teletype behind his glasses. Beads of sweat suddenly broke out across his wide, high forehead like fat raindrops.

"Do you understand?" Lyons repeated slowly.

"What?" Durmstrange said, growing red. "What do you want!" His voice almost reached to a shriek.

"You're going to take a little drive with me," Lyons explained. "And on that drive you're going to start naming names. You're going to start by verifying where Michael Klaus has gone. You're going to admit on tape how Agent Smith died. You're going to tell me every last thing I want to know."

Lyons reached behind him and pulled his silenced pistol out and set it on the desk. Any growing indignation Durmstrange might have been feeling at his rough treatment evaporated instantly.

There was a lethal promise about a silencer that could rattle the hardest man. A gun was a tool; it could have many purposes, some kind and others hard. A silencer existed for a single purpose: stealthy murder.

Lyons smiled at the frightened research scientist.

Amsterdam

HAWKINS SNATCHED THE PIN from the flash-bang grenade and let the lever spring free. There was a metallic boing as the coil spring holding the weapon parts together disengaged. Hawkins swung open the door and stepped through.

Skell stood on one side of the bar, his face registering only shock as he froze in midsentence. The bodyguard was spinning, his hand diving toward the small of his back under his designer-cut trench coat.

Hawkins lobbed the primed grenade in a gentle underhand, aiming for it to roll across the well-polished top of the wet bar. The bodyguard's mouth worked like a fish yanked clear of the water and tossed into the bottom of a boat. Hands free, Hawkins stepped back around the protective corner of the door. He drew a taser and snapped it on. With his right hand Hawkins pulled his Glock 17.

The woman screamed.

The bang was brutally loud and the flash blinding. Skell's stereo system abruptly shut down. Hawkins stepped back into the main room from around the corner, pistol held ready, snuggled safely in at his hip. He leaped forward and the taser came out like the fangs of a cobra as he struck. Skell backpedaled in the face of the sudden, incapacitating flash-bang, arms held up like a person expecting the impact of a car wreck. The bodyguard collapsed backward, sagging against the counter behind him.

Hawkins took two steps and went airborne. He landed on his hip on the bar and his momentum carried him sliding down its length. He whipped his taser around and tried to catch Skell in his ribs.

With almost unbelievable survival instincts the doughy lawyer shoved the woman screaming next to him into Hawkins and sprinted for the front door of the town house.

The electrical charge locked the woman up and then swept her to the floor, her eyes rolling up to show white. She made crude, inarticulate sounds deep in her throat.

As she went down and Skell ran, Hawkins spun. He cleared the counter, rolling off the edge, and came down next to the bodyguard. The European VIP protection specialist cringed in front of him, raising his hands and cowering like a child. Hawkins snarled and moved forward, weapon held up in each hand.

"Move!" he barked.

Hawkins took half a step forward and kicked the bodyguard in the hip, shoving him around the corner of the bar. He thumbed the power off on the taser and clipped it onto his belt. Following the stumbling bodyguard, Hawkins kicked him again, this time driving the man's arm into his side and spilling him onto the floor next to the incapacitated woman.

The bodyguard looked up, terrified. He saw Hawkins with pistol ready, looming above them. Hawkins's eyes gleamed in brilliant, angry counterpoints to the emotionless affect of his face. The bodyguard struggled not to let go of his bladder in his horror. The woman moaned, ineffectually, at his side.

In the entranceway Skell reached the door. He yanked it open in desperation. The hulking profile of Gary Manning filled the space. Skell squawked out loud. Manning floored him with a pistol butt to the nose.

Hawkins stepped past the cowering, ineffectual bodyguard and over to the edge of the bar, covering everyone in the room.

In the foyer Manning leaned down and thrust the muzzle of his pistol into Skell's forehead.

"Am I going to have to shoot you, little man?"

"What?" Skell was still shaking off the effects of his pistol buttings. "Who—?"

"I said, am I gonna have to shoot you?" Manning let the volume and cadence of his voice climb. He tapped the muzzle of his pistol against the bridge of Skell's nose.

"No," the lawyer answered, his voice surprisingly calm.

Already he was suppressing his fear and disorientation. His eyes sized Manning up and saw no escape there. Behind them Hawkins brought up his stun taser, clicked it on, then off and then on again. The device began to hum and crackle with energy. Any semblance of fight vanished from the bodyguard's eyes.

"Okay, both of you get up. Mr. Bodyguard, you slimy puke, I'm keeping my gun on you. Understand? You try anything, I shoot you. Skell tries anything, I shoot you. The girl over there, the one crying, she tries anything, I'm going to shoot you. No matter how this plays out, you get shot, understand?"

The man nodded, pale, as he climbed to his feet.

"I can't hear you!" Hawkins barked, never taking his eyes off the rising Skell.

"Yes! Yes, I get shot—I understand," the bodyguard babbled.

"Good. Now both of you get over into the living room. Sit your asses down in that couch."

Five minutes later Mr. Skell agreed to play ball and the information started flowing.

CHAPTER THIRTY

Dominican Republic

Durmstrange moaned and slumped forward in his chair before burying his hands in his face. Lyons had broken the intellectual's bluster within minutes of walking through his office door.

Lyons sat, giving Durmstrange an opportunity to collect himself. He carefully put the silenced 9 mm caliber pistol away, this time in the front pocket of his jacket. He felt no sympathy for the corrupt man.

Durmstrange's own refusal to face up to his personal demons had constantly put the lives of others in danger. Perhaps if Durmstrange had faced his addictions, sought help and struggled hard against his human weakness, he wouldn't be where he was now. In any event, this was not Lyons's problem.

"It can end with me," Lyons said. "It can end now. Tell me where Klaus is and there'll be no one left to blackmail you. You'll be free," Lyons lied. Durmstrange was going to end up in a numberless cell right next door to every other player in their vicious plan.

Durmstrange looked up, disbelief fighting with hope on his ruddy face. He didn't trust the frightening man in front of him, but Durmstrange desperately wanted to believe. He seemed to come to some internal decision and he straightened in his chair. He ran his hands through his thick, graying blond hair.

Lyons waited impassively for the man to control himself. The clock was ticking, but when wasn't it? His face was all over Klaus Institute security film. Rumford would know exactly who had been here when he left. Hopefully by the time the station chief got the footage it wouldn't matter anymore.

Lyons looked over at the video screen displayed on the second of Durmstrange's two terminals. A police car and then another pulled forward through the open security gate. For a second the camera panned inside the vehicle and Lyons quickly counted five men crammed into the midsize economy model.

I jinxed myself, he cursed silently.

"Time's up, Durmstrange."

The Dutch-Aruban opened his mouth, prepared to speak. "Shut up!" Lyons snapped, interrupting a now completely stunned Durmstrange.

Lyons looked at the video feed and saw five men with short hair, broad shoulders and trim waists entering the building. Each one of them was armed with a pistol and a submachine gun, and wore the uniform of local police officer.

On a second of the four video feeds Lyons saw a third car, identical to the first two, pulling in through the gate. Things were closing in around him rapidly now. Suddenly, Blancanales rammed the black SUV through the cop car and knocked it spinning off to one side.

"Shut up and stand up—you're coming with me."

"I can't—"

"Tell it to the gun, Durmstrange."

Lyons leveled the silenced pistol at the stunned man.

His eyes widened to ridiculous proportions behind his thick glasses. The effect would have been almost comical if the situation hadn't been so completely and utterly serious. Desperate, Durmstrange finished writing down the address on a piece of paper and shoved it toward Lyons.

"Here, here, take that. Klaus is there. I swear!"

"No good." Lyons crumpled the paper into his pocket. "Come with me or get shot."

"I'll come with you."

"Good choice."

Lyons looked at the video monitor, saw the police squad approaching Ms. Celeste's desk. He stepped around the desk and snatched Durmstrange up by the lapels of his coat. The confused research leader came easily and Lyons shoved him forward, directing him toward the corner of his office farthest away from the door.

Lyons whirled and put his foot against his chair, kicking out. The chair rolled smoothly across the short space and lodged with its back under the doorknob. He eyed the camera feed again and then turned his back on both desk and door. Durmstrange huddled, making more confused noises from his position in the corner.

"Pull the blinds," Lyons ordered.

"What?"

"Pull the goddamned blinds!"

Durmstrange turned to obey. Lyons didn't wait for the physician to complete his task. As soon as he turned his back Lyons lifted the 9 mm and pulled the trigger four times. The silenced, subsonic hollowpoints struck the glass and mushroomed out, spiderwebbing the floor-to-ceiling windows instantly.

Durmstrange gasped at the sound and spun. Lyons reached over and picked up the second leather chair sitting in front of the man's desk. He tossed it underarm into the already broken window, shattering the glass completely.

"Go. Go! Get out now," Lyons snarled.

Lyons took a threatening step toward Durmstrange and the man scrambled to obey. He stepped carefully through the hole to the outside Lyons had just introduced to his office. Lyons was behind him instantly, pushing the man forward into the parking lot. As he moved, Lyons slid the pistol into the waistband of his jeans.

Lyons stayed in close to Durmstrange as he hustled him across the parking lot. He kept one hand on the researcher's elbow and another close by the pistol butt sticking out of his waistband.

The black SUV slid to a stop in front of them. Schwarz disabled the police vehicles with quick bursts from his submachine gun as Lyons shoved Durmstrange into the back of the vehicle.

Blancanales slammed his foot down on the gas as police officers began spilling out of the building, weapons drawn. Rounds cut across the parking lot as the ex–Green Beret slalomed the big vehicle around parked cars and shot out the gate and into the street, sending the security guards flying.

Ten minutes after getting Durmstrange to the new safehouse, he started talking.

Stony Man Farm

BARBARA PRICE SWALLOWED the dregs of the coffee remaining in her cup, pulled a face and set the cup on her desk. She looked up as Carmen Delahunt and Kurtzman entered her office. The mission controller looked at them expectantly.

"Well?" she asked.

"Both Skell and Durmstrange have given us independent verification of Klaus's location," Kurtzman growled.

"Caracas?"

"Caracas," they answered together.

"And?"

"And our profile and hack program confirmed where Klaus is staying. He's in the presidential suite of the JW Marriott Hotel," Bear said.

"Security?"

"Besides his team of personal bodyguards, the Venezuelan government has assigned him a guard detail," Delahunt answered.

"That's going to be tough to get in."

"Well…" Delahunt began, then looked over at Kurtzman and the pair of them began to snicker.

"What's so funny?" Price demanded. "Have you all gone loopy?"

"Well, we got some details about Klaus's personal, um, predilections," Kurtzman explained.

"This was also verified by Durmstrange," Delahunt added.

"Don't keep me in suspense."

"We came up with a plan using Skell's connections. We think it'll work like a charm and that we can get a single operator past all the security without a problem," Kurtzman said.

"Well? What is it already?"

"Oh, man, is Carl going to be pissed," Delahunt said.

CHAPTER THIRTY-ONE

Caracas

Michael Klaus turned away from the view.

It was spectacular but he was hardly interested in some backwater like Caracas. It wasn't a proper city at all. Wearing only silk boxers by Madras he paused to study his body in the full-length mirror in front of his bed.

Things hadn't really gone his way recently.

"But I still look good," he told his reflection, and winked. He was trim and fit and tanned. He pulled the bottle of Dom Perignon White Gold Jeroboam out of the ice bucket. He poured the last of the expensive champagne out of the bottle sheathed in actual white gold into his crystal, long-stemmed flute.

When his whore arrived they'd switch to Cristal Brut 1990 Methuselah, which cost half as much and was more in line with what he thought about any prostitute he could acquire in Caracas.

He strolled out of his bedroom and through the sunken living room of his suite. He'd ordered the sale of his textile plant in South Africa earlier. He needed more liquid assets for the next phase of his plan.

He sipped the sparkling wine slowly and brushed his hand across his stomach. "I forgive you," he whispered to himself.

But he was still feeling cranky when the buzzer to the suite rang. He decided he was going to make his male entertainment for the night suffer a bit until he'd worked out all his frustrations about the failed operation.

Money was wonderful. If you had enough you could do what you wanted. Whatever you wanted. There were no consequences as long as you had money—and lawyers, he thought, grinning. He walked to the door, excited to see what present he'd been sent.

Yes, he thought, with enough money you could do whatever you want. He flipped back the security bolt and turned the doorknob. You could even thumb your noses at the Americans.

The door swung open to reveal a tall, muscular figure with clear blue eyes and close-cut blond hair. Klaus smiled.

"Oh, my," he purred. "You will do." Klaus turned and walked back into the suite. "Come in and close the door. Be sure to lock it, now. I hate to be interrupted."

"Whatever you say," Carl Lyons answered.

* * * * *